ALL

IS NOT

FORGOTTEN

ALL
IS NOT
FORGOTTEN

Wendy Walker

ST. MARTIN'S PRESS
NEW YORK

This is a work of fiction. All of the characters, organizations, and events
portrayed in this novel are either products of the
author's imagination or are used fictitiously.

www.stmartins.com

LIBRARY OF CONGRESS CATALOGING-IN-PUBLICATION DATA

Names: Walker, Wendy, 1967– author.
Title: All is not forgotten / Wendy Walker.
Description: First edition. | New York: St. Martin's Press, 2016.
Identifiers: LCCN 2016000031| ISBN 9781250097910 (hardcover) |
    ISBN 9781250097941 (ebook) | ISBN 9781250119681 (International, sold outside
the U.S., subject to rights availability)
Subjects: LCSH: Upper class families—Connecticut—Fiction. | Young women—Crimes
    against—Fiction. | Memory—Fiction. | Psychological fiction. | BISAC: FICTION /
    Suspense. | GSAFD: Suspense fiction. | Mystery fiction.
Classification: LCC PS3623.A35959 A79 2016 | DDC 813/.6—dc23
LC record available at http://lccn.loc.gov/2016000031

Our books may be purchased in bulk for promotional, educational, or business use.
Please contact your local bookseller or the Macmillan Corporate and Premium Sales
Department at 1-800-221-7945, extension 5442, or by e-mail at
MacmillanSpecialMarkets@macmillan.com.

First Edition: July 2016

10 9 8 7 6 5 4 3 2 1

For Andrew, Ben, and Christopher

ALL

IS NOT

FORGOTTEN

Chapter One

He followed her through the woods behind the house. The ground there was littered with winter debris, dead leaves and twigs that had fallen over the past six months and decayed beneath a blanket of snow. She may have heard him approach. She may have turned and seen him wearing the black wool mask whose fibers were found beneath her nails. As she fell to her knees, what was left of the brittle twigs snapped like old bones and scraped her bare skin. Her face and chest pressed hard into the ground, likely with the outside of his forearm, she would have felt the mist from the sprinklers blowing off the lawn not twenty feet away. Her hair was wet when they found her.

When she was a younger girl, she would chase the sprinklers at her own house, trying to catch them on a hot summer afternoon, or dodge them on a crisp spring evening. Her baby brother would then chase her, buck naked with his bulging belly and flailing arms that were not quite able to coordinate with his little legs. Sometimes their dog would join in, barking so voraciously, it would drown out their laughter. An acre of green grass, slippery and wet. Big open skies with puffy white clouds. Her mother inside watching them from the window and her father on his way home from places whose smells would linger on his suit. The stale coffee from the showroom office, new leather, tire rubber. Those memories were painful now, though she had turned immediately to them when asked about the sprinklers, and whether they had been on when she ran across the lawn to the woods.

The rape lasted for close to an hour. It seems impossible that they could know this. Something about the clotting of the blood at the points of penetration, and the varied stages of bruising on her back, arms, and neck where he'd changed his method of constraint. In that hour, the party had continued the way she'd left it. She would have seen it from where she lay, lights glaring from the windows, flickering as bodies moved through the rooms. It was a big party, with nearly all the tenth grade and handfuls of kids from ninth and eleventh making appearances. Fairview High School was small by most standards, even for suburban Connecticut, and the class divisions that existed elsewhere were far looser here. Sports teams were mixed, plays, concerts, and the like. Even some classes crossed grade boundaries, with the smartest kids in math and foreign languages moving up a level. Jenny Kramer had never made it into an advanced class. But she believed herself to be smart, and endowed with a fierce sense of humor. She was also a good athlete—swimming, field hockey, tennis. But she felt none of those things had mattered until her body matured.

The night of this party had felt better than any moment in her life. I think she may even have said, *It was going to be the best night of my life.* After years of what I have come to think of as adolescent cocooning, she felt she had come into her own. The cruelty of braces and lingering baby fat, breasts that were too small for a bra but still protruding through her T-shirts, acne and unruly hair, had

finally gone away. She had been the "tomboy," the friend, the con-
fidante to boys who were always interested in other girls. Never in
her. These were her words, not mine, although I feel she described
them quite well for a fifteen-year-old. She was unusually self-aware.
In spite of what her parents and teachers had drilled into her, into
all of them, she believed—and she was not alone among her peers in
this—that beauty was still the most valuable asset to a girl in Fairview. Finally having it had felt like winning the lottery.

And then there was the boy. Doug Hastings. He had invited her to
the party on a Monday in the hallway between Chemistry and Euro-
pean History. She was very specific about that, and about what he
was wearing and the expression on his face and how he seemed a
little nervous though he acted nonchalant. She had thought of little
else all week except what to wear and how to do her hair and the
color of polish for her manicure when she went with her mother Saturday morning. It surprised me a bit. I am not fond of Doug Hastings, from what I know of him. As a parent, I feel entitled to have
such opinions. I am not unsympathetic to his situation—a bully for
a father, his mother quite feeble in her attempts to parent around
him. Still, I found it somewhat disappointing that Jenny had not seen
through him.

The party was everything she had imagined. Parents out of town,
kids pretending to be grown-ups, mixing cocktails in martini glasses,
drinking beer from crystal tumblers. Doug had met her there. But
he was not alone.

The music was blaring and she would have heard it from the scene
of the attack. The playlist was full of pop mega hits, the ones she said
she knew well, the lyrics the kind that stuck in your head. Even
through the music, and the muted laughter that was wafting from
the open windows, she would have heard the other sounds that were
closer, the depraved sighs of her attacker, her own guttural cries.

When he was finished and had slipped away into the darkness, she used her arm for support, lifting her face from the brush. She might have felt then the air hit the newly exposed skin of her cheek, and when it did, maybe she had felt that her skin was wet. Some of the brush on which she had been resting stuck, as if her face had been dipped in glue that had since begun to dry.

Propped up on her forearm, she must have heard the sound.

At some point, she came to sit upright. She had tried to clean up the mess that was all around her. With the back of her hand, she wiped her cheek. Remnants of dried leaves fell to the ground. She would have then seen her skirt bunched up around her waist, exposing her naked genitals. Using both hands, it seems she got on all fours and crawled a short distance, possibly to retrieve her underwear. They were in her hand when she was found.

The sound must have grown louder because eventually it was heard by another girl and her boyfriend, who had sought privacy in the yard not far away. The ground would have crackled and popped beneath the weight of her hands and knees as she again crawled toward the perimeter of the grass. I have imagined her crawling, the inebriation hindering her coordination and the shock freezing time. I have imagined her assessing the damage when she finally stopped crawling and came to sit, seeing her torn underwear, feeling the ground against the skin of her buttocks.

The underwear too torn to wear, everywhere sticky with blood and dirt. That sound growing louder. Wondering how long she had been in the woods.

Back to her hands and knees, she began to crawl again. But no matter how far she moved, the sound grew louder and louder. How desperate she must have been to escape, to reach the soft grass, the clean water that was now upon it, the place she had been before the woods.

She moved another few feet before stopping again. Maybe it was then that she realized the sound, the disturbing moan, was inside her head, then in her own mouth. The fatigue came over her, forcing her knees, then her arms, to buckle beneath her.

She said she had always considered herself a strong girl, an athlete with a formidable will. Strong in her body and her mind. That was what her father had told her since she was a little kid. *Be strong in your body and in your mind, and you will have a good life.* Maybe she told herself to get up. Maybe she ordered her legs to move, then her arms, but her will was impotent. Instead of taking her back to where she had been, they curled up around her battered body, which lay upon the filthy ground.

Tears falling, voice echoing them with that horrible sound, she was finally heard and then rescued. She has asked herself again and again since that night why nothing she had inside her—her muscles, her wit, her will—had been capable of stopping what happened. She couldn't remember if she tried to fight him, screamed for help, or if she just gave up and let it happen. No one heard her until it was over. She said she now understands that in the wake of every battle, there were left conqueror and conquered, victor and victim, and that she had come to accept the truth—that she had been totally, irrevocably defeated.

I couldn't say how much of this was true when I heard it, this story of the rape of Jenny Kramer. It was a story that had been reconstructed with forensic evidence, witness accounts, criminal psychologist profiles, and the disjointed, fragmented scraps of memory Jenny was left with after the treatment. They say it is a miracle treatment—to have the most horrible trauma erased from your mind. Of course, it is not magic, nor is the science particularly impressive. But I will explain all of that later. What I want to express now, at the beginning of the story, is that it was not a miracle for this beautiful young girl. What was removed from her mind lived on in her body, and her soul, and I felt compelled to return to her what was taken away. It may seem the strangest thing to you. So counterintuitive. So disturbing.

Fairview, as I have already alluded, is a small town. I had seen pictures of Jenny Kramer over the years in the local paper, and in school flyers about a play or tennis tournament posted at Gina's Deli down on East Main. I had recognized her walking in town, coming out of the movie theater with friends, in a concert at the school that my own children attended. She had an innocence about her that belied the maturity she so coveted. Even in the short skirts and cropped shirts that seemed to be the style these days, she was a girl, not a woman. And I would feel encouraged about the state of the world when I saw her. It would be disingenuous to say that I feel this way toward all of them, the herd of teenagers that sometimes seems to have stolen the order from our lives like a swarm of locust. Glued to their phones like brain-dead drones, indifferent to any affairs beyond celebrity gossip and the things that brought them instant gratification—videos, music, self-promoting tweets and Instagrams and Snapchats. Teenagers are innately selfish. Their brains are not mature. But some of them seem to hold on to their sweetness through these years, and they stand out. They're the ones who meet your eyes when you greet them, smile politely, allow you to pass simply because you are older and they understand the place of respect in an orderly society. Jenny was one of those.

To see her after, to see the absence of joy that once bubbled up inside her—it provoked rage in me at all humanity. Knowing what had happened in those woods, it was hard not to let my mind go there. We are all drawn to prurient incidents, to violence and horror. We pretend not to be, but it is our nature. The ambulance on the side of the road, every car slowing to a crawl to get a glimpse of an injured body. It doesn't make us evil.

This perfect child, her body defiled, violated. Her virtue stolen. Her spirit broken. I sound melodramatic. Cliché. But this man ripped into her body with such force that she required surgery. Consider that. Consider that he selected a child, hoping for a virgin perhaps, so he could rape her innocence as well as her body. Consider the physical pain she endured as her most intimate flesh tore and shredded. And now consider what else was torn and shredded as he spent an hour torturing her body, thrusting himself into her again and again, perhaps seeing her face. How many expressions had she given him to enjoy? Surprise, fear, terror, agony, acceptance, and, finally, indifference as she shut down. Each one a piece of herself taken and devoured by this monster. And then, even after the treatment was given—because she still knew what had happened—every romantic daydream about her first time with a lover, every love story that swam in her head and made her smile with thoughts of being adored by one person like no other in the world. It was likely those things were gone forever. And then what was left for a girl as she grew into a woman? The very thing that preoccupies the heart throughout most of our lives may very well have been lost to her.

She remembered a strong odor, though she couldn't place it. She remembered a song, but it was possible the song had played more than once. She remembered the events that drove her out the back door, across the lawn, and into the woods. She did not recall the sprinklers, and that became part of the reconstruction of the story. The sprinklers came on at nine and off at ten, having been set to a timer. The two lovers who found her had arrived in the back to grass that was wet but air that was dry. The rape had been in between.

Doug had been with another girl, a junior who found him necessary to her plan to make some senior boy jealous. It is hardly worth the effort to elucidate the vapid motivations of this particular girl. What mattered to Jenny was that a week's worth of fantasies, around which she had wrapped much of her disposition, had been shattered in a second. Predictably, she began to drown her sorrows in alcohol. Her best friend, Violet, recalled that she had started with shots of vodka. Within an hour, she was vomiting in the bathroom. This had led to the amusement of some others, and then to her further humiliation. It might have been a script from one of those "mean girl" shows that seem to be all the rage now. Except for the part that followed. The part where she ran into the woods to be alone, to cry.

I was angry. I won't apologize for that. I wanted justice for what had happened. But without a memory, without any forensic evidence beyond the wool fibers under her nails because this monster had taken precautions, justice was no longer on the table. Fairview is a small town. Yes, I know I keep saying this. But you must understand that this is the kind of town that would not attract a stranger to perpetrate a crime. Heads turn when someone unfamiliar walks the two small strips of our downtown. Not in a bad way, mind you, but in a curious way. Was it someone's relative? Someone moving here? We have visitors for special events, sports tournaments, fairs, things like that. People will come from other towns and we welcome them. We are generally friendly people, trusting people. But on an ordinary weekend, outsiders are noticed.

Where I am going with all this is the following obvious conclusion: Had she not been given the treatment, had her memory been intact, she might have placed him. The fibers under her nails indicated she had grabbed at the mask. Maybe she pulled it off, or up just enough to see a face. Maybe she heard a voice. Or was he perfectly quiet for an hour of raping? It seems unlikely, doesn't it? She would know how tall he was, thin or fat. Maybe his hands were old or maybe they were young. Maybe he wore a ring, a gold band or a team emblem. Did he wear sneakers or loafers or work boots? Were they worn or stained by oil or paint or maybe they were perfectly shined? Would she know him if she stood near him at the ice cream shop? Or at the coffeehouse? Or in the lunch line at school? Would she simply feel him in her gut? An hour is a long time to be with another body.

Maybe it was cruel to want this thing for Jenny Kramer. Maybe I was cruel to pursue the wanting. It would, as you will see, lead to unexpected consequences. But the injustice of it all, the anger it provoked in me, and the ability to understand her suffering—all of it led me to a single-minded pursuit. And that was to give back to Jenny Kramer this most horrific nightmare.

Chapter Two

Jenny's parents were called just after ten thirty. They had been attending a dinner party with two couples from their country club, though the dinner was at the home of one of the couples and not at the club itself. Charlotte Kramer, Jenny's mother, had complained about this in the car on the way through town earlier that evening, how they should be dining at the club to use up their minimum and, according to her husband, Tom, because Charlotte liked the social scene there. Cocktails were always served in the lounge, so regardless of the company you had planned to keep during the dinner, there was a chance to mingle with other club members.

Tom disliked the club other than to play golf on Sunday with his usual foursome: a friend from college and two dads he'd met through Jenny's track team. Charlotte, on the other hand, was highly social and was aspiring to join the pool committee for the upcoming season. Any Saturday night not spent at the club felt like a lost opportunity to her. It was one of the many sources of marital discord between them, and their short car ride had ended with silence and mutual irritation at the making of the usual comments.

They both remembered this later, and how petty it had seemed after the brutal rape of their daughter.

One of the nice things about a small town is that people bend the rules when it seems appropriate. The fear of being reprimanded, or even sued, does not loom quite so precariously as it does in a larger community. So when Detective Parsons called the Kramers, he did not tell them what had happened, only that Jenny had been drinking at a party and was taken to the hospital. They had been immediately reassured that her life was not at all in danger. Tom was thankful for this, for being spared the few minutes of agony as they drove from the dinner to the hospital. Every minute after learning of the rape had been just that for Tom—unrelenting agony.

Charlotte had not been quite so appreciative, because the partial truth caused her to be enraged at her daughter's carelessness. The whole town would surely know, and how would that reflect on their family? On the way to the hospital, they had discussed punishments, weighing the impact of grounding or having her phone taken away. Of course, when they did learn the truth, it was guilt that found its way into Charlotte, and for that she was resentful of the misinformation. It is understandable, having been presented with a reason to be angry at your child only to then find out she had been so viciously assaulted. Still, I identified more with Tom on this. Perhaps it is because I am a father and not a mother.

The hospital lobby was empty when they arrived. There had been some attention given over the past several years to fund-raising and upgrading, and the results, while more cosmetic than substantive to many minds, were noticeable. Wood paneling, new carpet. The lighting was soft and there was classical music playing from the wireless speakers that hung discreetly in the corners. Charlotte "stormed" to the front desk (Tom's word). Tom caught up and stood beside her. He closed his eyes and let the music calm his blood. He was concerned that Charlotte would be too harsh, at least for what this moment called for, and he wanted to "balance her out." Jenny needed to sleep, to know her parents still loved her and that everything would be all right. The consequences could wait until they were all sober and clearheaded.

The Kramers knew their roles within the family. It was Charlotte's task to be the disciplinarian with their daughter. With their boy, Lucas, the roles were often reversed, likely because of his age (ten) and his gender. Tom described this arrangement as though describing a blue sky—it was as it should be, as it is in every family. And he was right in theory. There are always roles to be played, shifting alliances, good cops and bad cops. With the Kramers, though, the natural ebbs and flows seemed to have given way to Charlotte's needs, with the others taking parts she did not monopolize. In other words, the normalcy Tom attempted to ascribe to their family would prove to be quite abnormal, and untenable.

The nurse smiled at them sympathetically as she released the lock on the door to the treatment rooms. They didn't know her, but that was true of most of the support staff at the hospital. Lower-salaried professionals rarely lived in Fairview, coming in from the neighboring city of Cranston. Tom remembered her smile. It was the first hint that this was a more serious incident than what they had been led to believe. People underestimate the hidden messages in a fleeting facial expression. But think about the type of smile you would give a friend whose teenager got caught drinking. It would express a comical type of empathy. It would say, *Oh man, teenagers are tough. Remember what we were like?* And now think about the smile you would give if that teenager had been assaulted. That smile would surely say, *Oh my God! I'm so sorry! That poor girl!* It's in the eyes, in the shrug of the shoulders, and in the shape of the mouth. When this nurse smiled, Tom's thoughts shifted from managing his wife to seeing his daughter.

They walked through the security doors to triage, and then to another circular desk, where nurses processed paperwork and files behind computer screens. There was another woman, another worrisome smile. She picked up a phone and paged a doctor.

I can picture them in that moment. Charlotte in her beige cocktail dress, her blond hair carefully pinned up in a twist. Arms folded at the chest, posturing for when she first saw Jenny, and for the staff who she would imagine were passing judgments. And Tom, half a foot taller as he stood beside his wife with his hands in the pockets of his khaki pants, shifting his weight from foot to foot with increasing concern as his instincts fueled his runaway thoughts. Both of them agreed that those few minutes they waited for the doctor felt like hours.

Charlotte was very perceptive and quickly spotted three police officers drinking coffee from paper cups in the corner. Their backs were facing the Kramers as they spoke with a nurse. The nurse then caught Charlotte's eye, and a whisper later, the officers turned to look at her. Tom was facing the other way, but he, too, began to notice the attention they were drawing.

Neither of them would recall the exact words the doctor used to tell them. There was apparently a brief acknowledgment by Charlotte of knowing *of* each other—the doctor's daughter being one grade below Lucas at the elementary school—which then made Charlotte increasingly concerned about Jenny's now tarnished reputation and how it might trickle down to their son. Dr. Robert Baird. Late thirties. Stout. Thin light brown hair and kind blue eyes that grew small when he said certain words that caused his cheeks to rise.

Each of them remembered something about the man as he started to discuss her injuries. *The external tearing of the perineum and anus . . . rectal and vaginal lesions . . . bruising to the neck and back . . . surgery . . . stitches . . . repairs.*

The words left his mouth and floated around them like they were of a foreign language. Charlotte shook her head and repeated the word "no" several times in a nonchalant manner. She assumed he had confused them with the parents of a different patient and tried to stop him from revealing any more to spare him the embarrassment. She repeated her name, told him their daughter had been brought here for "overdoing it" at a party. Tom recalled being silent then, as though by not making a sound, he might be able to freeze time before the moment continued down the path he had started to see.

Dr. Baird stopped speaking and glanced at the officers. One of them, Detective Parsons, walked over, slowly—and with visible reluctance. They stepped to the side. Baird and Parsons spoke. Baird shook his head and looked at his black shoes. He sighed. Parsons shrugged apologetically.

Baird then stepped away and returned to stand before the Kramers. Hands folded as if in a prayer, he told them the truth plainly and concisely. *Your daughter was found in the woods behind a house on Juniper Road. She was raped.*

Dr. Baird recalled the sound that left Tom Kramer's body. It was not a word or a moan or a gasp, but something he had never witnessed before. It sounded like death, like a piece of Tom Kramer had been murdered. His knees buckled and he reached for Baird, who took hold of his arms and kept him on his feet. A nurse rushed to join them, offering assistance, offering to get him a chair, but he refused. *Where is she! Where is my baby!* he demanded, pushing away from the doctor. He bounded toward one of the curtains, but the nurse stopped him, grabbing his forearms from behind to steer him down the hall.

She's right over here, the nurse said. *She's going to be fine . . . she's asleep.*

They reached one of the triage areas and the nurse pulled back the curtain.

My wife has told me ever since we had our own daughter, our first child—Megan is her name, now off to college—that she projects scenarios like this one onto herself. When we watched Megan pull out of the driveway for the first time behind the wheel of our car. When she left for a summer program in Africa. When we caught her climbing a tree in the yard, what feels like a hundred years ago. There are so many more examples. My wife would close her eyes and picture a pile of metal and flesh twisted together on the side of the road, or a tribal warlord with a machete, our daughter sobbing before him on her knees. Or her neck snapped and body lifeless beneath the tree. Parents live with fear, and how we deal with it, process it, depends on too many factors to recite here. My wife has to go there, to see the images, feel the pain. She then puts it in a box, loads the box on a shelf, and when the nagging worry creeps in, she can look at the box and then let the worry pass through her before it can settle in and feast on her enjoyment of life.

She has described to me these images, sometimes crying briefly in my arms. What is at the heart of each description, and what I find so compelling for its uniformity, is the juxtaposition of purity and corruption. Good and evil. For what could be more pure and good than a child?

Tom Kramer set his eyes upon his daughter in that room and saw what my wife has only imagined in her mind. Small braids laced with ribbon falling next to the bruises on her face. Smeared black mascara on cheeks that were still puffy like a child's. Pink polish on broken nails. Only one of the birthstone stud earrings he'd bought her for her birthday, the other missing from a bloody earlobe. Around her were metal tables with instruments and blood-soaked swabs. The work was not yet done, so the room had not been cleaned. A woman in a white lab coat sat beside her bed, taking her blood pressure. She wore a stethoscope and offered only a fleeting glance before looking back at the dial on the black rubber pump. A female police officer stood unobtrusively in the corner, pretending to busy herself with a notepad.

Like life "flashing before your eyes" just before death, Tom saw a newborn in a pink swaddled blanket. He felt the warm breath of a baby on his neck as she slept in his arms; a tiny hand lost inside his palm; a full-body hug around his legs. He heard a high-pitched giggle come from a chubby belly. Theirs was a relationship unspoiled by the pitfalls of misbehavior. Those were saved for Charlotte Kramer, and in this respect, I could see that she had, however unintentionally, given them both a gift.

Rage at her attacker would come, but not then. More than anything, what Tom saw, felt, and heard in that moment was his failure to protect his little girl. His despair cannot be measured nor adequately described. He began to weep like a child himself, the nurse at his side, his daughter pale and lifeless on the bed.

Charlotte Kramer stayed behind with the doctor. Shocking as it may sound to you, she saw her daughter's rape as a problem that needed to be solved. A broken pipe that had flooded the basement. Or perhaps worse than that—a fire that had burned their entire house to the ground but left them standing. The key fact was the last bit—that they had survived. Her thoughts turned instantly to rebuilding the house.

She looked at Dr. Baird, arms crossed at her chest. *What kind of rape?* she asked him.

Baird paused for a moment, not sure what she was asking.

Charlotte sensed his confusion. *You know, was it some boy from the party who got carried away?*

Baird shook his head. *I don't know. Detective Parsons may know more.*

Charlotte grew frustrated. *I mean, from the examination. Did you do a rape kit?*

Yes. We're required to by law.

So—did you see anything, you know, that might indicate one way or another?

Mrs. Kramer, Baird said. *Maybe we should let you see Jenny, and then I can discuss this with you and your husband in a more private setting.*

Charlotte was put off, but she did as she was asked. She is not a difficult person, and if my descriptions of her indicate otherwise, I assure you most vehemently that it is not by design. I have great respect for Charlotte Kramer. She has not had an easy life, and her adaptations to her own childhood trauma are surprisingly mild—and reflective of the fortitude of her constitution. I believed she truly loved her husband, even when she emasculated him. And that she loved her children, loved them equally, even though she held Jenny to higher standards. But love is a term of art and not science. We can, each and every one of us, describe it in different words, and feel it differently within our bodies. Love can make one person cry and another smile. One angry and another sad. One aroused and another sleepy with contentment.

Charlotte experienced love through a prism. It's hard to describe without again sounding judgmental, or causing you to dislike her. But Charlotte desperately needed to create what was taken from her as a child—a traditional (I believe she even said "boring") American family. She loved her town because it was filled with like-minded, hardworking people with good morals. She loved her house because it was a New England colonial in a quiet neighborhood. She loved being married to Tom because he was a family man with a good job— not a great job, but great jobs pulled men away from their families. Tom ran several car dealerships, and it's important to note that he sold BMWs, Jaguars, and other luxury cars. I was informed that this is quite distinct from "peddling" Hyundais. Whether Charlotte loved Tom beyond all of this was not known to either of them. She loved her children because they were hers, and because they were everything children should be. Smart, athletic, and (mostly) obedient, but also messy, noisy, silly, and requiring a great deal of hard work and effort, which provided her with a worthwhile occupation and something she could discuss at length with her friends at the club over luncheon. Each piece of this picture she loved and loved deeply. So when Jenny got "broken," she became desperate to fix her. As I've said, she needed to repair her house.

Jenny had been sedated after arriving to the ER. The kids who found her described her as floating in and out of consciousness, though it was more likely the effect of shock than inebriation. Her eyes remained open and she was able to sit up and then walk with minimal assistance across the lawn to a lounge chair. Their description was that she sometimes seemed to know them and where she was and what had happened, and seconds later was unresponsive to their questions. Catatonic. She asked for help. She cried. Then she went blank. The paramedics reported the same behavior, but it is their policy not to administer sedatives. It was at the hospital, when the examination began, that she became hysterical. Dr. Baird made the call to give her some relief. There was enough bleeding to warrant concern and not wait for consent to prescribe the medication so they could examine her.

In spite of her outward appearance, Charlotte was deeply affected by the sight of her daughter. In fact, it was my impression that she came quite close in that first moment to feeling what Tom felt. Though they rarely touched outside their bedroom (and there only to perform the mechanics of intimacy), she took Tom's arm with both her hands. She buried her face into the sleeve of his shirt and whispered the words "Oh my God." She did not cry, but Tom felt her nails digging into his skin as she fought for her composure. When she tried to swallow, she found her mouth to be bone dry.

Detective Parsons could see them through the curtain. He remembered their faces as they looked down at their child. Tom's was contorted and sloppy with tears, his agony painted upon his flesh. Charlotte's, after the brief loss of composure, was determined. Parsons called it a stiff upper lip. He said he felt uncomfortable observing them in this intimate moment, though he did not look away. He said he was taken aback by Tom's weakness and Charlotte's strength, though anyone with a less simplistic understanding of human emotion would understand that it was actually quite the opposite. It requires far more strength to experience emotion than to suppress it.

Dr. Baird stood behind them, checking a chart that hung on a metal clip at the end of Jenny's bed.

Why don't we speak in the family lounge? he suggested.

Tom nodded, wiped his tears. He leaned down and kissed the top of his daughter's head, and this brought on a series of deep sobs. Charlotte brushed a stray hair from Jenny's face, then stroked her cheek with the back of her hand. *Sweet angel . . . sweet, sweet angel,* she whispered.

They followed Baird and Detective Parsons down the hall to a set of locked doors. Through the doors was another hallway and then a small lounge with some furniture and a TV. Baird offered to arrange for coffee or food, but the Kramers declined. Baird closed the door. Parsons sat down next to the doctor and across from the Kramers.

This is Charlotte's account of what happened next:

They beat around the bush, asking us about Jenny's friends, did we know about the party, did she have any troubles with any boys, did she mention anyone bothering her at school or in town or on her social media? Tom was answering them like he was in some sort of fog, like he couldn't see we were all just avoiding what needed to be discussed. I'm not saying that those weren't legitimate questions or that we shouldn't have answered them at some point. But I had had it, you know? I wanted someone to tell me something. I try really hard to let Tom "be the man" because I know I can be controlling. No one complains when the house is in perfect order and the fridge has everything they all need and their clothes are washed and ironed and put away where they belong. Anyway . . . I do try because I know it's important in a marriage for the man to be the man. But I couldn't take it. I just couldn't!

So I interrupted all of them, all of the men, and I said, "One of you needs to tell us what happened to our daughter." Dr. Baird and the detective looked at each other like neither of them wanted to go first. The doctor drew the short end of the stick. And then he told us. He told us how she had been raped. It was not what I had hoped— that it was some boy she liked and he got carried away. Oh God I know how bad that sounds. The feminists would have my head, wouldn't they? I'm not saying that that kind of rape isn't really rape or shouldn't be punished. Believe me—when Lucas is older, I'm going to make damn sure he knows the kind of trouble he could be in if he isn't absolutely sure he has consent. I do believe that men have a responsibility, that they need to realize that when it comes to sex, we are not on equal footing. And not just because of the physiology. It's the psychology as well—the fact that girls still feel pressure to do things they don't want and boys, men, have very little understanding about what girls go through. Anyway, it was not what I had hoped. And actually, it was what I had feared most. Detective Parsons filled in this part. He wore a mask. He forced her to the ground on her face. He . . . I'm sorry. This is hard to say out loud. I can hear the words in my mind, but saying them is another thing altogether.

Charlotte stopped to gather herself. She had a particular method, which she used without deviation. It was a long inhale, eyes closed, quick shake of the head, then a slow exhale. She looked down first after opening her eyes, then nodded in confirmation of the control she had wrangled.

I'll just say it, all of it, quickly and then be done. She was raped from behind, vaginally, anally, back and forth apparently, for an hour. Okay. I said it. It's done. They did the rape kit. They found traces of spermicide and latex. This . . . this creature wore a condom. They didn't find one hair either, and the forensic people who were brought in from Cranston later that night said he probably shaved himself. Can you imagine? He prepared for this rape like an Olympic swimmer. Well, he didn't get his gold medal, did he? Every physical wound healed beautifully. She won't ever feel any different from any other woman. And emotionally, well . . .

She paused again, this time more to take stock than regain her composure. Then she continued in a voice that was irreverent.

I remember thinking, thank God for the treatment. Everything he did to my little girl, we undid. So, I'm sorry for the bad language, but I thought—fuck him. He doesn't exist anymore.

Chapter Three

Charlotte and Tom Kramer did not agree on the decision to give Jenny the treatment. Charlotte won that fight.

The medical community is still learning about the formation and retention of memory. Studies have been on the rise, and new research surfaces regularly. Our brains have long-term memory, short-term memory, the process for storing memories and of locating and retrieving memories from the places where they are stored, which scientists now believe to be vast. Consider that for decades, neuroscientists believed that memories were stored in the synapses that connect our brain cells and not in the brain cells (or neurons) themselves. Now they have disproved this and believe it's the neurons that hold our history. We have also discovered that memories are not static. In fact, they change every single time we pull them from storage.

The treatment used to induce limited anterograde amnesia of traumatic events was found through a series of trials on both animals and humans over many years and in many variations. It starts with morphine. As early as the 1950s, doctors noticed a reduction in

PTSD from the early administration of morphine in high doses. The findings were inadvertent—the morphine had been administered to children who were victims of burning following a fire, purely for the intention of pain relief. Those who received the higher doses immediately after the fire had noticeably reduced symptoms of PTSD than the children who received less or no morphine. In 2010, a formal paper was written confirming the benefits of morphine for children suffering from burns. Morphine, along with other drugs, has been used for years to treat soldiers in the field, and researchers correlating records of trauma, morphine, and PTSD have found that high doses administered immediately after a trauma can significantly reduce PTSD in wounded men and women.

This is why: Every waking moment, we have experiences. We see, feel, and hear. Our brains process this information and store it in our memories. This is called memory consolidation. Each factual event also carries some emotional counterpart, and that triggers chemicals in the brain and those chemicals then place the events into the appropriate file cabinet, if you will. Things that capture our emotions are filed in the locked metal cabinets. They are not replaced by subsequent events and can be easily recalled. Other less provocative events, what we made for dinner last Thursday, might go into a manila folder somewhere. As time passes, these will get buried under other manila folders and at some point become impossible to find. They may even get sent to the shredder. Some researchers believe that morphine reduces the emotional reaction to an event by blocking norepinephrine so a "metal cabinet" event may get reduced to a "manila folder" event. This is the first component of the treatment.

Now, because the filing of any event requires the interaction of chemicals in the brain, you can see how interfering with those chemicals while they are trying to do their filing could interrupt the process. This is why a night of binge drinking results in a "blackout." It's also why drugs like Rohypnol (the date rape drug) enable a person to function "normally" but not remember anything that happened while the drug was in the system. The brain's filing staff is on a break. Nothing gets filed, and the events are presumably lost, as if they never happened. But this is during the short-term-memory phase. The second part of the treatment involves a revolutionary drug that claims to send the filers on their break during the consolidation of long-term memory—it stops the synapses from working at this stage by inhibiting necessary proteins, so the short-term memories are discarded. They call it Benzatral.

The tricky part with trauma is the timing. There is no exact time between short-term- and long-term-memory consolidation. Every memory involves different parts of the brain, depending on what the memory is made of. Was it a sight, a sound, a feeling? Was it music or math or meeting a new person? The brain is functioning while the trauma is occurring, so the filing is in process. The treatment has to be given within hours of the trauma, and even then it may not be completely effective if some of the events have already made it to long-term storage.

Jenny had the perfect set of circumstances. She was already inebriated when the rape began. She went into shock during the attack. Within half an hour, she was given a sedative. And within two hours, the treatment was administered. She awoke twelve hours later with only the small bits and pieces I have already mentioned.

Tom Kramer also recalled the conversation in the family lounge. I cannot fully capture the emotion with which he recounted it, so I will just give you his words and tell you that he did not cry. I think by this point he had no more water.

I don't remember exactly what was said. I just kept hearing the word "rape" over and over. I can tell you that it was a brutal, merciless attack. That they had no suspects. That he had been careful, wearing a condom and perhaps shaving his body hair. They thought, and this was later confirmed by the forensic investigators, that he wore a black wool mask—like one of those ski masks that covers your entire face and head. They said it lasted for about an hour. I have thought about that more than I should. When Jenny was back in the hospital eight months after the rape, when I knew this was not over, I went home and lay on the floor with my face pressed to the ground, my body positioned the way they said hers was. I lay there for an hour. An hour is a long time to be tortured, longer than any of us can imagine. I promise you that.

Anyway . . . the treatment. So they explained the process. The drugs that would be given. How it would put her into a sort of coma for about a day and that, if we were lucky, it might block her memory of the rape and at the very least, and this they said they knew for sure, it would reduce any PTSD she might suffer. They said the PTSD could be debilitating and require years of therapy. Dr. Baird asked if we wanted to speak with a psychiatrist to better understand the treatment and what life might be like for her without it. He said every minute that passed reduced the effectiveness.

Charlotte's eyes got so wide. "Yes!" she said without even looking at me. "Do it! What are you waiting for?" She stood up and pointed to the door like they should both rush out to follow her orders. But I grabbed her arm. I may not be the smartest man, but this didn't sound right to me. If she couldn't remember, how could she help them find this creature? How could she help put him behind bars, where he would get what he deserved? Detective Parsons nodded and looked at the floor like he knew exactly what I was saying. He finally confessed that it would be very difficult. That even if the drug didn't work completely, anything she did remember would be ripped apart in court as unreliable. Of course it would, right? I mean, come on. Game over. Look—I'm not saying I wanted this guy caught and punished more than I wanted my daughter to recover. But where her mother saw her recovery in forgetting and pretending this never happened, I saw it coming more by way of facing the devil, you know? Looking him square in the eye and taking back a piece of what he had stolen. And I was right, wasn't I? Jesus Christ, I wish I wasn't, but I was.

I asked him the next logical question. "If you felt so strongly, why did you agree?"

He thought about this for several seconds. I think he had asked himself this same question a million times, but he had never had to say the answer out loud. When he did, he looked at me with a blank face, as though it should have been obvious to me. Tom had not yet come to see that the dynamics at play in his marriage were anything but obvious—or normal, for that matter.

Because if I was wrong, if Jenny didn't get past it, I would be blamed. So why did I agree? Because I was a coward.

Chapter Four

What I haven't mentioned yet is the carving on Jenny's back. It didn't really become important to the story until now, and I should explain it before I go on. Everything happened so quickly the night of Jenny's rape. She was at the hospital within an hour of being found. She was then sedated. Her parents arrived within a half hour of that, immediately bombarded with the decision regarding the treatment. It had to be administered by the psychiatrist through the IV that the nurse inserted into the back of Jenny's hand. There were waivers and forms to review and sign, guarantees for payment. The treatment was not covered by insurance. And, finally, she was prepped for surgery to repair the damage from the rape, and for the thorough forensic examination.

Tom stayed with her until she was rolled away to an operating room. He said it was like watching his daughter in a manufacturing plant. He had visited one in Detroit years before, when he sold Fords. Metal parts, nuts and bolts, plastic and wires and computer chips, thousands of workers with busy hands and machines with moving parts putting things together. As he watched Jenny's limp body handled by five people, each with a job to do on her body, each concerned only with her body as her mind was manipulated with chemicals and forced to stay asleep, that was the image Tom recalled, and he was deeply disturbed by it, and by his own deferential behavior. He had wanted to lift her from the gurney, raise his fist in the air, and tell everyone to leave her the hell alone. But, of course, he did nothing of the sort.

Not to belabor their differences, but Charlotte had wanted to join her daughter in her sedation, fall asleep, and forget this ever happened. She did not watch the professionals do their work. Instead, she went home and relieved the babysitter, took a sleeping pill, tucked Lucas's blankets tighter around his body, and then curled up in the spare bed a few feet away. She listened to him breathe until she fell asleep herself. I would come to learn that she did this often to avoid being in the same bed with Tom.

When they were finished repairing the tears to Jenny's genitals and bowels, she was admitted to the ICU. Dr. Baird stopped up to see how Tom was doing. He was joined by Detective Parsons shortly after. It was then that Tom first learned about the carving on her back. Parsons explained it this way:

We had the preliminary report from the forensic examination. They had some samples of fluids and hairs that needed to be tested, but as we now know, nothing would ever be found. During the examination, they found the carving. It was more of a cut, really, in terms of how deep it was. It was only an inch long, but it required seventeen stitches. No one noticed it at first because she was so dirty and there were so many other superficial scratches that they didn't think much of it until they'd washed her. This one cut kept bleeding. The team that examined the woods where Jenny was attacked found a stick. It was sharpened at one end with some kind of knife like a small spear. The stick was only about a foot long. There was no skin on it except for Jenny's, but they did find some fibers that would turn out to be neoprene. That's the material used for sports gloves. They think he used the spear like a carving tool, slowly whittling away at the layers of skin.

Detective Parsons is a young man of thirty-one years, which explains the liberty he took when informing the Kramers about Jenny the night of the rape. With youth comes the inability to know what's going to happen as a decision is played out. It is one of the greatest shames of the human experience that by the time we know how to conduct ourselves in an appropriate manner, there's little conducting left to do.

Fairview doesn't have much use for detectives. The job here is either a stepping-stone up to a more "active" situation elsewhere, perhaps in neighboring Cranston, or a step down toward retirement. Parsons is not a bad detective. But with his relative inexperience came an awkwardness when he recounted the more "intimate" details of the rape. His eagerness to appear disinterested and professional actually served to reveal just how interested he actually was. It was unsettling. But as I've said, the gravitation toward the prurient does not make us evil. We still do everything we can to try to conceal it. And so Detective Parsons did just that as he continued.

When we consulted the rape specialists from Cranston, they had all questioned the time frame. An hour is highly unusual for a rape in a public setting. It would have been difficult to see them in the woods that night. There was little moon and significant cloud cover. But she was within hearing range of anyone out on the street coming or going from the party, and certainly of anyone coming into the yard like the two individuals who did eventually hear her and come to her aid. But they could not argue with the medical facts. Then when they learned about the stick and the scratch, they said it made

more sense. They think he stopped and started his various (there was
an oddly long pause here) *penetrations to whittle her. The carving
was low on her back. It's the place where girls like to get tattoos.
They think he was marking her, or maybe just enjoying the cycles of
relief and renewed fear from the starting and stopping, and then the
winces from the pain of the sharp blade in her skin* (another long
pause, this time reflective). *They think he may have gone through
his own cycles of arousal, perhaps needing to refuel his excitement
with the carving activity. This added a whole new direction to our
thinking. This perpetrator was more sociopathic than we had originally assumed. And we were already thinking pretty far down that
road.*

Jenny's physical recovery was not without its hardships. The
areas that were sewn are not easily "shut down" and so there was regular pain, daily pain. Jenny tried to stop eating to reduce the amount
of eliminating she would have to do. She lost over ten pounds in the
two weeks her body was healing, and that time was spent mostly in
bed or on the sofa loaded up with painkillers. There was some discord over the decision to send her back to school. There were only
three weeks remaining when she was well enough, and the school,
including all her teachers, had generously offered to provide her with
materials and allow her to take her final exams over the summer.

I was curious to learn how the Kramers came out on this issue.
Interestingly, it was Charlotte who wanted to keep Jenny home and
under wraps, and Tom who wanted her to "get back on the horse." I
wondered if Charlotte's real motivation had to do with the fact that
Jenny did not look well at this point. In addition to the weight loss,
she was pale, almost gray in color. She had dark circles under her
eyes that can come from painkillers. And, overall, she had lost her
"verve," her bounce, her smile. I think Charlotte would have seen,
had she been honest with herself, that she didn't want anyone to see

Jenny until the rape had been erased from her appearance the way it had been erased from her mind.

Charlotte won this fight as well.

The Kramers took a summer house on Block Island. It was a big sacrifice for Charlotte, who had to give up her spot on the pool committee at the club, but it had been her idea, a way of pressing the "reset" button. I imagine it was also a welcome break from one another. The fault lines in their relationship had now been stressed, and both of them feared the fracturing that seemed imminent. Tom came and went on weekends, then spent two weeks there in August. Lucas attended a local summer camp. He had been told about the attack (the word "rape" was not used), and he had not given it much thought beyond the impact it might have on his life. That is very normal for his age. Jenny finished her schoolwork and exams to complete tenth grade. She invited Violet to come for a week. They went to the beach and celebrated her sixteenth birthday. There were some smiles. Tom saw them as forced. Charlotte believed they were genuine, and as it had become her job to watch over Jenny carefully, journaling her moods, her eating habits, her disposition, her sleep, she felt very in tune with her daughter's emotional recovery. In either case, the summer ended without incident. Of course, this was just the calm before the storm.

Jenny was told about the rape by the counselor and psychiatrist at the hospital before her release. There had been very little follow-up with any mental health professionals. No therapy, no counseling other than routine checks. It had been recommended, but both Charlotte and Tom were against it. For Charlotte, what was the point of talking about the rape when they'd gone to such trouble to forget it? For Tom, who had not been in favor of the treatment in the first place, therapy sounded like another way of avoiding what needed to be done—and that was to find the rapist.

When the professionals and the Kramers convened at the start of the school year, there was a consensus that the treatment had been enormously successful. Jenny did not remember the rape. She had returned to her normal eating and sleeping routines. Her parents were hopeful she would join the flurry of college preparation that dominates junior year—SATs, AP classes, volunteer work, and sports. She showed no signs of PTSD, no flashbacks, no nightmares, no fears of being alone, and no physical reactions when she was touched by others. Her case was deemed so successful that a military doctor from Norwich, who was conducting an ongoing study of the treatment for combat protocol, had asked for her records.

There was just one thing—and that was the carving.

How was school?

Charlotte Kramer asked Jenny the question one evening in the following winter, eight months after the rape. The question broke an uncomfortable silence that was, apparently, present at any dinner when it was just the three of them. On this Monday night like the others all season, Lucas was at hockey practice. He was showing himself to be a natural athlete, and his mother had enrolled him in the holy trinity for suburban Connecticut—football in the fall, hockey in the winter, and lacrosse in the spring. This left Charlotte, Tom, and Jenny alone to bear each other's company, something that had not been easy since the rape. Without Lucas's adolescent chatter about the state of the boys' bathroom at school, which of his friends liked a girl, or his flawless sports performances, the silence that had infected their house was always sitting at the head of the table.

Jenny recalled that the dinner was her favorite, a roasted chicken, rosemary potatoes, French green beans. But she had no appetite—something she had been hiding from both her parents. She swallowed a small bite of food, then answered, *Fine.*

Her father stared at her. I'm quite certain he was unaware of this, but Jenny said he'd been doing it since they returned from Block Island. She said she could feel him studying every muscle of her face for clues. She became acutely aware of her expressions, knowing each one would result in some conclusion. Was that a slight smile at the corner of her mouth? Maybe something good had happened today. Was that a twitch in her eye? A grimace? Was she feeling annoyed by their questions like every teenage girl at every table everywhere? And mostly was there anything there to evidence the unrest that she had not been able to chase away? She had become very adept at hiding it.

She looked up to give him what he wanted—a benign smile. He smiled back, and when he did, Jenny said she could see the anguish that had lived in his eyes since that night in the woods. She wondered if he saw hers, too. If he did, they both still smiled at each other and pretended not to see.

What Jenny did not know was that her father was not studying her face. He was staring at her face, that part is true, but only to mask the fact that he had again noticed her hand twisted behind her back, rubbing the small scar where she had been engraved like a trophy.

Her mother continued the conversation.

I saw the cutest dress at Taggert's today! Maybe Saturday we can go and look at it? Unless you have plans with a friend? Any plans, sweetie?

Jenny believed, and I think she was mostly accurate, that her mother had moved on quite nicely. Though her frustration with the tension that Jenny and her father created could be deciphered by the slightly higher pitch her voice took on in moments like this one, she was living her life as she had before. Busy, social, upbeat. Yoga classes, luncheons, volunteer work at the school. She never noticed Jenny rubbing the scar, and even after it was finally discussed in the open, she claimed that she could not recall the behavior.

Jenny was not consciously aware of this behavior either, though Violet had asked her about it several times. It seemed to be akin to nail biting, or thumb sucking in small children. Something in her subconscious sent a signal to her hand to reach back for that place where she had been carved. I believed this to be the first indication that the treatment had not been as successful as the professionals believed.

The story of what happened that night in the woods had been carefully crafted, and the carving had not been one of the chapters. Everyone knew Jenny had been raped. No one knew for how long, or in what manner. Her memory loss was ascribed to shock and emotional trauma. This is the story Charlotte told. Tom said nothing to anyone, which he could get away with, being a man. And Jenny had no story to tell at all, except that she had received a treatment to make her forget. She had been uniformly diligent in keeping this to herself.

As tidy as everything had become, a different kind of monster had entered Jenny's mind and body, stealing everything good and putting in its place a gnawing anxiety that had become quite severe.

Sweetie? What do you say?

Her mother wanted to shop for a pretty dress. Her father glared at her mother. No one spoke of that night; but from how Jenny described things, it seemed as though that night could be heard on every breath that left their bodies. Her father, she knew, regretted what they had done to her—making her forget. He wanted revenge, justice, something more than what they had, which was, even after all this time, nothing. But her mother never looked back. To use the analogy I gave earlier, the house had been repaired, and that was that. Given the choice between the tension that stayed within the walls of their fixed-up house and Jenny remembering that night, Charlotte was happy to take the former.

Jenny had heard their fights from her room at night—fights that would leave her father in tears and her mother sounding "disgusted" and calling him "weak." She felt that all of this was her doing, from her inability to exorcise the monster and go shopping for dresses. She felt destroyed inside. And she felt she was destroying her family. Jenny had not noticed the fault lines that were there all along. Children never do.

She answered her mother. *Sure, Mom. That sounds good. Maybe we can get lunch first.* She forced another bite of food into her mouth.

Charlotte smiled. *Great!* Then she looked at Tom with smug satisfaction that things were all better.

When Jenny had eaten enough to convince them, she excused herself from the table. She took her plate to the sink and made a comment about needing to get online to chat with her friends.

She went to her room.

I think I've described Jenny in some detail. What have I left out so you can picture her? Long blond hair. Blue eyes. Slender and athletic. Her face was somewhere between youth and maturity—the cheekbones had started to protrude more visibly; her nose was becoming more angular. She had freckles and one small dimple on the right side of her mouth. She spoke eloquently, without the usual "um's" and "uh's" that teenagers use. And she was very natural in her use of eye contact, which is a skill that must be learned. Some people look too long before breaking away to look elsewhere. Others don't look long enough. She had it just right, which is something we grown-ups take for granted, as we have all—most of us, anyway—mastered this social acclimation.

Although she had lost her innocence (for lack of a better expression), she was still quite lovely and sweet. She described her thoughts like this. Her tone was flat and she was surprisingly unemotional.

I sat on the edge of my bed and started looking around. There

*were all these familiar things, things I had picked out or helped dec-
orate. I have rose-colored walls. They're not pink, because they
have too much red in them. That's what the lady at the decorating
store said. I can't remember the name of the paint color, but it's
basically a blush rose. The bookshelves are bright white and I have
all these books on them, though I don't really like to read much
anymore, and not just because of what happened. I stopped reading a lot when I was twelve. I think it's because I have so much required reading now, being in high school. And they used to have
reading contests, which they don't have in my grade. So most of the
books are either for school or they're really babyish.*

*I also have a collection of stuffed animals. I still pick one up from
every new place I go to. Well, I guess that's not really true anymore.
I didn't get one in Block Island. I can't explain why. I know why, but
I don't know how to explain it. If I had to explain it, I would say
that I felt like doing things that I used to do felt like a lie, like I was
trying to pretend I was someone I wasn't anymore. Like wearing
something blue because you used to like blue and you think you
still should like it, but you just don't now. Does that make sense? I
didn't like doing anything I used to do. I just did them, you know,
went through the motions, because I felt like if I didn't, then everything would just fall apart. Sitting on my bed with all these things
I used to love but not loving them anymore, I just wanted to set them
all on fire. That's when I knew I was never going to be all right again.*

She went on to explain her decision. It's shocking to me that
people ever make this choice. But I am not a religious person, so for
me, the only hope lies with living. Of course, the words "teenager"
and "choice" should not be in the same dictionary.

This is where I grow frustrated with the general lack of knowledge about the teenage brain. There is a reason teenagers shouldn't
drink or do drugs or have sex—or drive or vote or go to war. And it's

not because we tell them not to, or even because they're too "inex-
perienced" to make good decisions. The teenage brain is not fully
developed. It's hard to imagine this when their bodies seem so mature. I've seen sixteen-year-old boys with beards and body hair and
buff arm muscles. They look twenty-six. And girls with full breasts
and wide hips and enough makeup to work a Vegas trade show. I
won't even get started on the fights I used to have with my daughter
about what she tried to leave the house wearing, or with my son, who
swears he's not going to pick up six friends on the way to a football
game and try to buy beer with fake ID cards.

   In spite of their physical appearances, if you could look inside their
brains, you would not find a grown-up within a hundred miles. It is
not inexperience that leads them to make bad decisions. They simply
don't have the equipment. Consider Jenny's thoughts on that night
as she sat on her bed:

   *I closed my eyes and just let the monster in. I pictured him in my
mind. He was like a blob of darkness, and I couldn't really see his
shape, because it changed as he moved. But I could see the rough-
ness of his skin, with craters and bumps. I remember feeling him inside my stomach. It was like an explosion of that feeling when you're
really nervous, like right before a track meet, when I'm waiting for
the gun, but a million times worse. I just couldn't take it. I started
rubbing my scar. I remember doing it that night. I couldn't stop. I
wanted to scream, but I knew that wouldn't help. I had done that a
lot of times since the rape. I would tell my parents I was going for
a run and then I would run, but only until I was far from the house
in the field behind the tennis courts at the park. And then I would
scream and scream. As soon as I was done, like everything else,
running, sleeping, getting drunk or high—as soon as I was done, it
would come back. I wanted to peel myself off of me. This had been
going on for almost eight months. It was just too long.*

Jenny had started taking substances to relieve her anxiety. It had initiated with alcohol and progressed to marijuana and pills. The pills she would get from her friends' bathrooms—anything she could find. She'd been through all her own Oxycotin, even after the physical pain was gone. Her parents didn't know, which is surprisingly common. They had noticed the change in her friends and a fairly drastic decline in her grades, but they were "giving her some slack."

It is unfortunate—no, unforgivable—that the professionals who advocated this treatment for Jenny—or anyone, for that matter—failed to consider the following: that regardless of whether or not factual events are filed in our memories, and even if, at the time of filing to long-term memory, the emotions have been muted by morphine, the physical reaction that is experienced is programmed into our brains. The Benzatral does not erase it. I can explain it as simply as this: If you were to touch a hot stove and burn your hand, but later were made to forget how you got the burn, your body would still have the fear of being burned. Only it would not be activated only by heat, or a red-hot burner on a stove. It would come and go at its leisure, and you would have no idea how to stop it. This is why traditional PTSD therapy involves a process of pulling memories from storage and reliving them in a calm emotional state. Over time, the emotional connection to the factual memory begins to change, to lessen, so that remembering the trauma becomes less emotionally painful—and the emotional pain itself can be reduced But, of course, this is hard work. How much easier to just erase the facts? Like those vibrating belts from the 1950s that claimed to burn off fat without exercise or diet. Trauma cannot be cured by a pill.

Jenny had no memory of her rape, but the terror lived in her body. The physical memory, the emotional response that was now programmed into her, had nothing to attach to—no set of facts to place it in context. And so it roamed freely within her. The only tangible thing that was left from the rape was the scar from the carving.

It is easy to say that she should have sought help. But she is a teenager. And to her teenage brain, eight months was "too long."

She went to her bathroom, opened the drawer beneath her sink. She took out a razor, a pink disposable. Using the tools from her nail kit, she pried it open until the blades popped out. She set them on the sink counter, then returned to her bed, where she sat. Waiting.

Chapter Five

I feel I've gotten ahead of myself. Let me go back just a bit.

Tom Kramer was in his own kind of hell. The feeling that he had failed to protect his daughter haunted him day and night.

It was completely irrational. We can't watch our children every second of every day, and bad things happen. That's reality. As a society, we have gone through various trends of protective parenting. It seems to me that it was the proliferation of information over the Internet that resulted in the last wave. Any abduction, any molestation, any sexual misconduct, pool drowning, sledding accident, bike crash, or choking incident was instantly known by every parent from Maine to New Mexico. It felt as though these incidents were on the rise. There were campaigns and infomercials, new safety products and warning labels. Babies could no longer sleep on their tummies. Kids could no longer walk to school or wait alone at the bus stop. It makes me laugh to think of my mother *ever* driving me down the street and parking behind other cars to wait with me for the bus. She wasn't even out of bed when I left for school as a child. But that's what people do now, isn't it?

There has been some backlash, the "free range" movement, admonition of "helicopter" parenting. The conversation is starting to shift from the danger to children from negligent parenting to the damage done to those who are overprotected.

It's all just noise. If someone really wants to hurt your child, he's going to find a way to do it.

The summer after the rape, Tom became obsessed with finding the rapist. With his family gone to Block Island, he spent his time looking. He did not see friends. He did not go to the gym. He stopped watching television. From eight to six, he worked his job, but the obsession only followed him. Being in car sales exposed Tom to new faces every day. Cranston is a modest city, but it has over eighty thousand residents. Add to that the fact that his employer, Sullivan Luxury Cars, had the only BMW and Jaguar showrooms in a sixty-mile radius, and you can understand that every day brought a new face in front of Tom Kramer, and every new face, to Tom's mind, could be the face of his daughter's rapist.

The police had done all they could, within reason. Every kid who had been at that party was interviewed. The boys, in particular, were questioned formally and at the police station. Many were accompanied by an attorney. Tom had wanted all of them examined. He'd wanted DNA and skin samples. He'd wanted their cars and rooms searched for the black mask and gloves. He'd wanted them inspected to see if any of them had shaved themselves. Of course, none of that was ever going to happen.

The neighbors were questioned as well, families who had all been at home, or out together, or out with others. Every person had an alibi. Every alibi checked out. One of the neighbors, a twelve-year-old boy named Teddy Duncan, had gone outside at eight forty-five. His dog, a curious beagle named Messi (after the soccer player), had found a hole in the fence and escaped because that's what beagles do. They dig and hunt and chase things. It is likely he was in the woods just before Jenny was raped. But he would have been on the far right side, not deep in the back, given where his house was positioned. He'd popped back out onto Juniper Road to continue his search down the street. He said he remembered seeing a parked car that looked out of place. What that meant was that it was not high end, or a massive SUV with sports magnets on the back. With some help from Parsons and Google images, Teddy was able to conclude that the car was a Honda Civic.

For most of the summer, this navy blue Honda Civic became the focus of the hunt for the Fairview rapist. Records from the DMV were cross-checked with sex offender registries and other criminal records. There were thousands of blue Civics in the state of New York. And Teddy Duncan only "thought" the plates were New York white and blue. Incidentally, before your mind starts to go off in the wrong direction, Teddy found the dog at a neighbor's house and was back inside his own house by nine fifteen. And he is twelve.

Detective Parsons did an adequate job, given his skill level. He was not lacking enthusiasm in the beginning, and indeed seemed "civilian" in the way the facts of the rape piqued his interest. But his focus was always turned outside Fairview. He reached out to police stations across the region, inquiring about similar rapes—teenage girl, ski mask, no physical evidence left at the scene, blue Civic. And, of course, the carving on her back. Dozens of other rapes matched some of the fact pattern. None of them matched all of it. His colleagues in other departments promised to keep an eye out. The trouble was that the rapists who had been caught were all in prison. And the ones who were not caught could not be traced. It's hard to know how many women are raped, because it is the most underreported violent crime in the United States. But experts estimate that only 25 percent of reported rapes actually get solved. Things were not looking good for Jenny's case, and by Christmas, Tom was the sole driving force in his tireless quest for justice.

Tom's parents came for Christmas every year, and the family decided that this year should be no different. They arrived midweek, just as school was letting out. Tom's mother, Millie, was an intelligent woman with an exceptional sense of perception. This was disconcerting to Charlotte, who found it difficult to hide her secrets (we will get to that) when Millie was in town. Tom's father, Arthur, lived more in his head than in his heart. He was a retired professor from Connecticut College. He was a stoic and, in this regard, got along very well with his daughter-in-law.

Tom recalled the visit like this:

I felt like a child again, like I wanted to run into my mother's arms for a long cry and then sit on my father's lap watching a hockey game. I wanted them to tell me everything was going to be all right— my mother with some complex analysis of the situation, and my father with a look that would make me get my shit together, no matter how bad things were. They were so great with Jenny. My mother took her shopping and talked to her about the future, about colleges and careers. She asked her all sorts of questions about her activities and her friends and what she might want to do over the summer. My father was also helpful. He kept Lucas busy, took him skating one day, built a Lego in the basement. Guy stuff. But I was looking at it from the outside, you know. I couldn't be in it with them. It was too normal, too . . . calm. Inside, I was going wild. Kicking and screaming against the fate that the universe had handed my family. I would not accept it. I had failed to protect my daughter, and I would not fail at this. And yet I knew with every passing second that the chances of finding this creature were vanishing. I wanted to be a man. I wanted to feel like a man again. And I walked around silently and with a blank expression, looking like a strong man. But inside, I was a child having a tantrum. And part of me desperately needed my parents to see it.

It was during this week that Charlotte starting having her dream. She knew the origins—some wildlife documentary they'd watched a few weeks back about wolves. In one of the scenes, a lone wolf chased a lone impala through the woods to the edge of a cliff. The impala, being deft and sure-footed, slowly made its way onto the steep rocky side of the cliff, while the wolf frantically ran along the edge, looking down at his meal, so close but unattainable. He didn't give up for nearly an hour.

In the dream, Charlotte watched this scene from a distance. Though she knew the ending, each time, she relived it as though the impala might just get caught in the woods before making it to safety, or perhaps this time the wolf would venture off the side of the cliff onto the rocks and find his own footing. As it played out, always with the same ending, her heart would pound wildly and she would awaken to find herself tangled up in sweaty sheets and fear.

The dream was haunting in so many ways. The hunter and the hunted. Tom and the rapist. Injustice and Tom. The rapist and Jenny. Tom's family and Charlotte's secrets.

I asked her which character she was in the dream, the wolf who loses his meal, or the impala who cleverly escapes but will always be in danger on level ground.

I don't know. It wasn't clear in the dream. I mean, I always saw it from the distance, watching both animals. One running for its life. The other out to kill. So I can't say from any feeling or perspective I had. But, I did think about it. It tortured me nearly every night when the Kramers were here that Christmas, and it continued on and

off for weeks after they left. I suppose I could be the wolf, endanger-
ing my family and the entire life I've built. But then I think I'm actu-
ally the impala, running for my life. I do feel like that. Like I'm
always one step away from being found out. It sounds paranoid, I'm
sure, but I think Tom's mother knew. I could see it in her eyes. And I
hated her for it. I know she was helping Jenny. I should have wanted
her to stay longer. But all I could think, all through Christmas Eve
dinner and caroling and opening presents the next day and church
and another dinner, was that I wanted her to get the hell out of my
house.

Charlotte had her secrets, but I believed there was more to her dislike of Tom's parents, his mother especially. I mentioned her childhood earlier. I suppose this is a good time to elucidate, and I ask for
your indulgence.

Charlotte grew up in New London. For those of you not familiar
with this part of the country, New London is home to the United
States Coast Guard Academy and a naval sub base. The military is
strongly present. Her mother, Ruthanne, was a promiscuous young
woman who became a single mother at age twenty-three. She had
not attended college and worked at a small factory, making decora-
tive candles. Charlotte can remember vividly the smell of scented
wax that would follow Ruthanne through the front door of their
apartment after work. Ruthanne's family lived in town. Her parents,
after doing some readjustments to the dreams they'd had for their
youngest daughter, were helpful at first. But they were not healthy
folks—drinkers, smokers, verging on obesity. They were both dead
before Charlotte was ten years old. Two years later, Ruthanne finally married. His name was Greg.

This is Charlotte's first secret, and it was well kept. She did not
reveal it to me until I had earned her trust. And that was not an easy
task.

I was a beautiful girl. I had blond hair and blue eyes and my body was quite developed around that time. And my face, if you look at pictures, you can definitely see that Jenny is my daughter. My mother became the manager of the candle factory. They ran it twenty-four–seven, rotating the workers on day and night shifts. I guess they had enough customers that they needed to make all those candles. I'm sure it had something to do with the "illegals" they hired as well—maybe they knew there wouldn't be inspections at night. My mother used to talk about the two payrolls, the one on the books and the one that was cash. Greg worked on and off as a carpenter. He used to tell my mother to keep track of the cash, don't trust anyone. Especially the "illegals." He had several tattoos. One of them was on his neck. It was a snake and then some words under it. "Don't tread on me," they said. He wasn't a fan of the government. "The man" he used to call it. Anything that had any authority was "the man," like some kind of hippie. He was an idiot.

The first night it happened, my mother was at work. I was seventeen. We lived in this little shithole apartment with one bedroom and thin walls. The kitchen was nothing more than an electric burner and microwave. We didn't even have a proper oven. There was one bathroom with a tiny shower that ran out of hot water every morning because the neighbors were also "illegals"—they must have had six or seven people crammed into that place. Greg disliked "illegals" almost as much as the government. He used to walk around, talking to himself. He and my mother shared the bedroom and I slept on the sofa, so I had nowhere to go when he came out of there. I heard a lot of crazy shit coming from him.

Anyway, I would be lying if I said I didn't see it coming. Women just know. Maybe men do, too, but I'm not convinced of it. We can tell when there's a shift, when a man has decided he wants to fuck us. I've felt it with guy friends in college. I've felt it in crowded bars.

I've felt it with colleagues at work. And I felt it with Greg. I did my best to ignore him, stay out of his way. I started wearing more cloth-ing, pants instead of skirts, flat shoes, turtlenecks. It didn't matter. It never does, does it? Like I said, once a man has decided he wants to fuck you, there's no getting him off that position. So the night it happened, I had come home from work. I was a waitress at a diner a couple of nights a week. I remember being really upset about a cus-tomer. I truly can remember every minute of that night—how this customer yelled at me for bringing him pie with ice cream on it when he'd said no ice cream. He was right and I said I was sorry, but he asked to see my manager, kept yelling, wanting his meal for free. I started to cry. I thought I was going to be fired. My boss told me to go home. God, it sounds so stupid now. It turned out the guy did this every time to try to get a free meal.

"That would be upsetting to any seventeen-year-old," I told her.

I suppose. The point is, I came home crying. Greg was there. We sat on the couch and he listened to me talk for a long time. He got us each a beer. He told me everything would be okay. And I actually felt comforted by him. I let my guard down.

The rest of the story requires some graphic detail, but I believe it is important. I apologize if it is hard to read.

Greg smiled at her and stroked her hair. I imagine he had con-vinced himself that she wanted him as well, even behind the turtle-necks and the long pants. People believe what they want to believe. Her heart started to pound wildly, but she didn't move. He stroked her face. He moaned. It sounded like the word "ahhhh." He studied her eyes like a lover. He reached under her shirt and touched her breast. He moaned again and she felt his hot breath on her face as he leaned in to kiss her.

Charlotte remembers feeling frozen. He had comforted her and she wanted more. Not like this. Not with her body. But that was all that was on the table, so she remained still, frozen between her need to be comforted, to be loved, and her repulsion. She said he looked like a wild animal who had caught its prey. Exactly—the impala and the wolf. He bit her earlobe, hard, and reached his hand inside her pants and between her legs. He leaned her back until they were lying together on the sofa. She could feel his erect penis against her thigh. His finger went inside her. It felt good, like nothing she had ever experienced before. Charlotte had not yet kissed a boy.

You're wet, he said, laughing. *You're wet, you little whore.*

He seemed then to have the strength of two men and the arms of an octopus as he reached for her hair and slid off her pants, so quickly, like he had superhuman abilities. His knees were between hers. His erection on her stomach. And then, slowly, he teased her thighs apart and slid down, his erection running along the inside of her thigh. She remembered the "ahhhhh." His hip bones pressed into hers as he penetrated her. And when it was over (apparently in a matter of seconds), he pulled out of her and positioned his body so she was up against the back of the couch. He kissed her neck and moaned. Then he manipulated her clitoris with his fingers until she had an orgasm, which happened even through the repulsion. The body is a machine. We forget that sometimes.

They became secret "lovers." The need in Charlotte that was filled by these encounters eclipsed her conscience, her morality, her will. Greg bought her gifts and took her to the movies. They exchanged looks at dinner and "made love" on the sofa when Ruthanne was working the night shift. Charlotte knew it was wrong, and she was still, in many ways, disgusted by Greg. But, as she explains it, she could not stop herself.

I am ashamed of this. But it's the truth. Feeling a human body that close to me. Feeling skin against my skin. Being kissed and hugged and held. And then there was the sexual pleasure, which I could not control. I don't know. Maybe it was about the sex. Maybe I was a little whore. But at the time, it felt like love.

It took about six months for Ruthanne to admit to herself what she was seeing and feeling when she was in their company. By that time, Greg was fully unemployed and reliant on his wife. I imagine there was never any doubt about what would happen, though to Charlotte, it felt like her heart had been torn from her chest.

Ruthanne sent her daughter to live with Aunt Peg in Hartford. Peg was older than Ruthanne by six years and had managed to land a husband in the insurance business. They had three children, all away at boarding school, and they reluctantly agreed to do the same for their niece. Charlotte never went home again.

Tom did not know about her life with her mother and Greg.

You can understand now Charlotte's need to repair her house. I imagine there are those of you thinking more of this, that perhaps Charlotte's insistence on giving Jenny the treatment was because she had something in her past that was sexually perverse. But you would be wrong. Charlotte saw that night on the sofa as a seduction, an act of desire and the beginning of a love affair. Still, she understood that her relationship with her stepfather was "unconventional" and "morally questionable." It is for those reasons that she did not share this story with anyone—not even her husband.

But this is not the secret that Charlotte feared her mother-in law could see.

Chapter Six

Getting back to Jenny and the night she sat on her bed—

Tom's employer was Bob Sullivan. Bob owned twelve car dealerships throughout the state of Connecticut and had a net worth of over twenty million dollars. His face could be seen on any number of billboards on I-95 from Stamford to Mystic, and throughout every town that still allowed them. You would remember seeing him up there, his full head of black hair, determined eyes, big white smile, and rounded nose. Bob Sullivan was a self-made man, the kind whom magazines liked to write about. The kind who was so bursting with himself, it seemed a miracle he didn't explode like a struck piñata and litter confetti across the sky. Bob Sullivan lived in Fairview. He had a "plus-sized" wife and three sons who were being groomed to run the family business. He always drove the latest model of something, BMW, Ferrari, Porsche. He ate a paleo diet and drank red wine without constraint. He was generous but also ambitious, with his sights set upon a seat in the state legislature.

And he was having an affair with Charlotte Kramer.

We tend to think we know why people have affairs. Their marriage is bad, but they can't leave because of the kids. They have sexual needs that aren't being filled. They're victims of seduction, their self-control overcome by human desires. None of these were true for Charlotte.

Charlotte Kramer was two people. She was the Smith graduate with a degree in literature. She was the former assistant editor of *Connecticut* magazine and now the stay-at-home mother to two lovely children, the wife of Tom Kramer, whose family were scholars and teachers. She was the member of the Fairview Country Club who was known for her impeccable manners and extensive vocabulary. She had built her house carefully, and it was a good, moral, and admired house.

No one knew the other Charlotte Kramer, the girl who'd slept with her mother's husband and was forced to leave home. No one knew that her relatives were uneducated alcoholics who lived hard and died young. She was the girl who took off her clothes every night for a man nearly twice her age who smelled of cigarettes and poor hygiene. No one knew any of this—except for Bob Sullivan. Charlotte had put that girl in a cage. But over time, that girl had started to rattle the bars until she could no longer be ignored. Bob Sullivan was Charlotte's way of recognizing her, of keeping her calm in her imprisonment. It was her way of being whole as she lived half a life as Charlotte Kramer of Fairview.

When I'm with Bob, I'm that girl again. That dirty girl who gets turned on by bad things. Bob is a good man, but we're both married, so what we're doing is bad. I don't know how to explain it. I have worked very hard to live a "right" life. Do you know what I mean? To not think the bad thoughts and stop myself from having the bad behavior. But it's always there, this craving. Like a closet smoker, you know? Someone who's mostly quit and who would sooner die than have the world know she smokes, but then she sneaks one precious cigarette a day. Just one. And that's enough to satisfy the craving. Bob is my one cigarette.

You may judge Charlotte Kramer for her one cigarette. For having secret cravings that she cannot control. For not telling the whole truth. For not letting her husband know his whole wife. And for your judging of Charlotte Kramer, I shall have to judge you a hypocrite.

No one, not one of us, shows the whole self to any one person. And if you think you have, then ask yourself these questions: Have you ever pretended to like something awful your wife cooked? Or told your daughter she looked pretty in an ugly dress? Have you made love to your husband and faked a sigh as your thoughts ran elsewhere—to your grocery list, perhaps? Or praised the mediocre work of a colleague? Have you ever told someone everything would be all right when it wouldn't be? I know you have. White lies, black lies, a million lies a million times every day, everywhere, by every one of us. We are all hiding something from someone.

This may cause you to feel disheartened. Maybe it will make you pause when your wife tells you she believes you'll get that promotion, or your husband assures you that you are well liked on the PTA. The truth is, you will never know the truth, and if you did know, you would probably be fighting to save your marriage. I may appear a renegade. A miscreant. But no relationship can survive the naked truth, the whole truth. No. Once a couple have confessed their true feelings to each other, whether in private or in couples therapy or even to friends with big mouths, the game is over. Don't you see? Don't you know this in your heart of hearts? We love people for who they are and how they make us feel. We can usually tolerate their faults and even keep them to ourselves. But once we see any reflection of ourselves in their eyes that is not the one we want to see, that we need to see to feel good, the backbone of the love is broken.

Tom was never given a chance. No reflection Charlotte saw in his eyes could ever be trusted, because he knew only the one Charlotte who had been revealed to him. Bob Sullivan, and only Bob Sullivan, knew them both.

Charlotte and Bob met during the day in the small pool house at the very edge of the Kramers' yard. There was a dirt road that was used by the pool company and mostly concealed by trees. Even in the winter, it was possible for Bob to park and not be seen from the road. The yard was fenced. They had been very careful. They both had a lot to lose.

Jenny sat on the bed that night her mother made rosemary chicken, unable to stand herself for one more minute. She heard her mother leave to pick up Lucas. She heard them come home. She tried to wait for her parents to go to bed, but they had another one of their "talks" that would not end. She went to the stash of pills she had collected from the bathrooms of her friends' parents, and took a small white one. Those were always Xanax or lorazepam or Valium. She didn't know them by these terms, but I recognized them from the description she gave, both of their physical appearance and the effect they had on her when she took them. Twenty minutes later, she was asleep.

The next morning she went to school on the bus. Her mother waved good-bye. She went to homeroom and Chemistry and History. At lunch, she started to walk home.

I have said that Bob Sullivan was running for the state legislature. This is why his wife, Fran, hired the investigator to follow him and collect evidence. I have found that people know when something is not right. Even if the intimacy has already disappeared from the marriage, the other changes are simply too difficult to conceal. Happiness, in particular, does not like to hide in the shadows. In Bob's case, it was simply that his wife knew him too well.

That afternoon, after Jenny had walked home, Charlotte met Bob in the pool house. It was not a large structure—a twelve-by-twelve changing area with an attached bathroom. There was a sofa and tile floor, sliding doors with shades, and some shelves for towels and sunscreen and various pool things. And a small, sound-activated recording device installed by Fran Sullivan's investigator.

This is what it recorded:

[door closing, shades rattling, female voice laughing playfully]

"Shhh, come here, gorgeous."

[kissing sounds, heavy breathing]

"How much time do you have?"

"Half an hour, so take off your clothes and get on the floor."

[more laughter, sighs, sound of clothing being removed]

"You want my mouth today, don't you? You want me to lick you?"

"Yes."

[female sighs, male moans]

"If you were my wife, I would eat you for dinner every night."

[female sighs, arousal]

"Wait, stop. . . ." [female voice, worried]

"What?" [male voice, alarmed]

"The bathroom door . . . It's closed, but under the door . . . I think the light's on." [female voice, whispering]

[rustling, then silence]

[loud female scream]

"Oh dear Lord! Dear Lord!" [male voice, terrified]

[female screams]

"Help her! My baby! My baby girl!"

"Is she alive? Oh shit! Shit!"

"Grab a towel! Wrap her wrists, tight!"

"My baby!"

"Wrap them! Pull! Tight! Oh dear Lord! There's so much blood—"

"I feel a pulse! Jenny! Jenny, can you hear me! Hand me those towels! Oh dear Lord, dear Lord, dear Lord!"

"Jenny!" [desperate female voice]

"Call 911! Jenny! Jenny, wake up!" [male voice]

"Where's my phone!" [female voice, shuffling]

"On the floor! Go!" [male voice]

[footsteps, shuffling, female voice speaking to 911, giving address, hysterical]

"You have to go! Right now! Go!" [female voice]

"No! I can't! Dear Lord!"

Charlotte had trouble speaking about that afternoon. But, one morning, after I had found my way around the barricade, she gathered herself and managed to convey the following:

Bob was a hero when we found Jenny bleeding in that bathroom. I told him to leave after I called for help, but he refused. He didn't care. In that moment, I saw a man no one else sees. He may be greedy and whatever else people say, but he risked everything to save my child. He ripped a towel in half, slid it around her wrist. He told me to grab an end and pull. The towel was thick, and it was hard to get it tight. He screamed at me, "Pull!" and I did and finally it was tight and he made a knot. We did the same to the other wrist. God, we were both covered in blood. Soaked in it. My feet were slipping on the floor. When we had done both wrists, I called 911. I told him to leave but he refused. I cradled her head in my lap. I started to cry, not like before with the screaming cries, but just tears, you know? Bob was crying as well. He looked from my face to Jenny's face, back and forth like he didn't know which one was causing him more pain. He stroked Jenny's face and then he looked at me and stayed looking.

He said, "You listen to me! She is going to make it! Do you hear me? She will!" We heard the sirens coming. I yelled at him again to leave. I begged him. He kept saying "No!" but finally he understood. I didn't care about his career or his wife or his reputation. All I cared about at that moment was Jenny and my family. He could not be there when the police arrived. He cried harder as he stood up, stepping around the blood. "I love you," he said. And then he left.

Jenny did survive. And that is where I come in.

Chapter Seven

My name is Dr. Alan Forrester. I am a psychiatrist. In case you are unaware of the various credentials that exist among mental health professionals, I am the kind that went to medical school. I am a medical doctor, an M.D., graduated from Johns Hopkins University summa cum laude. I completed my residency at the New York–Presbyterian University Hospital of Columbia and Cornell. In my twenty-two years of practice, I have received numerous awards and distinctions, but I find no sanctuary in paper certificates, the kind you have undoubtedly seen hanging on the walls of your own doctors' offices. Cream stock, Latin words written in calligraphy. Fine wooden frames. They remind me of the trophies my son used to collect after each sports season. Cheap and reflective of nothing more than the need to secure future enrollments. Nothing attracts customers like the promise of an award. They are advertisements, and those who display them publicly are nothing more than human billboards.

Mine is a profession of constant challenges. Whatever has been achieved is, by definition, in the past, and it will likely have no bearing on the successful treatment of the next patient who walks through my door. Yes, it is true that experience makes us better at our various trades, and mine is no different. I am certainly a more capable diagnostician now than I was at the start of my career. But I have found that the diagnosis is the easy part. It's the treatment—the careful, balanced, meticulous management of pills and therapy—that poses the most significant challenges and requires as much humility as skill. Every brain is different. And so must be every course of therapy. I never presume to know what will work. And by "work" I mean help, because that is what we aim to achieve—the helping of a human being to escape the pain inflicted by his own mind.

You may conclude me a braggart, but I have been successful in helping every one of my patients with a single exception. This has been true in both my private practice at 85 Cherry Street in Fairview as well as my more gritty work at the men's correctional facility in Somers.

I am the only practicing psychiatrist in Fairview. The doctor who administered the medication to Jenny Kramer, Dr. Markovitz, lives in Cranston and does not provide therapy in private practice. There are far more psychologists, social workers, therapists, and the like in our town, but none of them can prescribe drugs, and none of them is trained in psychopharmacology. That is the first reason the Kramers employed my services.

The second reason is my work in Somers. Once a week, I travel upstate to volunteer a full day (eight hours that would otherwise be billable at four hundred dollars each) to treat mentally ill criminals at Connecticut's Northern Correctional Institution. This is a level five maximum security institution. So you are not confused, the men at Somers have been convicted of crimes and sentenced to prison. Some of them also happen to be mentally ill. Criminals who are found not guilty by reason of insanity are not sent to prison. They may face their own hell confined to state mental hospitals. Sometimes they are released after rather minimal and insufficient treatment. The irony is that there does not exist a perfect correlation between the degree of a criminal's insanity and his ability to utilize an insanity defense. An otherwise "sane" man who slays his wife's lover in the heat of the moment may be deemed temporarily insane and have a defense under the law, while a serial killer (all of whom, I would insist, are clinically sociopathic) will wind up on death row. Yes, yes, it's all more complicated than this. If you are a criminal attorney, you are probably jumping up and down in protest of my oversimplified rantings. But consider this: Was Charles Manson not insane for ordering his cult to murder seven people? Was Susan Smith not insane to drown her children? Even Bernie Madoff—was he not insane to continue his Ponzi scheme after he had made more money than he could ever spend?

Insanity is just a word. The men I treat are violent offenders, and they have illnesses ranging from depression to severe psychosis. I provide them with traditional "talk" therapy, though not the amount that is needed, and with medication. The prison would prefer me to focus on the drugs. In fact, the prison workers would let me medicate the entire population living within its walls if such a thing were allowed. Sedated prisoners make for easy prisoners. But, of course, it is not allowed. You can understand, though, why they are eager to send me anyone who meets their criteria. Hour after hour, they come and they go from a line outside the guarded metal door. Sometimes the line grows throughout the day and I feel the urge to cut the sessions short so I can get to all of them. I'm sure I do, and this weighs on my conscience. I see their faces on the long drive home, the ones I can't get to that week, and also the ones I sent away in haste with a few pills.

The bean counters come each quarter to scrutinize the spending on the prescriptions, but they can't argue with my rate. As unpleasant as it is to pass a day with violent offenders, I believe I am serving a vital role. Our prisons are overflowing with the mentally ill. Whether the illness led them to commit their crimes, or the prison environment created their illness, is not always easily determined. And for my purposes, largely irrelevant. In any case, I understand the criminal mind.

The third reason I was chosen to become involved with Jenny Kramer has to do with a young man named Sean Logan. I will get to that shortly.

After slicing her wrists open, Jenny awoke in the middle of the night. Her father was in the room and had fallen asleep in a chair. From her description of this moment, there was never any doubt in my mind that she had fully intended to end her life.

My eyes were suddenly open and I was seeing the curtain again. It's light blue and it hangs on metal rings from this bar that goes around the room in the ICU. They put me in the same room where I was the night they gave me the treatment. The night I was raped. I hate saying that. They tell me I should say it—and think it—because it will help me accept it and I guess get better. But it hasn't, right?

Jenny lifted her bandaged wrists in the air.

Whatever they gave me to sleep was still sort of there, so I felt pretty good. Like I was high.

"Like when you take the pills from your friends' houses?" I asked her.

Yeah. Then all these thoughts came at once, like a stream of bullets. I'm dead. I'm alive. This whole year never happened—it's still the night of the rape. I felt relief that this year had been a bad dream. But then I felt horrible that I would have to live it all again. And that made me come back to the most obvious thing, which was that

I had cut myself. And then more thoughts fired out at me. It was like this shock that I had done that, and even relief that it hadn't worked, because I must have been crazy to want to do it. But then all the reasons that had made me do it rushed in, and I was like, oh yeah, I wasn't crazy. I had reasons, really good reasons, and they're all still here. The bad stuff that I feel every day, all the time, was still there. It was like swimming up from the bottom of the pool and popping out of the water to find yourself exactly where you started before you dove in. You know what I mean? I was exactly where I was before. I tried to move my arms onto my stomach because that's what I do when I think about it, about the bad stuff I feel, but my arms were tied to the bed rails. Then I just thought how angry I was that it hadn't worked.

Jenny cried then. It wasn't the first time. But these were angry tears.

It wasn't easy, you know. I was so scared. I sat in that bathroom and I was crying and crying. I thought about Lucas mostly, and about my dad and what this would do to them. And my mom, too, though she's stronger than they are. I imagined she would be really mad at me. I almost stopped but then I told myself, just do it and get it over with! The blade was really sharp and it hurt way more than I thought. It wasn't the cutting that hurt, but the air when it went into my veins. It was like this horrible stinging and burning. I did both of them. Do you know how hard that was? With the pain of the first one, knowing how bad it would hurt again? They say you shouldn't look at the blood because it will make you try to save yourself out of instinct, but it was too hard not to look. And they were right. My heart started to pound like wild and "Stop it! Stop it!" was screaming in my head. I started looking around for ways to bandage myself, but I had removed everything before I started because of the instructions I read. I knew that would happen, that I would try to stop. I had to fight it so hard. You have no idea how hard it was. I had to close my eyes and lie down on the floor and focus on the dizzy feeling, which actually was kind of good. Like I was just letting go of everything. So I did. I just closed my eyes and ignored the voices that kept screaming at me and the burning pain. And I just let everything go. I did all of that. I went through all of that and it still didn't work.

"Are you angry?" I asked her.

She nodded, the tears flooding her eyes and running down her face.

"With whom?"

She took a while to answer. And when she did, she avoided saying the name but rather alluded to the target of her rage. *What was she doing there? Of all the places she could have been. The pool wasn't even open yet. There was still some snow on the ground. After everything! I mean, come on! Why did she have to be there?*

Jenny said none of this when she opened her eyes and saw her father. She kept her feelings to herself. But Tom Kramer had enough feelings to fill the entire hospital. He folded himself over her bed.

Thank God! I kept saying that over and over again. I tried to hold her, but she was so fragile, her delicate arms with layers and layers of bandages, tied to the bed rails. I pressed my cheek against hers, smelled her hair and her skin. It wasn't enough just to see her awake. I needed to feel her and smell her. . . . Christ, her face was so pale. It was different from the night of the attack. That night she looked lifeless. On this early morning, she looked dead. I never knew there could be a difference. But there is. There really is. Her eyes were open and she was looking at me and at the ceiling. But she wasn't there. My beautiful daughter wasn't there anymore. Dr. Baird came in with Dr. Markovitz. It was surreal, being back in the hospi-

tal with those two doctors again. I guess I had started to believe what my wife had been saying, that Jenny was better. That she would keep getting better, and that this dark moment in our lives was finally passing. I must have believed that. Thinking about it now, I must have started to take all my doubts and put them on myself. Like I was the one in the family who couldn't get past it. Like maybe I was projecting my despair onto my daughter and that she really was okay. I was the one who couldn't accept that this monster would never be found. And, God I can't believe I'm going to say this out loud. I think I was mad at her, at Jenny, for not remembering. For not being able to help the police find him and punish him for what he'd done. Is that crazy? To be so obsessed with vengeance?

"No," I assured him. "You are her father. It's instinct." I meant those words. And I fully intended to alleviate his guilt. I did so at the risk of encouraging his search for Jenny's rapist, and for this, I have some regret that I did not direct him away from embracing his instincts without reservation. An instinct may explain a reaction. But that does not mean the reaction is the best course to pursue. In any event, Tom was relieved.

That sounds right! Like I couldn't help myself! I found myself watching the news all day and every evening. I flipped between CNN, CNBC, Fox, waiting to hear about another attack. I had "rape" on a Google alert. Can you believe that? Part of me actually wanted this monster to strike again so there would be a chance to catch him. I'm a horrible person. I don't even give a shit anymore, you know? It feels good to admit it to someone, let it do whatever it's gonna do. Send me straight to hell. Send me to jail. Whatever. Being back in the hospital with those same doctors and my daughter again in the fucking ICU! Fuck it. Fuck me. I should have known she wasn't okay. I'm her father, for Christ's sake. But I know

*now from the shock I felt in that hospital that I had let myself be-
lieve it.*

What Tom didn't say on that day, but what he did finally admit to
me weeks later, was that he also vowed to stop deferring to his wife.
The first fault line had given way. The fracturing of their marriage,
their family, had begun. And so it was, on that morning after Jenny
cut herself open, that Charlotte became the new villain—both to
Jenny and her father.

This was not a surprise to me. But the art of therapy is to allow a
patient to come to his own conclusions. It must be this way, and as a
therapist, it requires great patience to nurture this process without
corrupting it. How easy it would have been for me to lead Tom to this
conclusion, that he was angry at his wife for making him believe
their daughter was recovering. A few carefully placed words. A sentence here and there. Reminders of the facts that would make this
case against his wife. It was, after all, Charlotte who insisted Jenny
have the treatment. And Charlotte who demanded they forgo therapy
and remove her to Block Island, where she would be in relative seclu-
sion. Charlotte who insisted and persisted in mimicking normalcy in
spite of Jenny's loss of interest in her life. Charlotte who reprimanded
her husband whenever he brought up the subject of their daughter's
rape. I said nothing of the sort. I was very careful. A therapist has
tremendous powers of suggestion. Tremendous powers, period.

I will not say whether or not Tom was justified in his feelings. Feelings do not require justification. On the one hand, Charlotte had
been adamant in her version of the truth. The rape had been erased
from her daughter's mind. And so it never happened. It is obvious now
to see that she was wrong. But she was not without the very best of
intentions. Nor was she entirely delusional. Dr. Markovitz had admin-

istered the drugs, and Jenny's memory had been compromised. She didn't remember the rape. Charlotte cannot be blamed for not understanding the human mind and the devastating aftereffects of the treatment. Those were just beginning to surface. And that brings us back to Sean Logan.

Chapter Eight

Sean Logan was a Navy SEAL. He'd grown up in nearby New London, the same town as Charlotte Kramer. His father had been in the navy, and his grandfather had died a decorated marine. He had six siblings, three older and three younger, making him the lost middle child. He was a beautiful man to look at. I don't care if you're a man or a woman, straight or homosexual, young or old. You could not look at Sean Logan and not be struck by his physical beauty. It was not one thing—his light blue eyes, his thick dark hair, the masculine bone structure of his cheeks and brow. These things together created a perfect canvas. But on that canvas was always painted some kind of emotion. Sean was not able to hide them. His joy, which I did not see until years later, was boundless. His wry sense of humor, infectious. He could make me laugh like no other patient I have ever treated, even in spite of my efforts to remain stoic. The laughter would erupt from my mouth like lava from a volcano. His love was deep and pure. And his pain was intoxicating.

Sean did not go to college, although he had earned a scholarship to Brown University. He was that driven, that smart. But he could not sit still within himself. We are all (most of us) at times overwhelmed by our feelings. Think about the first time you "fell in love." Or the first moment you saw your newborn baby. Perhaps you experienced profound fear in some kind of near accident, or extreme rage when someone hurt you or your family intentionally. You might go days without eating much, without sleeping through the night, without having control of your thoughts as they fixated on the source of the disruption to normal life. You might think you feel "happy" if the source of this disruption is positive—"falling in love," for example. But it is not "happiness." The disruption is created by the fear of not knowing how to assimilate this new situation into normal life, not knowing if it will stay or go. Your brain is actually in a state of adjustment, trying to figure out what it will need to do to accommodate the change in this new emotional environment. Actual "happiness" is when the relationship settles down and becomes stable. When you sleep through the night next to your new love because you know she is here to stay.

Imagine never getting to that settled place after a disruption, and instead feeling that new, powerful emotion all the time. It is not sustainable, and truly quite painful to endure.

We in my profession usually diagnose this affliction as anxiety in one form or another. Sometimes it lends itself to OCD. Other times we just call it generalized anxiety disorder. Anxiety disorders are on a continuum like all mental illness. We must have names for things so we can communicate about what we see, but it is not the same as diagnosing a physical ailment like the flu. There are no little bugs we can see through a microscope. All we have are our observations and, hopefully, intelligent deductions.

I have treated many patients like Sean, though he was an exceptional case. It can be a difficult choice to prescribe these patients with the appropriate medication. I can make them come back down to earth, but there they will remain. While the rest of us flow through normal patterns of these elevated emotions and then the return to normalcy, these patients have to choose. I suppose it's akin to addiction and the choice to be in recovery. Would you rather live a life of total sobriety or be in a constant state of inebriation? I would certainly choose sobriety.

I did not know Sean before he joined the navy. He was just seventeen years old and, as he describes himself, jumping out of his own skin. He cycled through girlfriends, drank and got high every day, even through school. His mother was overwhelmed. Two of the older siblings had returned home to live, one after graduating from college and the other after dropping out. The younger three were always in need of something, a meal or a ride or a clean shirt. His oldest sister got pregnant at twenty-three, unmarried. She sometimes dropped the baby off with her mother so she could go to her job as an office assistant. What I am trying to convey is that Sean did not know how to help himself, and there was no one else up to the task. After his senior year, he enlisted.

Military life was not a bad option for Sean. The physical demands of his training and the endless opportunities to strain his body afforded him a different kind of medication for his anxiety. Endorphins and adrenaline produced from anaerobic exercise are chemicals that cause the body to feel good. That's the simplest way to explain it. For someone with anxiety, extreme physical exertion can provide significant relief. Sean excelled, making it through the process in just over eighteen months. He did one tour in Iraq at age eighteen and returned home just after his nineteenth birthday. His parents were proud, his siblings conflicted by pride and envy. But without his regimen, and the constant natural high from being in danger, he was again reeling with his anxiety.

Have you ever done coke, Doc? He asked me this already knowing the answer. He was playful that way. *Well, you get real jumpy.*

I can still see him sitting on the couch in my office, legs straddled, hands in two fists. He began to shake.

It's like that. Like you have to keep moving some part of your body to get rid of your nerves. You can't sleep. You're not hungry. Could talk for hours about stupid shit.

"That doesn't sound enjoyable," I said.

Sean laughed. *I know, Doc. Cup of tea and a good book. We can't all be saints.*

"When did you use cocaine?" I asked.

Aw, not since tenth grade. I'm just saying that's what I felt like all the time. I'd forgotten what it was like before, you know, after being in the desert for so long. I slept like a baby there. Never thought about what was churning in my gut.

"And when you did come home, the times before that last mission?"

Fuck, man. It was like being in a cage. Like some wild animal in a zoo. I'd wake up and have like a second of peace. Then I'd feel it creeping in until I had a full belly of acid. I'd jump up and get the hell out of the house, go for a run until I was wheezing for breath. I'd kiss my ma on the cheek and grab a beer, take it to the basement to lift until my muscles were shaking. That'd do me okay for a few hours. Spent the rest of the day drinking. I don't touch the weed anymore. Can't risk it, you know?

"And Tammy, your wife? You said you met her on one of your leaves? How did she come into the picture?"

Sean smiled and winked at me. *Well, I'd put fucking right up there with drinking. Fucking and drinking at the same time—that just about got me through the day. I'd just be in some bar and then see some chick catching my eye. It was too easy. I sound like an asshole.*

But they were into it. I don't know. Never had that kind of luck in school. Maybe they felt sorry for me, having to go back.

I did not doubt one word of what he told me. Sean was a perfect cocktail for attracting women.

I guess I just got careless. Next time I came home, I had a kid and a wife.

In spite of his promiscuity, I am willing to say that I believe Sean Logan was a profoundly good man. And not simply because he married the mother of his child. Sean was a fighter. He fought for his life, for his sanity. For him, the only thing he knew that made life tolerable was being deployed, and so he came home when he was told, and he did his best to love his wife and know his child. But he feared this time—not like the men in the other stories you know, the men who are suffering from PTSD or who become addicted to the adrenaline high. Those men, for the most part, had been normal before leaving for war. For Sean, it was quite the opposite. He had sought war to escape himself.

Tammy described it like this:

I love him. Please don't doubt that. Seriously—I would die if he ever thought I didn't love him, from the first time I saw him, as stupid as that sounds, I did, I just loved him. You can't imagine what it was like that afternoon. It was a rainy day, hot and muggy. I'd gone with some friends to drink some beers and shoot pool. It was Saturday, you know? There wasn't much else to do. He was at the bar, had the whole place in fits of laughter, telling some story about some crazy thing he'd done to one of his buddies, some prank over in Iraq. He never dwelled on the bad stuff. He always wanted to make people laugh. He could lift the spirit of an entire room all at once, with one story and his enormous smile. So I walked in and he saw me. He stopped for a second telling his story, but his audience was waiting, so he continued, even though his eyes kept moving around the room, following me. I didn't know it about him then, but when he sets his mind on something, or someone, he's like a pit bull. He won't let go until he gets what he wants. And that afternoon, he wanted me.

Tammy was a pretty woman, short blond hair, big brown eyes. She was just twenty-four when I first met her, and I think she had been weathered by motherhood, but mostly by her marriage to Sean. I found it interesting that she used a pit bull as a simile in her story. Pit bulls, it is said, do not release their jaws until the animal clenched between their teeth is dead. I tried not to read too much into this. The pit bull has become a colloquial symbol, and most people don't fully understand what they're saying when they use the expression. Still, she looked as though life were being squeezed out of her. She was embarrassed to speak to me about the more intimate details of her relationship, but I felt it was important, and so I did my best to put her at ease.

Well, okay. So I guess I was flirting with him, too. I would meet his eyes and then look away. The usual things women do. It's so stupid, isn't it? Being married now, having a child. All that stuff seems ridiculous to me. But it did work. Tammy got a playful look on her face, and I could see the woman Sean saw that rainy afternoon.

When he was finished telling his story, he excused himself, took his beer and his shot of bourbon, and walked right over to our table. He had this shameless smile on his face, like "I'm here to get you to fuck me and I won't leave until I get my way." It sounds so obnoxious, but he was like a mischievous little boy and I was a complete goner. He asked me to dance. He put on a track from the jukebox— David Bowie, "Let's Dance." You know the song? "Put on your red shoes . . ." His hands were all over me, on my back, running down the side of my leg, through my hair. I had never felt that from a man before. It was like this desperate, raw need that only I could fill.

And believe me, I know anyone with a vagina could have filled it, but that's not how it felt. And even if it did, it wouldn't have mattered. After a while of dancing and drinking and laughing, he danced me closer to the small hallway that led to the back door, then outside into the alley. It was pouring rain. He started kissing me, pulling at my clothing. His face turned from playful to deadly serious. He was on a mission to satisfy this need. He looked like he would die in agony if he didn't satisfy it, and something about that just overwhelmed me. I became equally desperate to help him, to save him. And it turned me on, this power I felt I had. It was primal. I felt like an animal myself, tearing at his clothing until we'd removed enough to, you know, make it possible. He lifted me up against the brick wall of the building. It was, I don't know. I can't really describe it.

Tammy disappeared for a moment, as though she was reliving the experience. I gave her time to sit with her memories and the feelings they were evoking. She went on to explain how she'd taken him home. How they'd stayed in bed for the next two days until he had to leave for his third tour. Then she told me something that I let pass without much attention. There was much more for her to tell, and it was important to Sean's treatment that I hear the story. It was not my intention to treat Tammy. But many months later, when I became involved with the Kramers, this part of Tammy's story came rushing back into my mind.

It may seem strange to those who have not been in therapy how much intimacy is revealed in the process. I suppose this is why patients sometimes favor a therapist of the same gender, so there is less embarrassment. But there really is no need for this, no place for embarrassment in psychotherapy. I have the same reaction when my female patients speak to me about their sexual encounters as I do with the men. I am not listening out of some prurient interest, but as a clinician, a scientist. It is no different from speaking to a gynecologist or urologist. And our sexual lives are inextricably bound to our psyches.

I will make this sole confession: Hearing women reveal their sexual deceit with men has caused me to evaluate my own marriage, the intimate aspects of my relationship with my wife. It is not that I worry about the deceit. I know it is there. I have already discussed the fact that everyone hides and everyone lies. I do not expect my wife to tell me the truth about every experience she has with me in our bedroom. But I have gained insight and knowledge over the years that have afforded me the opportunity to ask the right questions at the right time, and to minimize the deceit to a tolerable measure, both for her and for myself, for my own male ego. I wish I could tell you that I go home and forget the things my female patients tell me. But that is no more possible than if I had an electrician for a patient who told me how to fix a broken circuit. We can't unlearn. It's not how we're built.

Tammy revealed to me that she did not have one orgasm during all those encounters. She said it cryptically because she is a modest person and because she was not my patient. This process was new to her, and she was a willing participant only inasmuch as it was helpful to her husband. The issue came up as we discussed the frequency of their intercourse, even for new lovers. She provided this fact by way of explanation, that perhaps she had pursued additional intercourse because she remained unsatisfied. I did not inquire further, except to ask her why she thought this had happened.

It was so intense, his need, and the way he was with me. It was so fast and powerful, even the way he kissed me. He made my lip bleed. I couldn't catch my breath. It was like I couldn't relax enough to make it happen. It would go on for an hour sometimes, and my heart would be pounding, and our skin was so wet with sweat, we were sliding against each other. I think my body spent every ounce of energy just trying to make sense of it. It was like trying to have sex while you're running a marathon. But it's different now. We know each other. I'm more comfortable. And the drugs are helping his anxiety. It's all good now. It really is. It was just a part of who he was back then.

That was where we left it. And I did not think about it again until I had a similar conversation with Charlotte Kramer over a year later. I suppose I should mention something about my work with the Kramers after they found me. I immediately began meeting with Jenny for two hours every other day. She would soon join my trauma group, and that, as you will see, would become a turning point in many ways. I saw her mother and father once a week, sometimes every other as it suited their needs. Jenny and Tom were open books. Charlotte was not. But her pain, and her guilt—both from her willful blindness to Jenny's despair and her relationship with Bob Sullivan— gave me powerful tools to dismantle her defenses.

It was perhaps three weeks into the therapy when I knew it was time. That she was hiding secrets had been obvious to me all along, and on this day, I decided to unearth them. I let a disconcerting silence come between us. I can't say how long it was. We think we know time, but in moments like this, one minute can feel like ten. It was when she nervously uncrossed her left leg from her right, then crossed the right over the left, that I finally spoke.

"Do you believe me when I tell you that I will hold your confidence? No matter what? That even the law cannot force me to betray you?"

Of course. I mean, yes. I know that.

I nodded. "Then why have you not told me?"

I did not know her secrets. And she is a smart woman. Before you begin to doubt this, it was not that I duped her into thinking I knew.

Rather, it was that she desperately wanted a reason to tell me. And so I gave her one.

I don't know. She said, *I didn't realize it was that obvious.*

It was on this day she told me about her affair. And it was on this day that I recalled the session with Tammy.

"Why do you think you're having the affair?" I asked Charlotte. We had yet to explore her past, her second secret, and the alter ego that needed to be fed. And so this question was still open.

I don't know.

I asked her if she wanted to know, if she wanted to discuss this, and if it would be helpful to her family. She was hesitant but agreeable.

"Okay," I said. "Let's start with the obvious. Is it the sex?"

She had to think about this before answering. *You know, it's strange. That's really all we do when we're together. And when we're apart, which is ninety-nine percent of the time, I find myself thinking about having sex with him. And yet, in the three years it's been going on, I haven't had one . . . you know.*

"Climax?" I said. I am used to filling in the words. Men always use the word "come." They use it routinely as though it were perfectly normal to talk about it that way. Come, cock, clit, ass, tits, pussy. Men are quite at ease with these terms. Women rarely know what words to use. They uniformly avoid the colloquial terms, but seem to find the clinical terms awkward as well. They usually pause and wait for me to rescue them. I have no problem finishing their thoughts and setting the appropriate boundaries for the conversation.

Charlotte nodded. *Yes. Not one.*

"And with Tom?"

Almost always. At least when we used to have sex. It was somewhat regular before all this started. Maybe three times a week. I think that's pretty healthy for a marriage as long as ours. Isn't it?

I nodded with a tilted head, not really agreeing but more taking a pass on the question. The health of their marriage was another topic altogether, and I wanted to stay focused on her affair with Bob.

But I don't enjoy it. I don't know when that stopped. Years ago. There's more to sex than the . . . you know. Maybe not for men. But for women, it's more than that. The dynamic between us changed somehow. It felt mechanical. With Bob, God help me, I could close my eyes right now and imagine his hands on my face and actually get a shiver down my spine.

This is where the conversation with Tammy Logan came rushing back.

"So what happens with Bob?"

It's just, oh . . . how can I describe this? I get excited and I want him. He's larger than life, his personality. Have you ever met someone like that? Someone who just dominates? He can walk into a room and take it right over. He just has this energy. And when he turns that energy my way, when we're alone, it's so intense that I lose myself in him. It is so clear in those moments that he is the man and I am the woman in this very primal way. I feel like I'm almost too excited. Like I've moved beyond the normal physical . . . you know, climax to something bigger. It's not like that with Tom. It feels awkward when I try to let go. When I try to feel that primal. It's like I can't feel him as a "man." Charlotte used her fingers to make quotations around that word.

And then I asked her the same question I asked Tammy. "But if you aren't satisfied physically, then what you are getting from him is not sexual. It's filling some other need. Is that what you're saying?" They both had the same response.

Yes. It fills a need. He's like a drug and I'm an addict.

Tammy started feeling nauseated about a month after Sean left. Her friends wanted her to have an abortion, but she couldn't get herself to do it. She wasn't against the idea on moral grounds. It was Sean, and the thought of him being with her, inside her, even though he was gone, even though she hardly knew him. She didn't have to explain it to me. You would understand if you could meet him. I can't do him justice with my words, and this is where the similarities between Bob Sullivan and Sean end.

Tammy wrote to Sean and told him she was pregnant. A few weeks later, a small engagement ring was delivered to her office, where she worked as a dental assistant. That was all. Just the ring. She wrote him back a long letter, explaining that while she loved the gesture, it was not necessary, that they could work something out. He wrote back three words on a piece of plain paper. *Yes or no?* She answered right away. *Yes.*

That is the kind of man Sean Logan is.

Still, this was not a romantic love affair. Sean returned to marry Tammy and be with his young infant son, Philip. But his anxiety, and the behavior he used to self-medicate, were not conducive to marriage and fatherhood. He had no patience with his child. And by that I don't mean that he lost his patience and was abusive. He just could not spend time with his family for more than an hour or so at a time.

I started to see that he wasn't normal. It was like he had this itch he couldn't get to and it tortured him. I wanted to just wrap him in my arms the way I did with Philip, wrap him so tight, he felt safe and would settle down. I loved him so much, but I couldn't help him the way I could help my baby. He was beyond that. I didn't understand about his anxiety back then. Neither did he. When his name came up again, we went to the base together, all of us. His mother was there, and two of his brothers. His father had said good-bye the night before. Everyone was crying, hugging him, making him promise to come home safe. I had the baby in my arms, and God help me,

*I couldn't cry. I wasn't happy to see him go, not exactly. But I was
grateful that he was leaving.*

Sean left for a fourth tour. He was on a sweep for a target in a
small village. There were eight SEALs on the mission. He was the
only one to come out. A platoon of marines found him unconscious,
his right arm blown to shreds. He was dragged to the safety of an
armored tank. His arm was amputated at a field hospital. It was there
that they gave him the treatment.

Chapter Nine

Sean Logan became my patient exactly seventeen months before I began my work with the Kramer family. He was referred to me by a physician at the Naval Health Clinic in Norwich. This is the same doctor who sought Jenny Kramer's records for her study of the treatment. She had followed Sean's case closely upon his return. She had supervised his therapy sessions, allowing the hacks assigned to his case to misdiagnose him with PTSD. The symptoms were not dissimilar. Anxiety, depression, anger, suicidal thoughts. But this young man had been given a drug protocol in the field that was new and unpredictable. It was meant to reduce PTSD, not create it. And no one bothered to factor in his history with anxiety. It was not even listed in his records.

People wonder what is wrong with our health care system that we have fallen so far behind the rest of the civilized world. People blame it on our laws, or the drug companies, on the areas that have become "socialized" or the areas that are not "socialized." Excuses, excuses. I don't care what you're getting paid or how hard you're being worked. A patient sits before you. He has lost his arm in battle. He has lost his memory of the battle. Or, more precisely, it has been stolen from him. And now he has lost himself to his own mind. Is this man not worthy of your time? Is he not worthy of you taking a proper history—the kind I know you were taught in medical school, and again and again throughout your residency? There is no excuse. None at all.

Sean was asked one question: *Have you or anyone in your family ever suffered from any mental illness?* Sean answered no. He had never been diagnosed or treated for his anxiety and had spent most of his life believing it was just "who he was." Until he came to see me.

I am angry. There is no use continuing the story without making this additional confession. I am angry that Sean Logan suffered for nine months before he was sent to me. I am angry that Jenny Kramer was given the treatment and that I was not employed to observe her in the months that followed. Surely the Kramers would have sought my help sooner had they known that right here in their little town a doctor was treating a man who had been given the same drugs and suffered as a result. What might have come to pass? I will tell you what. Jenny Kramer would have studied math instead of techniques for ending her life. She would not have taken a blade to her soft pink flesh and cut into her skin and then deeper into her veins until her blood spilled onto the floor.

Looking back on the months between the rape and the suicide attempt, it all makes sense to me now. Everyone in Fairview knew about the attack. But the use of the treatment to make her forget was not widely known. It was certainly not known to me. And yet, when I saw her around our town, the same way I had before, at the movie theater or the ice cream shop, I was surprised by her demeanor. Not that there is one way a rape victim should behave. I have treated victims of trauma for most of my career. I suppose it is odd, my work with the criminals in Somers and my work with victims of the same crimes they have committed—rape, murder, assault, domestic abuse. It makes perfect sense to me. Most of the men in Somers were victims before they were criminals. You would be surprised at how many people have been victims of trauma. Most of them (unless they have become criminals) seek help years later, when they have stopped moving and settled down into a family life. It is then, while they sit at their desks or drive their children to school, that the pain resurfaces. My practice in Fairview is thriving. The line outside the metal door in Somers grows longer each week.

I cannot pinpoint what it was about Jenny that did not ring true. Is it enough to say for now that after all my years as a psychiatrist, I know it when I see it? And while I am confessing things, I will add to the list that it bothered me. Knowing something was not right but having no business to inquire—it was not easy to sit with this. I wanted to know why no one was treating her. I wanted to know why she did not behave the way I would have expected. I wanted to know why I could not see the rape in her eyes. Not knowing was causing me to question myself and my professional competency. As angry as I was with the local medical community when I learned the truth, I was admittedly relieved that my observations had been correct. And I was beyond eager to help.

Charlotte Kramer came to see me while Jenny was still in the hospital. Dr. Markovitz had refused to release her without a course of therapy in place—a therapist on board and a plan for her care. Charlotte did not resist. Whatever responsibility any of us, including Tom and Jenny, might ascribe to her for Jenny's suicide attempt, Charlotte took it on tenfold. Soaked in her daughter's blood, she spoke to Detective Parsons about how she found her daughter. And while she managed to cover her tracks with regard to Bob Sullivan, I believe she was sincere about her feelings of remorse.

I sat with her in the family lounge. It was like déjà vu. I couldn't believe something else had happened to that poor girl. But Mrs. Kramer was different this time. I remember on the night of the rape, she was all dressed up for some dinner party. Even after hearing the news, she kept her composure. Tom Kramer was another story. Christ, was he a mess. Both times. Just a sloppy wet mess. Mrs. Kramer sat on the couch, crossed her legs, and folded her arms in a very ladylike way. But she was shaking. I remember watching her right hand as it lay over her left wrist, both of them resting on her knee. She was fighting it hard. I asked her to just tell me what happened, start to finish. She nodded and said something formal like, "Certainly, Officer." I mean, I'd been talking to this family for months, even before I found the blue Civic. Probably once every few weeks, you know, keeping them up to date on the investigation, asking about how Jenny was doing.

There wasn't much to tell before the car showed up again, what was it—ten weeks after the suicide attempt? But I knew Tom needed it, so I made the effort. I probably talked to Tom more than Mrs. Kramer, but still. There's a familiarity there now. But she addressed me like we'd just met. Anyway, she took this long breath and then . . . I'll never forget it . . . she used both hands to smooth out her blouse—this white blouse that was completely soaked in her daughter's blood. And then she reached up to her face to brush a piece of hair back across her forehead, and the blood, it just got smeared there across her forehead and she didn't even notice it. It was as if she was still going through the motions of normal behavior but she was so distraught that she didn't even see what she was doing—getting the blood all over her hands and then her face. I just wanted someone to come in and hold her until she finally let it out.

Detective Parsons continued, reading from his notes what Charlotte said to him:

She said she had seen a light on in the pool house bathroom. There's a small window and I guess she was out in the yard to check on some fallen tree branches so she could tell the landscaper what needed to be done. She caught a flash of light coming from the window. So she went to turn it off. That's when she found her daughter. She did not go into the details. She let out a little cough to clear her throat and said that she called 911 from her cell phone, which I guess she had with her, and then she wrapped Jenny's wrists in the towels. Probably saved her life. Hard to say, but at that stage, seconds counted, and it was ten minutes before the paramedics arrived. I was writing all this down in my notebook. At one point, she stopped talking. I thought she was letting me catch up with my writing, but even after I lifted my pen, she was silent. I looked up then, looked at her, and this very thin stream of tears was coming down both sides of her face. It was so odd because there was no other indication she was crying. I mean, Tom was like a contorted twisted ball of flesh, his eyes, his mouth, his brow all scrunched up and bright red. But Mrs. Kramer was just staring blankly with these little waterfalls coming down, dripping onto the bloody shirt. And she said then, when I looked up at her, and I'll never forget this either, she said, "This is my fault. I did this. And I'll fix it."

Dr. Markovitz immediately consulted with the Naval Health Clinic and the woman doing the study on the treatment. He said she had mentioned other trauma victims who had received the treatment and how she had been following their progress. She was, apparently, shocked that Jenny had tried to take her life. I find this disingenuous.

She knew full well what torment Sean Logan had suffered when he returned home without his right arm or his memory. She had followed his treatment at the clinic, the chronic insomnia, the rage attacks against his wife and in front of his son. He had withdrawn from his friends and family and cut off contact with everyone he knew in the navy. His symptoms were complicated by the underlying anxiety, which before had been self-medicated with exercise, drinking, and sex. The clinic had put him on Prozac and lorazepam, and these had muted the symptoms of the anxiety. Had he come to me before the mission where he lost his arm, I may very well have prescribed the same drugs. They could not understand why he was not getting better. But that's because they were missing two crucial pieces of information. First, his chronic anxiety predating the mission. They assumed his anxiety symptoms were a result of PTSD. Why, I might have asked them, would he have PTSD when he had no memory of the events? Wasn't that the whole reason for giving him the treatment? Infuriating. Second, they were unaware of the deleterious, anxiety-producing side effects from the treatment itself—from the dislodging of the emotional and physiological experience from the factual memories

Sean described his mental state like this. This was when he first came to me. His humor and lightness would not return for many months. He refused to wear a prosthetic. I think he wanted the world to see him as defective or damaged, because that was how he felt inside. You will surely notice the similarities to Jenny Kramer.

I lie in bed at night. The acid in my stomach is gone. The meds took that away—along with my personality, I'm told. I'm not that fun guy anymore. But I'd take that, you know. I'd fucking swallow that down and ask for another if I could stop this other thing. I look at the empty space where my arm should be, and then I close my eyes and try like all hell to remember that day. They gave me the report, but who the fuck knows? We were sweeping for this one bad guy. There was solid intel. Eight of us went in. We had air cover, and a corps unit was on its way. We moved through the streets, breaking off in pairs. The unit was ambushed right after I broke with this other SEAL, Hector Valancia. The corps found him dead next to me. Half his head got blown off. We took it from an IED. I was unconscious. Mangled arm. They got me out. Took off the arm. Then gave me the drugs. I can't blame them. I signed off on it. We all did. Shit, if someone asked you, "Hey, if you get fucked up in the field, do you want us to give you some drugs to make you forget all about it?" Fuck yeah, I do! But now, all of it is just a story. It's no more real or unreal to me as any other story. It feels like there's a ghost inside me— the ghost from that afternoon, and he's pissed off, just raging inside my body, searching for the story, not the words from the report, but the images of my buddy dying beside me, and the blood seeping from my shredded flesh, it rages for the memory of the pain that I must have felt when the bomb went off, even for a second. This ghost is a strong motherfucker. He just gets bigger every day and it's like there's no room for anything else. When I try to hold my son, when my wife tries to hold me, nothing can get in. Then there's just broken plates, a scared kid, my wife in tears. I'm a monster.

Charlotte Kramer called me after getting my name from Dr. Markovitz. As I've said before, she and her husband were eager to employ me. I met with her in my office before agreeing to take the case, although I knew I would be compelled to do so. How could I not? My involvement with Sean, my growing knowledge of the treatment, both its pathology and the potential countertreatment, my work with victims of trauma and crime and my proficiency with medications—I don't think I've ever been more suited to treat a patient than I was for Jenny Kramer.

And I will say one more thing on my proficiency treating survivors of trauma. It is an aside, really, but I was myself the target of an altercation when I was a young boy. I do not disclose this to my patients, because there must be boundaries. But there are times when they say things to me, things like *You don't know what it feels like* or *I can't explain how I feel now*, when I want to tell them that I do have some idea. Of course, few of us escape childhood without some bullying or aggression, or worse. Most of us can identify to a degree with these survivors of more serious crimes. Still, my patients cannot see me as anything less than a rock. I cannot cry with them. I cannot get angry with them. I cannot let them know they affect me in any way. They must be free to pound their fists into my gut without the fear that they will break me.

I know you have detected my soft spot for Charlotte. I recognized it myself the moment she walked into my office and sat elegantly on my sofa. Please do not misinterpret things. I am not, nor have I ever been, "attracted" to her in an inappropriate manner. It's simply that I knew, from everything about her, the way she held her back so straight, the way she spoke with a slight affectation, her neat clothing, the tucked-in blouse and pressed trousers, hair pulled so tightly in a bun, even the words she chose, that the story of Charlotte Kramer was going to be rich. I knew that it would be difficult but that I would uncover it, that she would reveal it to me, and that the extent of her emotional scars and the skill it would take to reach them would present a deeply satisfying professional challenge. I have no qualms admitting this to you or anyone else. It is no different from a lawyer relishing a complicated criminal defense. Or a builder reconstructing a home after a fire or flood. Is there empathy for the client? Of course. But legal, psychological, structural—whatever the problem the client has, the professional employed to solve it is not at fault for enjoying the task. That is why we joined the profession, is it not?

At our very first meeting, we spoke for an hour. During that time, she began to trust me to treat her daughter, and I would later use that to open her own vault of secrets. I could sense it. It is essential, and every competent practitioner has acquired the skill to do it. It requires strict adherence to boundaries, compassion, and an appropriate degree of distance. I did not flinch when she told me about the rape, the treatment, the strained year, and the attempted suicide, even though my thoughts were spinning with all the implications, which I have already described. Jenny Kramer had been a puzzle I could not solve, and now I had been given the pieces.

I met them all at the hospital the next day—Charlotte, Tom, and Jenny. I met with Lucas at my office sometime after that. He has gotten little of my attention as I recount the story. But I did speak with him and I did consult with both Charlotte and Tom frequently about how they should parent him during this crisis. It would take far too long to explore the deleterious effects events like these can have on siblings. Neglect, withdrawn love, and emotional denial are every bit as toxic as outright abuse. I made sure Lucas was spared that fate.

Jenny had been moved to the psych ward, where she was under a mandatory forty-eight-hour watch period before she could be released. There was recognition in her eyes when she saw me, and she even smiled slightly to acknowledge this. *I've seen you in town.*

She said this, and I realized that it was the first time I had heard her voice. She did not sound anything like what I'd expected. That may be a strange thing to say, but we all do this, we all impute certain missing variables to people we meet based on our preconceptions or past experiences. I was expecting Jenny's voice to be high pitched, maybe even childlike. But it was not. It was deep, slightly raspy, as you might expect from a middle-aged blues singer. It is not uncommon. Think about it—you will surely have before you one or two people from your life who have this type of voice.

She wore a hospital gown, tied in the back, and a robe her parents had brought from home. There was no sash, for obvious reasons, so it hung loosely around her in the wheelchair. I could see the white bandages poking out from beneath the sleeves.

Tom was eager to meet me. He stood and shook my hand vigorously, as though he could shake the cure for his daughter from my limbs. *We are so happy we found you.*

Tom was sincere. We all sat down and they looked at me, waiting for something brilliant to emerge from my mouth.

"I'm happy to help, if I can." I said, "But, Jenny. I have to ask you one very important question."

She nodded. Tom looked at Charlotte, who seemed to reassure him with the look she returned. They both nodded at me, and then I continued.

"Jenny. Do you want to remember what happened to you that night in the woods?"

I will never forget her face in that moment. It was as though I had solved the mystery of the universe, discovered the truth about God. She knew when I spoke these words what she hadn't known before but what was suddenly crystal clear. And her expression carried relief and gratitude so profound—I will never have a more satisfying moment in my professional career.

She nodded her head, choking back tears, but then they just exploded out of her. *Yes!* she said.

Then she said it over and over as her father hugged her, her mother wrapping her arms around herself.

Yes, yes, yes . . .

Chapter Ten

I suppose I should get to the blue Honda Civic and how it was found again in Fairview. If you recall, the Civic was spotted by a neighbor's kid on the night of the rape. He said it was parked on the street along the side that bordered the woods. He thought it had New York plates. But that was all. He could not narrow down the model year or anything else that might have helped to locate the car.

One thing I have to give to Detective Parsons is that he is very good at taking credit for things that are not exactly on his side of the scorecard. The blue Civic was one of them. Technically, Parsons was responsible for the acute awareness within the town to the importance of this car. Public notices appeared weekly in the local paper. Official police flyers were kept on community boards at every diner and coffee shop and nail salon. And Parsons reminded the force at every staff meeting. I pitied anyone who dared enter our borders with a blue sedan. There had been over two dozen false reports during the course of the year. Officers were pulled from their posts to drive by the pharmacy parking lot, or the line for the car wash, or someone's driveway, only to find a blue Chevy or Saturn or Hyundai. Not one Civic.

As you have likely ascertained, Detective Parsons worked not only for the Town of Fairview, but also for Tom Kramer. Tom's single-minded obsession with vengeance, as he put it, had stripped him of any social inhibitions, and he hounded Parsons relentlessly. And Parsons was a nine-to-fiver at heart. Some people just are, and you can't shake it out of them. He treasured his free time. He did not have a family and I did not know whether or not he had a girlfriend. Or boyfriend, for that matter. I had not been able to discern his orientation. He liked to play sports and stay fit. Recreational soccer, softball. He was an avid swimmer. Tom's demands interfered with his life. It wasn't just with the blue Civic. At Tom's insistence, Parsons and the Fairview police force had reached out across the country, not only through various computer-based systems, but through actual personal contact as well. Tom advised me once that there are about 12,000 local police agencies in the United States. He said it was his intent to have Parsons call, write, or e-mail every single one of them.

Rapists rarely strike just once. And this guy—well, he left some calling cards, didn't he? The black mask. The way he shaved himself, wore a condom. And that thing he did with the stick.

Tom spoke with a strained professional tone, like he had transformed from the victim's father to a police investigator. He did this sometimes in our sessions, particularly when he would first arrive and was bursting at the seams to give me a status report. Still, it was telling that he would not use more precise language to describe the carving on his daughter's back.

I did not learn about the carving until I began treating Jenny and her parents. Detective Parsons had given me a copy of the entire police file, and so I first came upon it in a written document. This was very disconcerting to me. The scar from the carving was the only external physical manifestation of the rape. And it was the scar that Jenny reached for when the emotional memory from that night broke free inside her. It was in our second office session that she first showed it to me. It was nothing, really. Just a vertical, one-inch straight-line discoloration to the right of her spine. It was nothing. But it was the only thing.

Getting back to Tom and the story of the Civic:

You would be shocked by the inadequacy of our country's interagency communications. No one can agree on one system, so not every agency has a system that's compatible with any one sharing service. There's no real Interpol equivalent, even after 911, when it became so clear that this type of sharing was necessary. I mean, efforts were made. But there are just too many cooks in the kitchen, twelve thousand agencies across fifty states. And there are even more that are nonlocal special forces. I get that it would be impossible to track down a hundred thousand car owners, and that even if we did, it's not like any of them would ever admit to raping a teenage girl. But this was different. You put a few guys on it, have them spend an hour each day, calling, e-mailing . . . five days a week, and it gets done, you know? Now every department has the facts, specific facts, and maybe, just maybe, something similar happened in one of their small towns. Think about that. I mean, what do Fairview cops do all day? They find clever places to hide with their speed radars. Parsons gave me a hard time at first, but then he could see I was right. An hour a day on the phone instead of catching up on Facebook. That's a small price to pay, compared to the reward. A very small price.

I have to tell you that I felt proud of Tom. I have mentioned his anemic ego, as well as his deference to his stronger-willed wife. Anytime I see that dynamic in a relationship, I am compelled to investigate the subject's childhood. My findings are not uniform, but they do tend toward a finite group of childhood experiences. Tom was no exception. I have named his type of childhood "misguided intellectualism."

If you are a parent, I'm sure your eye catches the latest fad parenting book on the bookstore shelf or popping up on your Amazon page along with every other thing the headless beast knows you need. Wrinkle cream, hair-loss gel, diet plans, Cialis. I have had more than a few good laughs comparing pop-up ads with friends at dinner parties. One of my friends is named Kerry. He's a man, but the Internet won't believe it. You can imagine the folly that results. Reading parenting books—and all self-help books, as far as I'm concerned—is the equivalent of learning math from a dog. They should be gathered and burned. Every last one.

Tom's parents are educators and intellectuals. His father taught literature at Connecticut College for thirty years. His mother worked in the alumni office. They lived and breathed academia and prided themselves on being learned. This translated into everything they did and everything they were. Much of it was benign, or perhaps even beneficial for Tom and his younger sister, Kathy. Their vacations consisted of family camping trips. They were not allowed to watch television without supervision, and only on the weekends. You can imagine the dullness of the permitted content. They were required to read ten books every summer and did not attend camp. There were no sleepovers, strict curfews, and church every Sunday, although religion was discussed in terms of theory and sociology rather than passion and faith. Everything was evaluated and analyzed, stripped of the emotional influences that could lead to the belief of an untruth, or a misguided course of action. You have known people like this. For those less disciplined, they evoke the urge to shake them senseless until some emotion is set free. They seem inhuman, even in the presence of their extremely good behavior.

What did this mean for Tom? When he brought home straight A's on his report card, there was no elation, no hugs and kisses and calls to grandparents. There were no quarters handed out for his piggy bank or extra dessert or a pass on piano practice. The paper was not hung on the refrigerator. No—it was evaluated and discussed, and Tom was reminded that his grades were a reflection of his hard work and that he should not come to think he was somehow better or smarter than anyone else. And when he sang in the school play or hit a sloppy single at his Little League game or produced a painted clay animal from art class that only slightly resembled a giraffe— everything Tom ever did was given a dispassionate and honest re- view. *You sounded a little off-key in the second chorus, Tom. You had a little luck getting to first, Tom—don't think it will happen again, you need to practice more. Well, it sure looks like you had fun mak- ing this thing.*

Yes—exactly. They were ahead of their time, weren't they? Ahead of the parenting advice that has been shoved down our throats in the last decade. We shouldn't be proud of our children; they should be proud of themselves. We shouldn't give false praise, because they will stop trusting our opinions. We shouldn't send them into the world thinking they are better than they are. This will only lead to disap- pointment. True self-confidence comes only from truthful parenting.

I have been an outlier in my rejection of these absurdities.

We are small, inconsequential beings. It is only our place in the hearts of others that fills us up, that gives us our purpose, our pride, and our sense of self. We need our parents to love us without condi- tion, without logic, and beyond reason. We need them to see us through lenses warped by this love and to tell us in every way that just having us walk this earth fills them with joy. Yes, we will come to learn that our clay giraffes were not masterly. But when we pull them out of our attics, they should make us cry, knowing that when our parents saw these ugly pieces of plaster, they felt ridiculously misplaced pride, and they wanted to hug us until our bones hurt. This is what we need from our parents, more than the truth about how small we are. We will have more than enough people to remind us of that, to give us dispassionate evaluations of our mediocrity.

It is not surprising to me that Tom felt small and acted small. Or that he married a woman who made him feel small and worked for a boss who treated him like a small man. It is our destiny to re-create our childhoods in our adult lives. Then we wonder why we're not happy. This is why I have a nice house and drive a nice car.

What I came to admire in Tom was that he did love his children beyond reason. And while he subconsciously chose to subject his own ego to ongoing degradation, he did not do the same with Jenny and Lucas. His instinct to show them how much they filled his heart had not been beaten out of him. Nor had it been injured by Jenny's rape and attempted suicide. In my mind, when I picture Tom at home, I see balls being thrown and caught, video games, laughter. He does all this with a clenched jaw and a broken heart. But he does it.

To this end, Tom was not anywhere reasonable when it came to finding his daughter's rapist. In spite of his guilt after the attempted suicide and the reconstructed reality he created, Tom never let up. He may have persisted with less conviction or a lowered emotional attachment to the process as he was lulled into believing that his wife was right about Jenny's recovery and the need to "move on," but he did persist. As far as anyone in the town could detect, Fairview remained fully committed to finding Jenny's attacker, and the reports about blue sedans came in nearly every month.

Now, the only things that resulted from those reports were distracted cops and a few moms getting away with speeding on their way to a school pickup. Until a year later.

The car was spotted on a street adjacent to the high school by a pair of senior girls making their way to town. It's only a half-mile walk, and the kids like to gather for milk shakes and mischief, though there's not much trouble to be found in downtown Fairview. Still, this path is well traveled. The driver of the car obviously had no idea a virtual posse had been enlisted to secure his capture.

Jenny had not yet returned to school. That made two spring terms in a row that trauma had caused her to abandon her life. Still it was my advice that she immerse herself in the therapy and acknowledge the gravity of what had occurred both recently and last spring. I hate the armchair psychologists who postulate that the best remedy for trauma is getting back to normal life. It's nothing more than a wives' tale, for lack of a more politically correct expression. At some point, that would be the right course for Jenny. But not until she had completed her work with me. It had not served her well thus far, agreed? Have you ever tried to concentrate on work after receiving devastating news? Or exciting news? What do you do? Do you go outside for a smoke or to call your wife, or cry or jump up and down? You do not sit at your desk and return to your work.

Officer Steve Koper took the call. The girls had tried to be discreet, turning the corner before dialing 911 from a cell phone. The school had sufficiently scared the student body and their parents after the rape. E-mails went out monthly, reminding parents about the blue Civic, and about warning kids not to venture out alone in secluded areas. There had been speakers about rape and abduction, and pamphlets with safety measures children should take. And, of course, news of Jenny's attempted suicide had gone "viral," bringing everyone's mind back to the rape and the blue Civic. I'm quite certain this is why the girls noticed the car. Everyone was again talking about Jenny Kramer.

It's a funny thing, teen culture. As ruthless as it can be, teenagers still take their cues from the adult world. Had Jenny not been raped, her story from that night would have resulted in merciless ridicule. She'd been jilted by Doug Hastings. She'd puked in the bathroom. She'd run away crying, alone into the woods. I have no doubt she would have lost some friends over it, been forced to turn off her social media for months, maybe even the year. I have several teenage patients. This is mostly what they talk about. But Jenny was raped, and the seriousness of her rape was made clear by the police, the school, and the local media. Jenny was suddenly the girl everyone had to be nice to. She was invited to parties, sleepovers, ski weekends in Vermont. She was asked to join the school paper, Model UN, acting club. Everyone wanted kudos for showing kindness. Even Doug Hastings, who (can you believe this?) asked her to the movies.

Jenny had floated through, accepting invitations, putting on an appropriately happy face, stealing pills from bathrooms.

It felt like I was a celebrity or something. Like I had done something special, so now everyone liked me. What had I done? I was stupid to run into those woods. To get so drunk. To get so upset over a guy. Over a jerk like Doug Hastings! All the teachers and those people who came to talk to us, everyone was basically saying, "Don't do what Jenny Kramer did. Don't be stupid like Jenny Kramer." I felt like saying to all of them, "If I'm such a stupid loser, why do you want to be friends with me?" It shouldn't have been both ways, you know? And the thing is, if I had done something good, like made the Olympic track team, no one would want to be my friend. They would all be jealous and would find reasons to hate me. That happened to this guy a few years ago. He won some national math thing. He met the president and everything. He might as well have had Ebola. Everyone called him a geek, made fun of everything he wore and said and did. I don't even know what I did or didn't do. I don't know if I fought him off or just lay there and let it happen. I don't know, so they can't possibly know. Except for one thing: That he won and I lost. That's the bottom line, right? That I lost that fight.

You can see the strength in this young woman, can't you? Her irreverence, her sense of perception, which is well beyond her years? She even had a sense of humor. Remarkable.

Officer Koper drove past the Civic and around the corner to where the girls were waiting. I'm sure his heart was pounding just a little faster after he saw the logo on the back of the car. They told him what he already knew, that they'd spotted the car a few minutes before calling the police. Koper took their names and numbers and told them to get home. Then he called Detective Parsons.

I didn't believe it at first. We'd had over, what? Twenty-six false alarms? That's a couple every month. You get numb to it after the first few. Honestly, I wanted to catch this guy. I really did. Not just for the Kramers, but selfishly. This is the kind of collar that makes a career, you know? But you gotta be realistic, too. Tom Kramer, he had no choice. As a father, you sit there and you live with that guilt. He used to say to me all the time that he failed to protect his little girl. I'm sure he said it to you and everyone else who would listen. So, yeah, he's gotta do everything he can do until he gets past it. Or maybe he dies trying after forty years. I never told the guy to leave us alone, to stop calling. Nope. Never. I always said, "Yes, Tom. No problem." Had guys calling departments all over the country. It wasn't enough to cover the Northeast. And those ads and flyers. I just put it on our rookies. Made 'em pay their dues. It became a joke in the department. We gave the list a name. Called it "the bitch list." Oh . . . wow, I guess that could be taken the wrong way. It was because we'd become Tom Kramer's bitch. I know—it's a horrible expression. But these guys are young. Anyway, when this call came in, I was like, "Yeah, right. Probably a Ford this time." But Koper swore it was a Civic. Sitting there by the school, no less, empty and in the spring again. I started to think that maybe this guy had come back to relive the moment, or maybe repeat the ritual. Can you imagine? Now, that would be a story. . . . I drove up there in an unmarked car. Had my partner with me. And we just sat across the street, a little down from the Civic, between two other cars. We sat there for two hours and twenty-one minutes. Then we see this guy walking down the street. And I knew just from looking at him that we were gonna be making an arrest.

Chapter Eleven

The driver was a young man named Cruz Demarco. He was arrested in Fairview for selling marijuana. He picked up an additional felony charge for selling drugs within 1,500 feet of a school. Of course, that was just the beginning.

I have two observations. First, while it may seem absurd that the presence of a modestly priced sedan on a residential street in Fairview would arouse such suspicion, it is actually quite logical, and in this instance, it paid off. It was profiling. There's no way around that. I don't disagree with our decision as a community to curtail its use. There are unfair consequences to innocent people, and that is unacceptable. However, that argument does not diminish the statistical facts. By example, there was a very low probability that the Civic, with New York plates, under those circumstances, belonged to a resident—maybe 1 percent. This is a fact—not an opinion. Checking Civics in Fairview was the first thing Parsons did after interviewing the kids at the party. There was a larger probability that it belonged to a housekeeper, landscaper, nanny, caregiver, relative, or the like.

Consider also that no one came forward to report anything like this. Given the time of day and where it was parked, the largest piece of the pie chart would contain outsiders. And why would an outsider be parked outside a high school party, at night?

The second observation I have is how everyone in this town was so eager to believe Jenny had been raped by an outsider, how they clung to this Civic like a life raft of hope. Parsons was first and foremost among them. His excitement at finding this car felt desperate to me.

My heart was pounding when we approached the car. Man, I was so glad we waited for a transaction to go down. I was ripe for a bad search. No way I was letting this guy go without questioning him and searching that car. I kept thinking, "Holy shit. We got him! We got him!" But we didn't have probable cause till we saw the sale go down. Thank God my partner was there, holding me back.

An unwitting sophomore named John Vincent had emptied his mother's wallet earlier that morning in anticipation of Demarco's return to Fairview. He walked nervously to the passenger side of the Civic.

This poor kid. What an idiot. He was trying to be discreet, you know, looking around but pretending he was just taking a stroll. Then he bends down at the side of the car. We can see the money going in. A small package going out. Right out of some cheesy cop show. We waited long enough to let the kid run away. You know, did one of those "Hey, you! Stop!" but then didn't really make an effort to chase him down. My partner was already at the driver-side window. Had Koper pull the squad car into the intersection. Guy had nowhere to go.

This part of the story amuses me in a silly way. Officer Koper—it's pronounced with a long *o* but still, it looks like it could be "copper."

And Cruz Demarco. That was his actual name, as ridiculous as it sounds, given to him by his nineteen-year-old mother, who probably thought it sounded cool. Or maybe it was some character from a video game, or one of the men who could have been the father. Cruz had his sob story. Single mother. Poverty. Shitty childhood in Buffalo. All I could think when I heard about him was that he would get eaten alive up in Somers.

I feel as though I am at the top of a roller coaster. I despise roller coasters, so I suppose I have been stalling. I have been a bystander thus far, an observer passing my judgments and rendering opinions. Everything started to happen that very early spring. My involvement with the Kramer family, treating Jenny as a patient, Sean Logan, and then the arrest of Cruz Demarco. The collision was coming, and I didn't see it. With all my brilliant powers of deduction, I didn't see it coming at all.

They found close to three pounds of marijuana in the blue Civic. That was more than enough for the arrest.

We got him down to the house. Impounded the car and called in forensics from Cranston. No way I was messing around with that. Can you imagine? If they found dirt matching the stuff behind Juniper Road? Or the black mask with the same fibers that were found under Jenny's nails? I was like a kid on Christmas morning.

Demarco was an unpleasant human being. He was twenty-nine years old. Barely stood five feet four inches. Weighed under 120 pounds. If you're a woman, you know what that looks like. He was skinny, and his pale white flesh hung from his limbs like an old woman's. His black hair was long in the back and the front, shorter at the sides. It was slick from excessive hair gel. He moved with various twitches, in his walk and his speech, even his eyes. And he smelled of cheap soap. I did not meet the man in person, but he was described to me in great detail by Detective Parsons. From the photos in the local paper and what I was able to find on the Internet, he did not quite bow to the level of repulsion ascribed to him. But this is common. We want to hate someone, assign guilt or blame, impose punishment, so we see them in the worst possible light and impose upon them the worst possible traits. Or perhaps he was all those things. There was no doubt he was a criminal. But drug dealing and rape are two very different crimes.

He didn't ask for a lawyer. I went so far as to have him sign a waiver. No way I was gonna risk a Miranda question. Got a camera wired up. Two cops watching from the outside. Me and my partner inside. We gave him his cigarettes and an orange soda. Started out making him feel comfortable, you know? See if that would work before we even let him know why he was really there. I just started the conversation while we were waiting for his sheet. I was like, "Yeah, tough break. This stuff is pretty much legal now. Maybe we can work something out. Really just want to keep our kids from getting off track, you know?" He shrugged. He said it was his brother's car and he didn't know anything about any drugs being in it. My partner got a little "bad cop" on him. Reminded him we saw him make a sale to the kid. He smiled. Said, "What sale? That kid was just asking me if I was lost or something. Reached in to help me read my map." Seriously? I mean, yeah, there was a map in the glove compartment. But who the hell uses maps anymore? That thing was probably ten years old. Then we get a knock. They had his sheet. Bingo.

Demarco had a long relationship with the criminal justice system. All of it was related to drugs. Much of it was misdemeanor stuff, possession, use. Now, that doesn't mean that he wasn't selling.

What's on a conviction record and what the original arrest was based on are not necessarily one and the same. I'm sure you've watched enough television to know the kind of wheeling-dealing that goes on between prosecutors and defense attorneys. Trials take time and cost money. And no one cares about pot these days. So while his sheet went back over a decade, there was just one distribution conviction. June of last year. Two weeks and four days after Jenny's rape.

Demarco had spent six months in a level four facility in Bridgeport. I imagine it was not a pleasant experience for such a slight young man with that soft white skin. Is this aberrant? I fear that the time I spend at Somers has imbued me with knowledge that should not be shared so casually with the rest of the world. I am normally quite cautious about the assumptions I make—even the jokes I laugh at or don't laugh at, in social company—out of fear of being misunderstood. Surely I would not have prison rape pop into my thoughts just from a discussion involving a small man with soft white skin. But if you spent eight hours a week hearing about life behind bars in a level five institution, you would also start to connect these things. My wife has scolded me on more than one occasion.

You did it again, sweetheart, my wife would say. She always uses that term of endearment, even when she's angry. *A catcher is the guy behind home plate. That's it. No one finds it interesting.*

I don't know if that's true or not true. I think there's enough empirical evidence in our media and entertainment to suggest otherwise. Still, it is not always appropriate dinner conversation. (The catcher is sometimes used to describe the person "receiving" when two men engage in sex.) I suppose that's why I find dinner parties so excruciatingly dull.

The good news for Parsons was that he now had something to use for leverage. He had two felony charges in his pocket. Adding those to the prior conviction made Demarco a repeat offender with mandatory sentencing triggers.

I go back in with the sheet. And I'm, like, "Oh man, tough break. This prior, and now two felony charges," and he starts to squirm a little. "Maybe you should take that PD," I say to him, "get yourself a lawyer." His feet start shuffling around on the floor. He's got his fists clenched together. Then my partner pulls me in, whispers some bullshit. It was all for show. Just wanted it to look good, you know? And then I say, "Listen . . . any chance you were in town last May? You might be able to help us out with something." He shrugs his shoulders as if to say he might have been if there's something in it for him. I figure, we get him to admit he was in town, and then we go from there. But he doesn't budge.

I did not understand the logic of this. If Demarco was the rapist, he wouldn't go anywhere near an admission of presence at the scene of the crime. Still, Parsons got back on the right track.

We had enough to lock him up. He got a PD from Cranston. Guy who knows his way around, but no way he's gonna want a full trial at PD rates. It was time to go back to that night. Now that we had a face. First, to Teddy Duncan. That kid who was chasing his dog. Second—now that we had something to use to shake up those kids, we could go back at them. None of them, not one kid from the party, admitted to seeing a blue Civic. But if it was Demarco, he was probably there selling drugs. Sees Jenny stumbling into the woods. Easy prey. And those kids, not one of them was gonna cop to buying drugs. But now that we knew, had the car, had the driver—we had a chance to roll one of them and get the ID.

Parsons was optimistic, gleeful even. So were the Kramers. I did not share Parsons's conclusions about Demarco. But it was not my place to dissuade him from his plan of action. He had been kind enough to keep me apprised so I could be helpful to Jenny and her family. What was I going to say? This is not your man. Don't go back to interview those kids or Teddy Duncan. Don't go down this road. I wished him good luck and waited for the next report. My regret is profound.

Chapter Twelve

The resurfacing of the blue Civic had two immediate repercussions. The first was the interference with my treatment of the Kramer family. The second involved my son.

Jenny and her parents had been seeing me on an individual basis for several weeks. My work with Charlotte and Tom was not complicated. The primary purpose was to have them fill in the blanks about Jenny and the year leading up to the suicide attempt. But our sessions quickly shifted focus to address their own pain from this horrible chapter in their lives. This, of course, led us into the underlying problems in their marriage, and further back to their childhoods, where all marital problems begin.

I have already espoused my disapproval of couples therapy, specifically, of seeing a couple together where too many truths are told which cannot be untold. Things may need to be said, but not necessarily heard by the other spouse. The Kramers' issues collapsed before me like a house of cards, and I was working to sort them out. But I was doing this with each of them, alone.

Tom was a virtual case study. Textbook. He needed to get in touch with his anger at his wife for dominating the decisions with Jenny, and then for dominating their marriage. Then he needed to get in touch with his anger at himself for allowing this to happen, to recognize that Charlotte was merely filling in the giant chasm of indecision that resulted from his own diminished self-confidence. Finally, we could get around to his parents and the cause of his diminished self-confidence. Understanding, acceptance, forgiveness, and then a course of action for change.

This is not about whining or not taking responsibility. I know what many people say about talk therapy. They are wrong. Tom had to train himself to recognize when he was creating a chasm, acknowledge why he was doing it, then step in and be decisive, confront his wife if he felt she was wrong. He needed to own his strength and his intelligence. He needed to be a man again, for himself and his wife, who no longer wanted to touch him. It would not be easy. We call this type of "retraining" cognitive behavioral therapy. I had a patient once who asked me to explain what we were doing. She complained that it felt dishonest, that she did not want to stop herself from telling her husband how much she disliked his sister. When I told her our ultimate goal, she said, *Oh, you mean fake it 'til you feel it.* That's CBT in a nutshell. Unlike the memory-recovery process, which is highly controversial, CBT is the white bread of psychotherapy.

Charlotte was more complicated. I knew immediately why she had married Tom. I think I've already elucidated these facts. Tom was part of her perfect house, the one she longed for as a child. Bob was the beam she used to keep the house from caving in. Now you will see why I bothered you with the details of her sexual experiences with him and the conclusion that Bob was her drug. All of these things are like strands of sugar in a cotton candy machine, spinning fast for now so they don't get stuck to each other, until it's time to wind them onto one stick—one perfectly formed stick of sugar threads.

Bob was Charlotte's drug. Sean was Tammy's drug. And Jenny would be Sean's. There is a reason people are drawn to others in this way, in a way that makes them feel like they are addicts. It is not healthy. In fact, it is by definition unhealthy from an emotional standpoint. I'm sorry to disappoint, but a healthy relationship is usually quite dull. I had started to make great progress with Charlotte on this issue until the arrest of Cruz Demarco.

Charlotte did not go home when she left the hospital the second time. After speaking with Detective Parsons, her clothes soaked in blood, the blood now smeared on her forehead as Parsons described, she drove two blocks and called Bob. He agreed to meet her.

I don't know why I didn't go home. Lucas was with our neighbor, so I couldn't curl up in his room. But that's not it. Maybe it's more accurate to say that I didn't go home, because I couldn't bear it— and the part I don't know is why I couldn't bear it. When Jenny was raped, I went home. I wanted to hold my son and crawl into the bed in his room and watch him sleep until the pill kicked in. As upsetting as that was, I felt I could handle it, that I was handling it. They were giving her the treatment. They were fixing her. And she wasn't suffering. She was asleep, and she would sleep through it all and wake up as if it never happened. Have you ever been in a near accident, where you slip on ice or don't see a car in the blind spot? There's that moment of panic and then relief, and then you think, Okay, I dodged a bullet today. Next time I'll be more careful. That's how I felt. Scared but relieved. In control of the future. But this time, it was different.

Charlotte talked for the entire hour that day about her meeting with Bob. She was disturbed by her decision to call him rather than go home to be with her son. She was disturbed by her behavior when she was with him. And she was disturbed by how she felt when she left him.

We met in a parking lot between Fairview and Cranston. It's the one with Home Depot and Costco on Route 7. You know that one? It's enormous. He got in my car and we drove to the back, where the deliveries are made. We were just going to talk. He had changed his clothes, and I think he was a little shocked that I hadn't been home yet—that my clothes were still so dirty. He asked how Jenny was and I told him. He hung his head in his hands and rubbed his forehead so hard. . . .

Charlotte demonstrated how Bob had rubbed his forehead. She said she had this thought that he was trying to erase the memory of what had happened that afternoon, like trying to erase a pen mark with a pencil eraser. His skin started to get red.

It was late. Bob had stopped at one of his showrooms to change his clothes. No one had seen him come in the back door. He said he didn't know what to do with the bloody ones, if he should throw them out or burn them or try to wash them. He said he felt paranoid that someone would find them and that they would be caught.

I was so unsettled inside. Like I said, this time was different. We were parked between two semis. It must have been close to ten thirty. It was dark out. I remember not being able to see his face very well. He kept talking about logistical things, his clothes, my clothes, what I was going to do with mine. He made suggestions about how to clean the bathroom, how I shouldn't go in there again. "Just call a service. Tell them there was an accident and give them the keys. There are agencies that do that. . . ." Blah blah blah. I could feel myself unraveling. I can't describe it any better than that. Like a thread had been pulled, and now it was working its way out of the seam, inch by inch.

I asked her what she had wanted him to say. She was staring at the small tulip plant on the table in the corner of my office. I bought it at the grocery store and had not removed the white sticker from the pot, which had the price and description. TULIPA "MONTREUX." I had no preference. These were the only ones they had, and my wife had insisted I have a spring plant in the office. Charlotte was staring at the sticker. It was the one thing she could find that was out of place, and she was subconsciously fixated on it. Naturally, I drew my own conclusions. I made a mental note to leave the sticker.

"What did you want him to say? What did you need from him?"

Silence. Thinking.

"If you could go back in time and rewrite that scene in the car, what would Bob have done? Start from the beginning—he gets in the car and . . ."

And he looks at my face and then at my clothes, at the blood still all over me. And he doesn't look around nervously to see if anyone has noticed us. He doesn't care.

"He just sees you and he knows what you need. You don't even have to tell him. So he does what?"

He . . . he takes my face in his hands and he . . . Charlotte closed her eyes then, placing her own hands on her face. She became emotional.

"What, Charlotte? What does he say?"

He tells me it's all right. That my baby girl is going to get through this.

"No. That's not what he says. Dr. Baird said that at the hospital. Think harder, Charlotte. What does he say as he looks at you, sees you, and holds your face in his hands?"

I don't know.

"Yes, you do. You called him for a reason. Take a breath and let it out. Go back to that night. It's just you and me here now. No one else will ever know what Bob says to you in that car. You're safe here,

Charlotte. Just let it come out. He's holding your face, looking into your eyes. What does he say?"

He says I love you.

"No, Charlotte. He says that all the time. You're not being honest. You know what he says to you."

Charlotte was crying. You are probably surprised to learn this. It was not the first time she had let herself go in our sessions. Remember that I was the only person who knew about her affair with Bob. I had fought very hard for her trust, and I had become a safe place for her to hide her secrets, and her tears.

"You know what he says, don't you?"

She nodded. Then she took a breath and opened her eyes. The tears stopped and she spoke calmly. *He takes my face in his hands. He doesn't care who can see us. He looks into my eyes, and he says, "This is not your fault."*

"Yes." I said. "That's right. Bob is the person who gives you what you need when the others can't. He fills in the gaps. He doesn't judge your past. He has no vested interest in you being one Charlotte and not the other. You're not raising his children. You're not his wife. Your past will never reflect poorly upon him."

I always felt like I could tell him anything and that he would just love me more. He used to tell me that I was just a victim of my stepfather. That my mother was a desperate, selfish girl who never grew up. She did what she had to do to survive.

"And this made you feel better about yourself?"

Yes. And then he would fuck me and leave and I would wash him off me before my husband came home.

"And then you felt bad about being with him."

Of course. Whatever he did to make me feel better about my past was always replaced with feeling bad about my present. And then I would miss him until he came back.

This is what we do. We do not want to change. In our natural core, in our guts, we want to feel the way we did as children. More strands of spun sugar that need to be woven in.

But that night in the car, he didn't make me feel better. He didn't know what I needed. We talked about all those things, about the logistics. Maybe he told me he loved me, how relieved he was that Jenny was okay. I don't even know. I had stopped listening to him as the seam kept pulling apart. I could feel it, you know? That thread just giving way, and then finally I just came undone. I know I started to cry and pull at him, at his coat and his shirt. I reached my hand between his thighs. I needed him to do something. . . . I didn't even know what I wanted exactly.

"It sounds like you wanted to have some kind of sexual contact with him."

Yes, maybe. Anything.

"So you could feel different from how you were feeling."

Yes.

"Like a drug. You've said that before. That he was like a drug for you."

Yes. I wanted him to change the way I felt inside. Like a drug. That's right. But he just pushed my hand away and looked at me like I was some sort of deviant. Like I was depraved. "What are you doing?" he said. "We need to have some respect for the situation." He went on and on. How could I want sex hours after what we had witnessed? I felt like this wall just slid down between us. Our connection was broken, and he was looking at me the way I saw myself when I thought about my past. It was humiliating.

This was tremendous progress. We went on to discuss this event in the car, and how Charlotte had been using Bob to feel better about her past, but then to feel worse again. An upper, then a downer—always leaving her in the same place. The upper lost its potency while the downer grew stronger. She started to need more of the upper, exchanging sex for his love, his acceptance. She would ask him about the things his wife wouldn't do, or things he'd seen on the Internet. Bob had a large appetite. Charlotte did not climax with Bob, if you recall. Yet she was preoccupied with thoughts of having sex with him. The sex got her the words, that was the piece she didn't understand until weeks into our work. Like Pavlov's dogs salivating at the sound of a bell. They did not get any satisfaction from the bell. But the bell meant that there would be food. And they were very hungry for food.

But on that night, Bob did not have the right words. For the first time, the drug was totally impotent, and Charlotte went home soaked not only in her daughter's blood but also in her own self-loathing and humiliation. It was here that we were interrupted by the arrival of the blue Civic.

I remember quite clearly the moment I learned that the blue Civic had resurfaced in Fairview and that an arrest had been made. I had spent the entire day in Somers and was driving home. I don't enjoy music while I drive. I find it provokes emotional responses that then distract me from my thoughts, and driving is an excellent time to think deeply about things we often shortchange. Sporting events, fast-moving ones in particular—basketball, hockey—on the other hand, stimulate these thoughts. The action and chaos float in and out of my brain, mostly providing background noise that helps me focus.

I was thinking about a patient I had seen that day. He was serving his second year in a term of three to five years for a home invasion over in Lyme. The patient came to see me for anxiety and depression. In my practice at Somers, this is, invariably, an attempt to get meds. I sometimes prescribe them out of compassion. It is a miserable experience to be in prison. I give these drugs to patients in Fairview who are going through divorce, a job change, mourning the loss of a parent—life events that can be upsetting. Certainly, by that standard, a person spending ten years in prison should warrant the same degree of compassion. But in that practice, I have to be extremely prudent with my compassion. Patients have sold their meds—pretending to swallow them upon their administration, sometimes even regurgitating them. They dry them out and sell them one at a time. Other patients—well, it's better to just let them adjust to their new lives. They can't stay on these meds for ten years. The prison won't allow it, for one thing. They are also addictive over time. We don't need to be creating drug addicts in the prison system.

I did not face this dilemma with the patient I saw the day I learned about Cruz Demarco. There was no doubt he intended to sell the pills and that I was, therefore, going to refuse to prescribe them. As the session carried on, and as he began to sense my hesitation, he started to toy with me. This is extremely common, and as much as it disproves any claims of chemical disorders like depression, bipolar disorder, schizophrenia (we call these Axis I disorders), it actually serves to confirm my diagnosis of the other types—the Axis II disorders. (Axis I disorders are, simplistically, malfunctions in the brain's chemistry. Axis II disorders are personality disorders. They are caused by the absence of, or malformation of, normal human personality traits such as empathy and the ability to form healthy attachments. They fall along a spectrum that starts with borderline personality disorder and ends with sociopaths. The definitions, in my opinion, are somewhat amorphous. Many of them are immune to treatment.) This patient was a sociopath.

My stories from Somers would fill several volumes of textbooks. And I must humbly confess that I was not always this proficient at detecting the truly gifted Axis II patients. They do not walk in off the street in places like Fairview. In fact, they rarely seek treatment to get well. They do not believe they are ill, but they do come to realize that others perceive them as different. They can be very cunning in hiding their behavior in order to blend in and, more important, to get what they desperately need. It is only in the correctional facilities, prisons and psychiatric units, that a doctor can find them in sufficient volume to hone the necessary skills to both identify and treat them.

When I first started my work in Somers, I was not up to the task. It is difficult to accept the mistakes that I made over the first year. Perhaps longer. My worst transgression was with a patient named Glenn Shelby. I had treated him for about six months, ending the fall before Jenny's rape. Glenn had been serving a short sentence for robbery. He suffered from two primary mental conditions, neither of which would ever be apparent to you. Coming upon him in the normal course of life, he would present as warm and curious. He would show a deep interest in you and anything you chose to share with him. On more than one occasion, even I found myself further down the path than I had intended to wander with Glenn. He would ask questions like a teenage girl gossiping with her friends, detailed questions that would lead you to disclose more than what was reasonable under the circumstances of your meeting. He would pursue you as a friend, and although it would feel uncomfortable at times, as though he were desperate to grow close to you, he would also sense this before you cut him off. He would then adjust his behavior just enough to keep you on the hook. Eventually, your discomfort would outpace his ability to make the adjustments because his need for intimacy with you, as a friend or lover, was driven by his borderline personality. That was the first condition.

Glenn also had a form of autism. I say "form" because he was never assessed by a trained professional before his borderline symptoms began to surface. Autism is also a spectrum. I detected the characteristics from his mannerisms. He was a brilliant man, very adept at mimicking normal behavior. But I was, thankfully, skilled enough to make this diagnosis. Intelligence, by the way, is often seen in patients having either of his conditions.

His parents had an abusive, explosive relationship. He was beaten himself, and subjected to witnessing the beatings of both parents by one another. His mother was tall and strong, as was Glenn. They had neither the time nor the inclination to notice the ways he was different from other children. His aberrant behavior was the trigger for much of the punishment his parents inflicted.

Before landing in prison, Glenn had been self-medicating the overstimulation caused by his autism with a variety of street drugs. When he ran out of money, he used a toy gun on a cashier at a bodega in Watertown. Glenn could not hold down a job for long. His intelligence was appealing at first, but he made people uncomfortable and was typically fired within a few months.

I had done my best for Glenn. My very best. He refused to accept medication. He did not think he was ill. What he sought was therapy—a chance to have a safe connection with another human being, which can be a dangerous endeavor in prison. I was eager to provide this to him. He was the subject of abuse by other inmates because of his odd disposition and how he sought emotional intimacy in an environment where such a thing is perceived as deceptive. I imagine some of the inmates had succumbed to his talents, confiding more than they should about their crimes to this strange man. He was frequently accused of being a "rat." I believe it was his physical size and strength that kept him from being killed.

Glenn Shelby was the one patient I was not able to save. His life ended with suicide. This is certainly why I have dwelled on him here. Why I dwell on him, period. The several months I treated him was not enough time for me, in my ineptitude, to understand the depths of his conditions.

I was thinking about the patient I had just seen on the drive home

that day, and trying to get myself around the profound disappointment it triggered. Disappointment in myself. How easy it was for me
now to see through this sociopath. He was beyond help. But Glenn, I
do not believe that about him. If he walked through my door on that
same day, I would have been able to help him. Save him. The world
is not a fair place.

You may wonder why I choose to immerse myself in such filth
every week. My wife believes it has to do with my upbringing. My parents used to take in foster children. I think it was because they had
only two children themselves, and for ten years only me. My sister
was a miracle, they said. The doctors had believed that my mother's
uterus was damaged by my difficult delivery and could no longer hold
a fetus. She suffered many miscarriages. We were given a great deal
of information about this so we would understand why they opened
our home to strangers. I do not even remember all of their names or
even their faces. I did not enjoy sharing my home with these strangers. I resented them for taking resources that should have been
mine—the love of my parents, money, food, space. But I was just a
child, and children are selfish that way. And yet my wife tells me, as
do my parents when we see them for our annual visit, that it is their
generous spirit that lives within me. I think about that every time I
drive up north to Somers.

The radio was on. A Knicks game had just ended, and a newscast
was airing. I heard the name, but it did not mean anything. Then
I heard the description of the car and the reference to the rape in
Fairview last spring. They did not mention the Kramers, as that is
the policy of the media with regard to rape victims. But everyone
knew. There had been only one rape. There was only one blue Civic.
And now they had the driver.

My distress over Glenn Shelby and the injustices of the world were
instantly gone from my mind, and I was listening to every word. I

called in to my voice mail. I had several messages waiting, which is very common, and I usually wait until the evening to listen to them, as I am sometimes required to take notes. Changes in appointments and the like. Today they were all about the arrest—Tom Kramer, Charlotte Kramer, Detective Parsons—they all called to tell me what had happened. The Kramers said that they were anxious to see me to discuss what this could mean for Jenny, whether we could use Demarco's face or clothing to try to recover her memories. The thought of that was horrifying, and I listened impatiently because I wanted to call them back and urge them to keep Jenny away from any images of this man. The power of suggestion was anathema to our work. It would undermine everything. But then I got the last message, and my thoughts shifted one last time. It was from my wife.

Chapter Thirteen

My wife's name is Julie Marin Forrester. I love my wife. It feels disingenuous to use this phrase after I have proselytized to such a degree about how nebulous love is. How it means nothing except in the context of the person who is "feeling" it. How it means something different to each of us and is therefore meaningless in some respects. How else can I describe it? I do not admire her. She is not particularly skilled at any one thing, though she is highly competent at running our family. She attended college (I won't say which one, so as not to offend any of you who may be alumni), but I don't think she learned much. She was very social. Lived in a sorority. Majored in English, which basically means she read a lot of novels. It was mostly a passive exercise for her.

It is strange having to think about it for this long, my feelings for my wife. If I ask myself the same questions I ask my patients, it certainly does not sound like love. I feel intellectually superior to her. There's no point hiding that truth. I rarely have patients who don't know how they feel on this subject. I make all our decisions that involve reasoning and the weighing of costs and benefits. How much of our retirement to invest in the stock market. When to refinance our mortgage. Which contractor to use to fix the roof. She makes the decisions that involve the likes and dislikes of our family. What kind of flowers to send my mother on her birthday. What color ski coat our daughter would like for Christmas. What movie our son might like to see on his birthday. I make the decisions involving discipline and motivation of our children. That falls squarely in my court.

She is very attractive. We met in New York when I was doing my residency. She worked as a waitress while she interned at a publishing house. She would read manuscripts all day in a windowless office, then serve wealthy businessmen at a Midtown steak house until 2 A.M. Julie made an excellent living for a young college grad in those days. She was not above using her looks to boost her tips. She was not above an occasional hand brushing her behind as she passed by a table, or a stroke of her arm as she leaned over to clear a plate. I am not disgusted by her Machiavellian attitude. I believe it correlates with the simplistic way she approaches nearly every aspect of life. She never gave a second thought to the unwanted touches of self-entitled assholes with wedding bands and deficient consciences. It was just easy money to her.

Perhaps that is what I mean when I say I love her. She is simple. She sees things simply. I never wonder if she is hiding a secret agenda or manipulating me in ways I won't understand for months to come. All day, I hear about lies, secrets, plots, and distrust. And those are just my days in Fairview. When I walk through my front door, feeling pride for a day of hard work, feeling satisfied that I have provided this house and all these things for my family, Julie is there, tending to our kids, tending to our house, tending to me. She generally ignores me until the kids are fed and their homework is done and we've done the dishes together. But then she sits with me for a glass of wine and she tells me about her simple day and I see that she is happy. The comfort this provides me is indescribable. I, in turn, feel happy in her company. I feel appreciated and cared for. And so I love her.

Before you think I am stuck in the 1950s, my wife spends her days teaching a class at the community college in Cranston, seeing her friends to play tennis or have lunch, and treating herself to a few hours of reading or a pedicure or something else that she finds enjoyable. She is not a servant in our family. She is free to do whatever she wants. In fact, I have encouraged her to pursue a master's degree so we might engage in more sophisticated conversations.

There is one aspect of life that is not simple for my wife. I have mentioned before her fear of bad things happening to our children. How she makes herself feel the worst possible outcomes before she can move past the fear. My wife lost both her parents when she was in her thirties. They'd had her when they were in their midforties, so their deaths were not untimely. One went to heart disease. The other to a stroke. I have considered the possibility of genetic weaknesses, as these would affect my own children and might be cause for some early precautions. But I have concluded that these ailments were more a result of time and the sedentary lifestyle her parents maintained. The loss, however normal from an actuarial standpoint, was difficult for Julie. Her one brother lives in Arizona with his wife. They have no children. Our immediate family is all she has, and her parents' deaths have made her acutely aware that people we love do in fact die. It's amazing how we all lose sight of that. Maybe life would be unbearable if we did not.

I knew right away from the tone of her voice that she was worried. It was breathy and of a higher pitch than usual. She was trying, but failing, to hide her panic.

Hi, sweetheart. Hope your day is going well. Just wanted to know

if you'd heard the news about the arrest. I'm sure you have, it's been
all over the TV. Probably on the radio as well. Anyway . . . apparently
they now want to speak to all the kids again, you know, the ones
who were at the party that night. I'm sure they just want to see if
any of them can confirm that the man they arrested was the same
one parked out on Juniper. No big deal, right? Call me, though.
Laura Lyman said they might hire a lawyer to go in with Steven.
Mark Brandino is his name. Maybe we should think about that for
Jason? Anyway . . . call me, okay, sweetie? I love you. Drive safely.
Give me a call. Okay . . . bye-bye.

Her words were like a cold shower. I had not thought much about
Jason being at the party that night. There were over a hundred
kids there, nearly half the school, including most of his varsity swim
team.

Jason is a swimmer. He's an excellent swimmer, actually. There's
been talk of an early college offer from Michigan, maybe even Penn.
He's going to need the swimming, being a B+ student. He works
hard, so this really is his limit academically. I knew it might be an
issue when I married Julie. I would put her IQ at around 100 to 110.
I have found a negative correlation between exceptional IQ levels and
emotional stability. The same is true with nurturing instincts. There
seemed no point in having brilliant children if their mother couldn't
give them the proper amount of affection. And, indeed, my children
are well adjusted, attractive, popular, athletic, and highly competent
intellectually. I believe this will give them a kind of happiness that
always evaded me.

Jason is a wonderful young man. You can believe me or not believe me. It is the objective truth. If I told you he was the greatest
seventeen-year-old kid on the planet, then you could call my objec-
tivity into question. And you would be right. I do not believe he is
the greatest seventeen-year-old kid on the planet. I just feel like he is,

and like everything he does and says (almost—he is a teenager, after all), is precious, and I find myself soaking it in so I have a full reserve of it when he goes off to college in a year, as my daughter did two years before. That is the parent in me. The objective person in me sees that he is a wonderful young man.

He is kind to others. He sits with us at dinner and talks about the world with compassion and understanding. We discuss everything from the Middle East and terrorism to the economy. Sometimes I smile at the conclusions he's come to because he is so young and has so much to learn. But at least he cares enough to think and draw conclusions. He gets up every morning with a smile on his face, cracking jokes at breakfast, humming some new song he's downloaded. He goes to school, goes to swim practice, comes home for dinner and then to study and sleep, only to start all over again. Yes, he is sometimes glued to his phone on the social media or video games, but this does not alarm me the way it does some people. This is their world, and they might as well become acclimated to it. It will not serve them well to treat their technology like a vice and limit their exposure. They will end up without the skill set that is already becoming necessary for the workplace and social environment of their generation.

I know I belabor this analogy, but I have come to see these teenage years as a construction project. I tell my young patients, and my own children, that this is not their life. Not yet. What they are doing now is building a house. It is a house they will have to live in for the rest of their lives, so they'd better get it right. They will be able to remodel, redecorate, and repair. But they can never rebuild. Everything they put into this house, every emotional scar from a bad relationship, every sexual perversion they give in to, every opportunity they secure for themselves, every drug they allow to interrupt the maturing of their growing brains, will be forever in the foundation of that house. The neuroscientists keep moving their conclusion, but the human brain winds down its developing around age twenty-five. What happens between puberty and the midtwenties in the brain, while it is finishing its development—its hardwiring—involves increased risk taking and peer influence. The reward center is trying to sort out what behaviors lead to rewards so it can lay down some wires, some bricks. Those bricks become part of the foundation, and they are there to stay. If those bricks tell you to like alcohol or cocaine or deviant sex acts, you will be fighting those cravings for the rest of your life. And of course, a child who blows off her grades and winds up at a subpar college will have to move to the back of the line when it comes to finding a job. It all matters.

If I have a patient who can't get an erection with his wife, my first question is whether he uses pornography. My second question is when did he start. Invariably, when he was a teenager. If I have a patient who is an addict, my first question is when did she start. Answer—when she was a teenager. If I have a patient who is abused by a spouse, my first question is when was she abused by her parent? Answer—before she left home at eighteen.

My son is building a solid house. I know he drinks on the weekends. I am certain it is moderate. He does not use drugs. I know this because I know drug users. I can tell in thirty seconds when someone is high. I see them enough to know. It's not rocket science, just experience. My daughter, whom I also love deeply, built her own good house, though she is more like her mother. She doesn't want to be bothered thinking about things that do not have an immediate impact on her life. But she is funny and fun loving and brought a lightness to our family before she left for college.

My wife keeps a close eye on our son. She is more suspicious than I. If he is doing something to undermine his house building, she will find it. So far, her covert operations have revealed nothing more than some Internet pornography. She set up various Internet restrictions. I had a long talk with Jason. That was that. Julie's diligence gives me great comfort. And when she is worried, I know there is cause.

I turned off the radio and let my wife's fears enter me. I felt them trickle in and then multiply until my mind was reeling. Jason had already been interviewed by the police. We had spoken to him as well about that night and what it meant and how he needed to be safe—both from being harmed and from harming others. We spoke to him about consent and about being with girls who are intoxicated. When it happened, when we learned of the rape of Jenny Kramer, my wife was thinking about our daughter off at college, and what we would do if this had happened to her. I had not thought about this until Julie put the idea in my head, and it stayed there for weeks as a most horrific, unbearable thought. She was also the one who was thinking about Jason, and what if he knew who did it but didn't want to say, or what if he was falsely accused? This thought had been less troubling. I knew my son. He would be the last person on anyone's list of suspects. Still, my wife's fears were contagious.

There is one kind of love that is not amorphous, and that is the love of one's own child. I spoke about this when discussing Tom Kramer's childhood, if you recall. Both from an experiential standpoint as well as a clinical one, I know—it's not just a belief—that we are genetically designed to die for our children. And if we are willing to die for them, we must feel in our bones that they are worthy of our death. And by the course of reason, we must see them as more worthy than everyone else we are not willing to die for. For most of us, with the exception of soldiers who are trained to die for others, that "everyone else" is truly everyone else in the world. We say we would die for our spouses, or at least some people say this, but I do not believe it is true. I do not believe, in that moment of truth, there is any husband who would throw himself in front of that proverbial bus to save his wife. Nor is there a wife who would jump out to spare her husband. Only for a child.

Only for a child.

This is what I was thinking as my wife's fears grew inside me. Jason. I have to protect my son. From what, I did not yet know.

Chapter Fourteen

I did not call my wife. Instead, I called Detective Parsons. I have his private cell phone, and he always picks up when he sees my number. For the first time, I lied to him.

"I heard you've made an arrest. That's wonderful news," I said. He confirmed the reports. He was beside himself with relief.

"I was hoping you could fill me in on everything you know. I'm sure you can imagine how important this could be for Jenny."

This was not untrue. The lie was in the motivation my words implied. I was not unconcerned with Jenny. But my wife's fear was raging inside me.

Parsons told me about the arrest, about Cruz Demarco and how he'd "lawyered up." They were waiting for him to get an assignment from the public defender's office. I told him I did not want any of the Kramers to see his face, either in person or in a photograph. He said there'd been no release of Demarco's name or picture. He promised to speak to the Kramers before releasing any information to the press. I agreed to call them as soon as we hung up to take added precautions. Jenny could not have her memory compromised by suggestive influences.

Then he told me about his reinterview of the neighbor's kid, Teddy Duncan, who'd spotted the blue Civic the night of the rape.

Teddy. What a piece of work. But then you meet his mother and you get it, you know? He was a brat last time I met with him, but now that he's a teenager, what a little asshole. Thinks he's some kind of celebrity because he spotted a car while chasing his dog. Sat there like I was doing an interview for People *magazine or something. Anyway, the kid tells me the same story as last time. His parents got him a puppy for Christmas. A little beagle. The mom says the thing's been a nightmare, chewing up all the furniture, pissing and shitting all over the house. The deal was that Teddy was supposed to take care of it. That was the whole point. Kid's been getting in trouble at school, bad grades, skipping classes. The whole nine. Counselor suggested getting him a pet that he is responsible for. Convinced them it would do the trick. But little Teddy couldn't give a shit, you know? They got a fence around the property. Mom doesn't believe in the electric ones. Says it's creating force fields that will give them cancer. I didn't have the heart to tell her the extra fifty pounds on her ass was more likely to kill her than a doggie fence. So the dog keeps digging holes under the fence and getting out to chase things, squirrels and shit. The day of the party, the landscaper comes and fills the holes, so they think they're good to go. Mom lets the dog out, and an hour later, he's gone again. Guess there was a hole that had some dead leaves and stuff covering it. So the mom yells at Teddy to find the dog. And that's when he goes out looking.*

Now, that was around eight forty-five. Kid is in the woods maybe a few minutes calling for the dog, but he doesn't come. He listened for rustling. I guess that sometimes works, you know, he can hear the dog running around. But that night he can't hear anything, because there's all this noise from the party next door. Music, kids laughing and cheering. They were playing drinking games, so that all made sense. So he gives up and heads back to the road, to Juniper. He walks on the inside of the car line, so he's in the middle of the road, walking toward the party house. That's when he saw the Civic. Said it stuck out because it was "ghetto." Can you believe that? What a little prick. I asked him if he looked inside. He swears there was no one in the car. Said he could see just fine because he saw two kids "mashing" in the back of a Suburban, which was also parked on Juniper. They have streetlamps on Juniper. They were all working that night. Then we showed him photos of blue Civics from the back, with different plates and slightly different colors. He picked Demarco's. Said he remembered some of the plate numbers.

"Which he couldn't do before, right?" I asked.

Yeah, but I guess seeing them jogged his memory. We showed him ten cars with ten plates.

"Were they all blue? The cars? If the others were the wrong color, surely that could have been why—"

Fuck that, Doc. Let the PD come up with the defense. We have a kid who saw his car and no one inside, right around the time of the rape. The car was there but empty.

"But even if it was this guy, Demarco, he could have been inside, selling drugs. I'm sure that's what he's going to claim."

It's starting to sound like you don't think this is our guy. Did Jenny remember something?

Parsons was defensive. Too defensive, like he had some kind of personal stake in nailing Demarco. I had never seen him as an ambitious man. I suppose he wanted this to be over, the relentless badgering from Tom, the lingering suspicions that the rapist was walking around Fairview in plan sight. But his eagerness appeared to be affecting his attention to detail. I wanted the charges to stick. I wanted this all to go away. But even I knew how many holes this story had.

I had to stop myself from answering the question about Jenny. She had remembered some things, but that was not why I had asked the question.

"No—and I have no opinion on this man except to foresee the next steps in the investigation. You'll have to verify where he was, inside or outside the house, I imagine."

We've already started. Every kid is getting a fresh interview. Even if he never stepped foot in that house, someone had told him about the party and that he should come by to sell them shit. Only way this guy knows where to be and when. And I'd bet he made a few sales before he saw Jenny in the woods. That's the other thing. Teddy showed us about where the Civic was parked. You can't see into the woods from there. There's a row of bushes. He would have had to have been walking to or from the house or, worse, looking out from inside the house, to see her going across the lawn. But I'm not giving up on him. No way! Last thing I want to do is have this lead go away.

"I see." I was lost then, in my thoughts and my wife's fears.

Alan? You still there?

"Yes. Sorry about that. I'm on the road. I thank you for your time. I should call the Kramers now."

Parsons said good-bye and hung up. I cleared his number, then made a call. It was not to the Kramers.

The phone rang. A woman answered.

"Law office of Mark Brandino. Can I help you?"

I almost hung up. My heart was pounding. The thoughts were absurd. The fears irrational. None of that mattered. This was my child.

Chapter Fifteen

You want to know what happens with my son. But you would not understand anything that happened without knowing about Jenny's therapy. And for that we must start again with Sean Logan.

I began working with Sean a few months before Jenny's rape. It was toward the end of winter. Sean never wore a coat. He said he was always hot. Yet when he came through my door the first time we met, he was shivering. I remember this with exceptional clarity.

Sean had come to me out of desperation. As you already know, Sean had lost his right arm in a bomb explosion in Iraq. His comrade died beside him. He was given the treatment, and he now had almost no memory of the event. He suffered from severe depression and anxiety, which were exacerbated by his underlying anxiety condition. He did not have the traditional PTSD pathology that most people have been made aware of through movies and magazine articles—the overreacting to stimuli reminiscent of combat. Do you recall how I explained to you the brain's filing system? How emotional responses to events cause the brain to categorize memories?

Simply put, the extreme emotional experience of combat causes the memories from that event to be filed in the metal cabinet—with neon lights and alarm bells. It's the brain's way of telling you, *Do not forget that when these things happen, you could die!* And so any stimuli that enter the brain that remotely resemble combat trigger the fight-or-flight chemical response, the flood of cortisol and adrenaline that make you react, or overreact. And when you are placed in a constant state of chemical panic, your "nerves fray." That's the colloquial expression. Your body is physically altered—heart pounds faster to get blood to muscles, pupils dilate to focus attention, sugar is produced for immediate energy consumption. It is physical stress. We need not get more complicated than that.

The course of therapy is not a walk in the park, but it has a methodology and a path involving desensitization—in a sense, refiling the memory. Every time we recall a memory, it is altered and then returned to storage in the altered state. This is called reconsolidation. Soldiers are exposed to combat stimuli in a setting that is safe and comfortable. Over time, they can make their brains take down the neon lights and alarm bells and recognize the difference between a balloon popping and sniper fire. The patient's brain actually begins to recall the memory in a different way that does not associate the facts of the memory with pain or fear.

This was not possible for Sean, because he was not dealing with a response to a filed factual memory. He was dealing with a physical and emotional response that had no "remembered" facts. I have had clients who believe in reincarnation. They tell me that they feel things that they should not feel, given the course of their lives. They tell me the only explanation is that they experienced things in their prior lives that left these feelings in place.

I will not go further afield to comment on my views of the supernatural. I have developed a tolerance for the views of others so that I do not inadvertently disparage them. It takes tremendous effort. However, I think these clients serve as a fine comparison to what Sean and Jenny experienced. Powerful feelings that do not have a file. *Why am I so afraid of the water? Why do I gag when I smell grass? Why did I feel déjà vu when I went to New York City for the first time?* These are some of the questions from my clients. Of course, I usually get to the answer without resorting to the absurd, but we do not need to concern ourselves with that.

Sean had different questions: *Why do I want to pound my fist into the wall when I'm holding my son? Why do I want to throw my wife across the room when she touches me? Why do I feel like screaming all the time, for no reason and at no one?* The triggers were benign and held no resemblance to anything he would have seen on his mission. He called them ghosts—the feelings that roamed inside him, looking for a place to rest.

And Jenny: *Why do I feel like my skin is crawling? Like I want to peel it off my body? Why do I keep rubbing my scar where he carved my skin with that stick? Why is my stomach always burning with acid?* Like Sean, her body was producing chemicals in reaction to an emotional response that had no particular trigger, and certainly no trigger that resembled her attack.

There is a world of controversy around memory recovery. Some researchers (and I use that term loosely because the people who have inserted themselves in this arena range from celebrated neuroscientists to convicted sex offenders) claim that memories cannot be recovered and that any so-called recovered memories are necessarily false. Indeed, I am sure you have heard about cases of emotionally damaged adults receiving treatment from therapists and suddenly "remembering" that they were molested by a parent or a teacher or a coach. There is even an organization dedicated to stopping memory-recovery therapy.

There are just as many researchers on the other side, and they, too, have compelling stories about successfully recovered memories that are later verified by confessions or physical evidence.

I have read every research study, news article, anecdotal story, and legal brief that has been made public over the years, and I am comfortable with my conclusions. There are two issues: The first is that memories are stored. The second is that stored memories must be retrieved to be "remembered." Both processes involve brain hardware and brain chemicals. Memories can be stored and subsequently lost or erased. Memories can also be saved but misfiled and therefore difficult to retrieve. Both these events are forms of "forgetting." I believed, and still do believe, that the treatment given to Sean and Jenny and now countless other trauma victims does not "erase" every memory from the trauma. Some are saved but misfiled, and are therefore capable of being found and retrieved. And remembered.

I did not presume to know which memories were hiding in Sean's brain, or Jenny's. It was a fact-finding mission, and it had to be done carefully. I have alluded to my concerns about suggestions becoming memories themselves during reconsolidation, and how this can corrupt the process of true memory recovery. You can see how this could happen, can't you? What if I told Sean his friend died in his arms before he himself lost consciousness, how blood was flowing from his mouth as he tried to speak, and how terror flooded his eyes? A hand reached out and grabbed hold of his left arm, and maybe a cry of pain made him shiver with his own fears of death. And then he looked down and saw his right arm mangled, flesh spilling out between shattered bones and ligaments, and he knew he would never be whole again. You can see how he might come to think these to be true and then to wonder if he witnessed them and finally to feel and see them as actual memories.

Sean and I gathered the facts. We collected reports from the field, interviews with other soldiers who served in that area and had been inside that town. Sean spoke to the marines who saved him and the interrogators who eventually captured some of the insurgents and could describe what they looked like. We even had pictures of some of them, the ones who were killed. Sean had low-level security clearance. But the soldiers were willing to bend the rules for him. I believe the process of talking to these soldiers, of reconnecting with "his people," was therapeutic in and of itself. He felt he had them on his side. He also had his wife and his son and his family. Now he had me.

Soon, he would have Jenny.

We were able to reconstruct the mission from the original plan. Sean remembered much of the plan, and we presumed that he had followed his orders in the field. We used a computer program to construct a virtual image of the town—like a video game. It is amazing how realistic these images are now. And then we worked, sometimes for hours at a time, walking Sean through the virtual village, his comrade beside him. We played audio taken from documentaries, the sound of the dirt crunching beneath his boots, the short, concise messages coming through the radio. The audio re-created what was heard during his actual mission. Sean would fill in the blanks with actions he knew he would have taken. I would read from the script we'd re-created using every piece of information we had gathered. Nothing else was added.

"You turn the next corner. There's one shot heard in the distance."

The audio would play the shot being fired.

"Medic! Medic! Oh fuck! Fuck! Miller down! Miller's down, man! Medic! Oh, fuck no! No!" I would read the script.

My heart jumps out of my chest, but I keep my shit together. Stop dead, back against the wall. Look up to the rooftops, look in windows. Shooter couldn't be this close, but there could be another one.

They know we're here. Maybe knew all along and were just wait-ing. That thought must have come. Valancia would be shitting his pants. This was his first real mission, and he was a little bit of a pussy. We keep moving.

The session would go on like this until we got to the place where the bomb went off. We had an actual image of that street and the red doorway where he and Hector Valancia were found. The marines did not find any debris indicating where the bomb had been hidden. There was speculation that it had been cleared before they arrived. It had taken close to twenty minutes to secure the area. They were both presumed dead.

"There are people on the street. You're getting close to the red door. The red door is the location of the insurgent you've come to capture or kill. It's just you and Valancia now. Six men are down. The ma-rines are on the way."

Valancia's telling me to pull back. I know he is. I can picture him, his face. He'd be tugging at my sleeve, saying something like, "This is no good, man. No good."

"Let's be clear, though. You don't remember him saying that, but it's likely he would have wanted to leave."

Yeah. More than likely. We'd been in there for five minutes, and we had six men down. Valancia would cut and run. I know what I'd be thinking.

"What is that?"

Kill this motherfucker or die trying.

"And Valancia would follow you?"

Sean would pause here, close his eyes, and swallow it down. *Yeah. He would follow me. And then he would get his fucking head blown off.*

We would go through the data we had, reliving each moment the best we could. Looking for these memories, these files, was maddening at times. It was like looking for lost car keys in a cluttered house. You retrace your steps, try to recall the last time you used them. You tear up the place, looking under couch cushions and carpets and in the pockets of every jacket and pair of pants. Sometimes we found traces, the equivalent of loose change. He remembered Valancia tripping in a small hole along the dirt road. And the smell of meat cooking, though he could not recall looking for its source, something he surely would have done. An open window, perhaps. But the big event had evaded him. Evaded us. At least with car keys, you know they didn't "vanish into thin air." With Sean's memories, and later Jenny's, there was always that possibility, and so we never knew when it was time to stop and give up the search. I will just say that the process of looking seemed to help both of them, and this made it easier to continue the work.

There were fifteen seconds between Sean's radio report that they had a visual on the red door and the next communication. That second report, the last one, indicated that there were seven civilians in the street, women, children, old men. Sean said this would have made him extremely nervous. That he would have been tempted to turn back then.

I would have thought it was off, you know. Every other street empty after the sound of the gunfire. But on this street, the street where our target was supposedly hiding, no one's afraid? Mothers don't bring their babies inside? Even after they see us, they don't run and hide? I reported it, so I must have seen it. And if I saw it, I would have thought about leaving.

"Would you have? Or would you have died trying to kill that motherfucker?"

This was the question he couldn't answer. His conscience wanted to believe that he had tried to retreat; that he hadn't let his ego and his anger at knowing these people had killed six men in his unit cloud his judgment and put Valancia's life on the line. That he would have considered his wife and son and even the war, because surely he was not going to get inside and complete his mission if they knew he was coming. He would be another dead soldier to drag through the street. A dead soldier can't fight. Yet, he could feel himself charging for that door, screaming and firing his gun and not caring how many of those people he killed. He could feel that rage. And he had been found there, by that door and not several yards away.

We were stuck in this place, and I became convinced that it was this place we needed to stay in until he remembered enough to know what had happened. Would he have to learn to forgive himself for leading Valancia into a death trap? Or would he have to learn to live with his decision to retreat, and not take out some of the insurgents who had killed his friends? I came to believe that his anger, his rage at his wife and son, was grounded in guilt. He felt unworthy of being loved, of having these gifts, and so being with them triggered self-hatred. Without knowing, without remembering, the "ghosts" would keep roaming.

The look on Jenny's face when she heard him talk of the ghosts was beyond satisfying to me professionally.

They met in my therapy group for victims of trauma. We meet every week. Sean had been coming to the group for several months, which was about a year into his treatment. He had been far too volatile before then. The decision to allow Jenny to come had not been easy, but I knew from the onset of her therapy that I would advocate for this course. Yes, her circumstances were complicated, but she was still a victim of trauma, and it is my experience that every victim of trauma needs a community of support.

Tom had objected. He was concerned that she would be exposed to "adult" content and language. He was not wrong about this. The conversations can be graphic and crude at times. But it is a group of mixed company, and this tends to keep the tone more civilized. Charlotte thought it would be helpful. She told Tom he just didn't understand that women needed to talk, to tell their stories and listen to others tell theirs. Two of the other patients in the group were rape survivors. This disagreement had taken place before I started my work with the Kramers, before Tom had found his voice within their marriage, so Charlotte had prevailed. This was one time I was thankful for her dominance.

I had told Jenny about Sean and Sean about Jenny. They were eager to meet in this setting. Because Jenny was new, she spoke first. She was not at all afraid, even though she was half the age of most of the patients in the room. She said, simply and concisely, *I'm here because I was raped. I'm the girl you probably all read about. I was given some drugs to help me forget what happened, and now I don't remember it. It was hard not remembering. Too hard. I tried to commit suicide.*

I did not press her to say more. Instead, I let each patient speak to make an introduction, which is our policy when we have a new member. Sean was somewhere in the middle. He was jumping out of his seat to tell his story to her. After he recited the facts, he admitted to his own suicidal thoughts. And then he explained about the ghosts, roaming inside him.

I know I can't live with them. The only reason I'm still here is because I choose to believe that I can get them out. Kill them or scare them or satisfy them somehow. If I didn't believe that, I would be dead.

Jenny's hand slowly rose to her mouth, and her eyes grew wide. As Sean went on, explaining about the ghosts, about how he needed to remember what happened in front of that red door, I could see the hope rush in her, almost plumping up her veins, filling her with the blood she'd spilled on that bathroom floor.

I do not have a strict policy against patients meeting outside the group. But I do advise that boundaries be established. I suspected that Sean and Jenny would connect somehow to share their stories in more detail. We can get sidetracked in group, with so many people and so many urgent needs. What I did not foresee was the depth of the connection and the series of events that would unfold. Jenny and Sean shared something unique, something no one else in this community shared. The treatment was not widely used then. There was no open forum to find others who had received it, who might be suffering in its aftermath. They understood something about each other that I could not; that their families could not; that the group could not.

"What about the other rape survivors?" I asked Jenny. "Do their stories, their feelings, resonate with you at all?"

Jenny shrugged. *I dunno. I guess. A little. But I don't get a lot of it. I mean, I get it, but I don't think I have the same problems. I mean, I don't really feel afraid of guys. I don't feel ashamed. Not even for cutting myself. I feel mad about it. I feel mad that I feel so bad all the time that I want to die. But not the way they do. I dunno. It's different.*

"But it's not different with Sean?"

She smiled and looked at the floor. I feared she was embarrassed. I feared it because it meant she was developing a crush on him.

It's like we get each other. And he makes me laugh.

"He's very dynamic. Very expressive, isn't he?"

Yes.

"How do you communicate?"

Texts mostly. Sometimes we Skype. He doesn't have iChat. He's too old.

"Ouch."

Sorry . . . I didn't mean . . . you know, it's a teenage thing.

"I'm kidding, Jenny. I know what you meant. How often do you text and Skype?"

Most days I wake up to something he's written in the middle of the night. He has trouble sleeping. It's usually really sad. I text him back before I get out of bed. I tell him to come back from the dark side. It's an inside joke we have. We have a lot of them. Mostly about the treatment and not being able to remember. He calls me Grandma. Stuff like that. Then it just depends on what we're doing. It's just kinda normal, like with Violet. Only Violet doesn't get a lot of what I say.

"But Sean does."

Yeah. He gets everything. Like, every single thing.

"You sound relieved when you say that."

She didn't answer except to nod her head. I could see she felt like crying, but she held it back. *I want to work now. Can we start?*

The human desire not to be alone in the world is powerful. More powerful, perhaps, than reason or conscience or fear.

I should want to take it all back, to support Tom Kramer in his objections and reconsider my plan to put Sean and Jenny in the same room. I should want that. But I don't. That image of Jenny, of the hope, the life rushing back inside her, is not something I would ever wish to be gone.

I started the memory-recovery process with Jenny soon after she met Sean. He had shared with her the small progress he had made and how he believed he was going to remember more. Jenny came into the process with high expectations, which I tried to mitigate to some extent. I had no idea what we were going to find.

Still, we forged ahead. First, we focused on our plan, on how we were going to collect our data from every source we could find. Her friends. The kids at the party who saw her, spoke to her. The couple who found her in the woods. And, of course, the forensic report. We discussed how we would walk through the night, starting with the parts she did remember. We would get the playlist from the kid who hosted the party and we would play the music. I would let her smell the drinks she consumed, and we would get the exact ingredients. Vodka, we knew, had been in all of them. She would bring the body spray she wore that night, and the cosmetics and even the clothes. And then we would walk through each stage. From the party to the lawn. From the lawn to the woods. And then, the most difficult part, each stage of the assault. The report was quite detailed. And there was a trail of blood and clothing.

I know this sounds morbid. You must get over it. The process is no different from what I did with Sean. It's no different from searching for your car keys.

Jenny was scared but eager. Her parents were terrified. But on the day we got the first memory back, they could all see I was right.

Chapter Sixteen

This is how that day unfolded.

Detective Parsons called me that morning. Cruz Demarco had finally been assigned a public defender and had his arraignment. Bail was set at fifty thousand dollars, and he was in the process of getting the money together with a bondsman. He had nothing to offer as collateral, and his mother was done with him. Two arrests in two years. She couldn't find it in herself to get back on that horse. Very sensible. Of course, it would have been more sensible to consider this twenty years earlier, when she was shooting heroin in front of a seven-year-old.

Forty-eight hours had passed since my drive back from Somers. My wife and I had met with Attorney Brandino. We gave him a five-thousand-dollar retainer, in exchange for which he agreed to speak with Jason and appear at any interview he might have with the police. He said he would instruct Jason on what to say and what not to say and stop him in the interview if he crossed any lines that could not be uncrossed. He was representing two other boys who had been at the party, and we had to sign a conflict waiver. One of them had already had the interview. They were looking for confirmation that Demarco was there that night, and nothing beyond that. I felt relieved. He was very reassuring.

Something else had transpired in these two days. The kid who'd bought the drugs from Demarco just before he was arrested (his name was John Vincent, if you recall) had been brought in for an interview. Parsons had used the leverage from that day to get the kid to identify Demarco from the night of the rape. Once he had that ID, he went back at Demarco.

Demarco has a story, and he didn't mind telling it to a point. After the Vincent kid gave him up for the night of the party, he admitted to being there. Said he was "invited" by a senior he'd met at some club in New Haven. Said he came to "hang out." Wouldn't cop to selling drugs, but there was some indication he might be willing to give up some of Fairview's self-entitled punks in exchange for a deal. I didn't tell him yet that wasn't what we were looking for. Didn't tell him he was being looked at for a rape. And the idiot PD didn't put those pieces together until it was too late.

Parsons danced around the subject. Said he needed verification Demarco was really there so he could nail Vincent—made it seem like a favor that might be the start of some quid pro quo on Demarco's charges. Asked him to describe the party, where he was parked, what he saw and heard. Told him they needed to make sure he wasn't bullshitting about being there that night.

He looks at his PD, who nods. Sure, go ahead and dig a deeper hole. What an idiot. I don't care what it costs you—hire a decent lawyer. You didn't hear that from me.

Demarco described some of the kids he saw coming and going. His account included the couple who went into the Suburban to have sex—which was consistent with Teddy Duncan's story. He also saw a teenage boy pass by his car and disappear into the woods.

So he says this, and I'm like, What the fuck? Is this for real? My head is spinning now. Is he playing us? If he did the rape, there's no way he cops to being there just to position himself for a deal on the drugs. No way. It made me start to think that he was just there selling dope, and that maybe this kid he saw did the rape. But then I thought, what if he wants us to think that? What if he's making this whole thing up about seeing this kid go into the woods because he knows we have kids who will place him at the party, he knows about the rape—maybe did the rape—so why not get out in front of that? Maybe the PD is really some do-gooder from Yale who's outsmarting us. Fuck.

Demarco told Parsons that the boy had been wearing a blue hoodie with a red bird. He couldn't remember what kind of bird or if there was writing as well. The boy had short hair, light brown, average height, average build—athletic looking. That described about 50 percent of the boys at Fairview High School.

I don't know what to make of this. I haven't said anything to the Kramers, but you know what Tom will do when he does find out.

"He'll want to ask Jenny."

Yep. And so do I.

I told Parsons that I could try to find a way to ask Jenny this without compromising our work. But, honestly, I did not see how I was going to do that. Since my work began with both Sean and Jenny, I had immersed myself in memory-recovery research, and there were new reports coming in every week. There was one that had caused alarm. A neuroscientist in New York reported being able to reconsolidate memories to make them false, simply by providing detailed facts that were interwoven with strands of reality. People were told

they had been lost in the mall when they were little children—
something that never happened. The mall was one that they knew
well and the story included specifics, like how their mothers yelled at
a clerk, what they'd been wearing, what they ate for lunch. The details had all been taken from true stories. It was just that last detail—
that they had gotten lost—that was added. Their brains added that
last detail into the real memories of going to the mall and, voilà—
they had a whole new reconsolidated false memory that they could
not discern from the truth. Some of them cried as they "remembered"
their fear when they couldn't find their mothers.

It is one thing to reconsolidate memories in a way that lessens the
emotional attachment. I see no harm—indeed, only good—in that.
But changing the facts is altogether different.

You can imagine the implications for my work.

I saw Jenny later that day. We began our therapy as we always do,
by talking about any new feelings she'd had, her state of mind, her
general disposition. I always make sure she's not slipping back into
the darkness that made her suicidal. And I always make sure she's
not using any substances beyond the mild anxiety meds I'd prescribed. Lately, I had added to our session inquiries about Sean because their developing relationship was having a profound impact on
her. And because it was beginning to concern her parents. We moved
on from there with a significant pause and reconfirmation that she
felt prepared to do the memory work. She always has, without fail
and with visible enthusiasm. I could see her mood lifting as she pulled
from her bag the prompts we have been using to go back to that horrible night.

"Where do you want to start today?" I asked her.

With that smell.

How good is your memory? I know I've mentioned that one of the
few things Jenny remembered was a strong odor. I obtained sam-

ples from a physical rehabilitation center, a variety of "scratch and sniff" patches that are used for patients with anosmia (loss of smell due to brain injury). They use them mostly to test—to see if there are any particular odors that are recognized by the patient. Any recognition prompts hope because if there is none within six months, the condition is considered permanent. It is a terrible condition, but that does not concern my work with Jenny. The patches were extremely useful to us.

Jenny always held her clothing in her lap. They are not the actual torn and bloodstained articles from that night, but new ones her mother purchased—exact replicas. The short black skirt, the ballet slippers, the cropped sweater and underpants. All exactly the same. She rubbed some makeup on her face and lips, the same makeup she has always worn and wore that night. It has a fruity smell. We now know which songs were playing during the party and the entire hour of the rape. I won't bore you with the list. It was what you would imagine. Demi Lovato, Nicki Minaj, One Direction, Maroon 5, et cetera, et cetera. With closed eyes and the room dark, we played the music and took her back to that night. I did the initial prompts until she knew them herself.

I'm so happy when we walk in. I feel pretty. I feel excited. All I can think about is Doug Hastings. I walk with Violet through the kitchen. We're looking for kids from our grade. People say hello to us. We get a drink. My eyes are scanning every doorway, looking for a glimpse of Doug. Violet pokes me. She tells me to stop being so obvious. I try to talk to a girl we know who's already drunk. She sounds like an idiot.

I placed the paper strip that smells like vodka under her nose. She inhaled and let the smell sift through her brain. The music was playing. We know what song it was. "I Knew You Were Trouble" by Taylor Swift. Jenny remembered this all very well. She explained to me that this song is about a boy who breaks a girl's heart and how the girl is singing that she should have known better. This song was still playing when Jenny and Violet walked into the family room and she saw Doug there with another girl. They were definitely "together." We discussed briefly the irony of the song.

I felt dizzy. It wasn't the drink, either, because I'd just had a couple of sips. I felt like the world had just exploded, my world. My entire world.

Jenny and I have discussed this many times. I am an "old man" by her standards, but I can remember what it felt like to be rejected by a girl when I was fifteen. We all know that feeling, don't we? Don't you?

Violet stares at me and then Doug and then back at me. She tries to make me laugh by saying she's gonna go kick his ass. She says she heard he has a little dick anyway. She makes fun of his hair, how it's sticky with gel. She calls him metro. None of it matters. I could not sit with the feelings I had, so I went to the kitchen and started chugging vodka.

Jenny had begun to adopt "therapy speak." It's very common. We talk about "sitting" with our feelings. Being able to process them and redirect them with thoughts so they lose their power over our bodies. It is then that we are able to live our everyday lives.

Jenny continued with the parts she remembered. They ended with her vomiting in the bathroom.

Violet was holding my hair. I could hear people talking about me, laughing at me. Someone was pounding on the bathroom door. Violet yelled at them to go away. She told them to fuck off. This song was playing, and I hate this song.

"Moves Like Jagger" was playing when they were in the bathroom. It was playing in my office as she was talking about the bathroom. It is here that we stopped to smell the strips. It was my suspicion that the strong odor she recalled was something in that room—the vomit, or bathroom cleaner, or one of those toilet disinfectant disks that turn the water blue. I had strips for the vomit (yes, they do have those) and for the cleaners. I have an actual blue disk—the same brand used by the family in that house on Juniper Road. None of them had a greater reaction than any other beyond what would be expected (the vomit strip making her cringe).

But on this day, I had added one more. Bleach.

I had not thought of it originally. I do not clean our bathroom. It was my wife who had this thought when I was confiding in her our failure with the memory of the odor. I went through the list of things we'd been working with. The family had given me a list to the best of their recollection. But remember, nine months had passed. My wife thought about it for a few seconds and then blurted it out—*Bleach!* The irony of this will soon be apparent.

I went through our strips and the blue disk with Jenny. Then I introduced a bleach disk. Bleach smells the same (unless it's scented) in all forms—liquid, powder, granules, pressed-powder disks. She looked startled and opened her eyes.

"It's something new. Just let it come in," I said.

She closed her eyes, then inhaled deeply. The reaction came in a matter of seconds, but I can recall the progression as if it were happening right now in slow motion.

It started in her shoulders. They rose almost to touch her ears. It reminded me of a cat when it becomes afraid, how its back arches up and its hair stands on end. Her face then contorted, forehead collapsing into her eyebrows, lips pursing together, then her open eyes, wide with terror. She jumped from the chair. Her arms flailed, fists closed, swinging at my hand holding the bleach and then at me. She caught me in the face, sending my glasses to the ground. My cheek began to swell instantly. I would have a bruise for several days.

But it is the scream that I remember most.

She stood in the middle of my office, holding her stomach, buckled over in half. Her back rose and fell with the overpowering heaves of her breath as the cries of agony poured from her body.

I have treated hundreds of patients and I have seen breakdowns of all kinds. Men have punched holes in my walls. Women have sobbed. Men have sobbed. Teenagers have yelled at me with obscenities that rival my patients in Somers. This was something beyond anything I had ever witnessed. And I knew Jenny was back in those woods.

I did not hold her. That would not have been appropriate. But I did grab hold of her arms to steady her. She pushed me away; her arms were still swinging wildly.

Stop it!

She screamed at me over and over. She was looking at me but not at me. I kept trying to grab hold of her until she finally let me. I walked her to the sofa and helped her lie down in fetal position. I texted her mother that we were ending early and to please come back from her errands.

"Jenny," I said cautiously. "Where did you go? Can you tell me?"

She held herself, still crying, but calmer. Her hand was on her back, rubbing the scar.

"Close your eyes again. Take a deep breath. Let's not lose this moment. What are you feeling? Can you tell me? Do you want to stop or keep going?"

She took a breath. She closed her eyes. Tears were streaming, pooling on the leather beneath her skin. She was so strong. So incredibly determined. And when she spoke, the way she said the words, and the raw emotions that were escaping the confines of her body and filling the room—I felt not only that I understood her. I felt like I *was* her that night.

I feel him. I feel his hand on my shoulder, pushing me to the ground. I feel another hand on my neck , like I'm an animal and he's riding me. Oh God!

"Okay, Jenny." I could barely get the words out. "What else do you feel? What else do you see? Do you smell the bleach?"

She shook her head. *There's nothing else! Where did it go! I want to see him. Who did this? Who did this to me?*

Rage seemed to have taken over her body. She got up from the sofa and looked around the room, frantically.

"What do you need, Jenny? What is it?"

Then she found it. The bleach disk. She picked it up and pressed it to her face. It made her gag—it's too strong to be that close.

"Jenny, stop! It can burn you, your nostrils and throat . . ."

She breathed it in again and then dropped to her knees. I could see it on her face then. It was beautiful but also profoundly devastating. We had found it. She had found it. One small memory of that night.

"What is it, Jenny? What are you remembering?"

It hurts so much. I can feel him, he's tearing me, pushing harder and harder. I can smell him. I smell it on him. He's on me like I'm an animal. Oh God! I feel him! I can't stop him! I can't stop it from happening! I feel him inside me. I can't hear him, but the way he is, I don't know! The way he's moving. I'm an animal and he's just riding me and it's making him . . . I don't know!

"You do know. What is it you know about him right now, at the moment he's inside you?"

Oh God! Oh God! I can't say it!

"Just say it. I already know, Jenny. So just say it."

I know he feels satisfied.

I had no more words that day.

Chapter Seventeen

By the time Charlotte came for Jenny, we were both emotionally exhausted. I told Charlotte that it had been a productive but difficult session and that we would talk about it later. I suggested Jenny take a pill and get some sleep.

Tom and Charlotte met with me the next day. In the eleven weeks I'd been treating the Kramer family, I had conducted just one session with both parents, and that had been to discuss Jenny's treatment. Seeing them separately had proved immensely useful to their family, and to each of them individually, and I fully intended to stay this course. I have already told you how I feel about couples therapy. However, I made an exception, given the extraordinary progress Jenny and I had made in recovering this memory of the rape.

Tom's primary concern was with the search for the rapist and how we could use this new information in the investigation. He also wanted to know why I had not asked Jenny about the blue sweatshirt with the red bird. Charlotte was more concerned with what this memory was doing to Jenny. After her breakthrough about her meeting with

Bob and her acceptance of the guilt she was carrying for not seeing Jenny's death march during the months after the rape, she was keeping her eye on that ball.

I explained to Tom, to both of them, that I was not about to introduce the blue sweatshirt into the memory-recovery process with Jenny after what had happened. I had come to believe three things after her sudden recall of the moment the rapist penetrated her. First, was that the memories had not all been erased. Of the different scenarios for "forgetting" that I have explained, it was clear that Jenny's "forgetting" had to do with the inability to *recall* the memories from that night. The treatment she was given, the combination of drugs, had caused the memories to be filed in a place that was disconnected from any emotion, and from the other memories of the party. Without having these trails of crumbs to lead her back, the memories of the rape were lost inside her brain. The missing car keys.

The second thing I believed was the deduction that if the memory of this one moment had not been erased, none of them had. The events from that one hour were so close in terms of spatial proximity and emotional significance that there was no reason to believe that only some would have been spared the treatment. My own thoughts were spinning that day, thinking about what this meant for Jenny, but also for Sean. I wanted to tell them both to clear their schedules, to work with me day and night, until we found every last detail of what had happened to them. But I am a patient man, and I respect the process of therapy. Too much too soon could cause more harm than good. It's like inputting data into a computer. I didn't want the hard drive to crash.

The third thing, and the most important to convey to Tom, was that Jenny was like a patient having surgery. She was, metaphorically, on the table, cut open, exposed. Given the reconsolidation research and the uncertainty about memory recovery, we had to keep the operating room perfectly sterile so our patient did not become infected with harmful germs. Her brain was starting to find the missing files and put them back into the right place—the place with the story about that night, the songs and the clothes and drinks and Doug with that other girl. How easy it would be to allow a false fact to be added to that story while it was being reconsolidated. Like the subjects who were made to "remember" being lost in the mall.

"Do you understand, Tom? If I ask her or even suggest that a man in a blue sweatshirt might be a suspect, she could put that with other memories of that night and believe it to be true even if it's not—and then we'll never know. If we can just be patient—"

Charlotte understood. *She might remember it on her own, and then we'd know for sure. My God. It's been almost a year. Unless she remembers his face, I don't see how any of this is going to help.*

"Well, even then, please don't lose sight of the fact that the treatment has compromised her ability to serve as a witness. And all the work I'm doing here, well . . . it's very unconventional."

Tom rubbed his forehead with the palm of his hand. *I don't care about all of that. I just want to know who it is.*

"Even if the way you find him means he can't be punished?"

Oh, he'll be punished. Don't doubt that. Don't ever doubt that.

Charlotte looked at him, and then at me. We both had the same thought, I imagine. Tom seemed to be indicating that he would take matters into his own hands if a conviction were not possible. But we were so far away from that point, I didn't give it much pause. Nor did Charlotte. That did not prevent her from using Tom's false bravado to lash out.

Seriously, Tom. Can we just stop this charade? You have put all our lives on hold while you—do what? Look for pictures of boys in sweatshirts? Why can't you get past this? Why, for God's sake, can't you be man enough to let it go!

"Charlotte . . ." I said, trying to stop this runaway train.

On hold? What the hell has been on hold? Huh? I coached Lucas's lacrosse team. I had record-breaking commissions. I'm home every goddamned night and every weekend playing with our son and studying with our daughter so she can get back on track. What should I be doing? Playing golf? Would that make me more of a man, if I played more golf and spent less time searching for this monster?

This is why I don't believe in couples therapy.

"Charlotte, Tom . . . let's stop right there. Everyone is emotional today. Saying things that cannot be unsaid is not going help anyone. Least of all Jenny."

Fine, Charlotte said. She could no longer look at her husband. *Can we please discuss what this means for Jenny? You said she has found one memory from the woods. The man smelled of bleach. . . .*

"Or she could smell bleach in the woods somehow."

Okay. She smelled the bleach. She would have smelled it for the entire time. For the whole hour it was happening. And yet the one memory is the moment he . . .

"Penetrated her. Yes, that's right."

But he did that for the whole hour. And in different ways . . .

"I believe the memory was from the beginning. I imagine it was that moment that was most shocking to her. When she realized what he wanted to do. What he was going to do."

Charlotte exhaled loudly and slumped back against the sofa cushions. Her eyes were on the sticker on that tulip plant. *So now she knows what it feels like to be raped. So now what? Is this going to make her feel better?*

I proceeded with caution. Knowing about Charlotte's first sexual experience, I felt I needed to be respectful of her secret. I had been suggesting to her that she tell her husband. It was the only way to finish breaking the bond she had with Bob Sullivan, and unless that bond was broken, her marriage was going to fail. Charlotte did not want her marriage to fail. She just did not see that she was on that road.

"I know it sounds strange. But yes, this is going to make her feel better. She is going to be able to attach her emotions to this memory. Even if this is the only one we get back, it may be enough."

Tom was not paying attention. I could see him obsessing on that sweatshirt. And I knew he was going to go home and ask his daughter about it.

"Tom?" I said, getting his attention. "We need to be on the same page. All of us."

I don't know. This all sounds like a bunch of voodoo nonsense to me. You let her smell bleach and she remembered being raped. What if we show her a sweatshirt and she remembers something else about that night? How can you say the bleach wasn't suggestive? Huh? You didn't know if there was bleach. You thought she was remembering a smell from the bathroom. How do we even know where she smelled the bleach?

"I don't know for sure. But she had an organic memory of a strong odor. She's smelled over sixty odors during our work together, and this was the only one that triggered that response. She doesn't have any memory of colors or clothing or the red bird. If I introduce something like that, she'll know there must be a reason, that we have some suspicions, and that knowledge could trigger a false memory. Her brain will send it to the place where it holds the story of that night, and it will arrive in that place with a seal of approval. I don't know how else to explain it to you."

Then show her sixty shirts and coats and sweatshirts. It's safe to say the guy was wearing something on his body. She can't assume anything from that. Right?

Tom was relentless. And he had Parsons breathing down my neck about this sweatshirt. If they could all just give me more time to work with the bleach and this one little memory. It was like a little newborn chick. I just wanted to keep it safe and warm and see how it progressed. I agreed in the end to have her look through catalogs of men's clothing, from suits to T-shirts, while we were doing our work. I promised to do it later that week.

I would not keep that promise.

Chapter Eighteen

The Kramers went home to Jenny. I went home to my wife, who was crying in our bed, holding a blue hoodie with a red bird.

The Kramers did not speak in the car or in the house, partly because they were angry at one another, and partly because they were each lost in the new reality Jenny's recalled memory had created. They were two trains leaving the same station but heading in opposite directions.

Tom went to his computer and pulled up photos from the high school Web site. He was looking for pictures of students. He was looking for blue sweatshirts. Charlotte went to Jenny's room. She found her daughter reading a history textbook. The tutor had just left, and Jenny seemed calmly engrossed in an assignment.

It was the kind of moment that would have gone right by me before the rape. My eye was trained for abnormal behavior, misbehavior. If I saw her on her laptop but couldn't see the screen, for example. I'd go in and pretend to be opening a shade or putting away some laundry so I could get a peek at what she was looking at. Or if she was speaking too quietly on the phone, I'd check our account to see what number she'd called. Things like that. I guess you could call it spying, but it's just what we do. We all do it, the mothers. We talk about it at lunch sometimes, share our notes. But now, it's the normal behavior that stops me in the hallway.

Charlotte went into Jenny's room. Jenny looked up and smiled at her. It was not a happy smile, but it wasn't fake either. Jenny asked if I had told them. Charlotte nodded. She did not press Jenny for details or offer any opinions or advice.

I walked to her bed and climbed in beside her. She looked at me strangely at first, but then it was as if she remembered how I used to do this with her, how I would climb into her bed and she would lay her head on my chest and I would rub her back. When she was a little girl, I would read to her. Sometimes we would just talk. That probably surprises you.

"Why do you think it surprises me?" I asked her.

Because of how our relationship changed. How she grew closer to Tom and more distant from me. But it seemed normal. I think it was normal. She needed to distance herself from me to grow up. Isn't that what girls do?

"Yes, it can be very normal. You didn't get to experience that, did you?"

How do you mean? I couldn't have been more distant from my mother.

"But you didn't get to separate in a safe environment. Where you knew you could go back to being a little girl if you needed to."

Charlotte thought about that and nodded with ambivalence. *Well, in any case, I climbed into her bed and she put her head on my chest. I kissed her hair and I ran my hand up and down her back. I kept thinking about her scar and how I wanted to reach under her shirt and touch it.*

"Why?" I asked her, though I knew the answer.

I guess I wanted her to know that I knew it was there. Well, of course she knew that. But that I really knew it was there. That I knew . . . or that I felt it.

Charlotte couldn't find the words to explain herself.

"What did you feel?"

It took her a long moment to answer.

When you told us what she said, how she felt like . . . like she was an animal being ridden and how she could tell it satisfied him when he'd finally, you know . . . it's not easy the first time. He had to work for it, didn't he? He had to put in some effort and listen to her screams, didn't he?

"Yes, I imagine that's true."

And maybe she thought he wouldn't be able to, that maybe it wasn't possible for it to happen like this. That maybe the fight she was putting up . . . every muscle working to keep him out, to keep him from succeeding . . . There's this moment when he breaks through and finds his way in, all the way inside you and then his body just shakes with ecstasy and yours with pain and this feeling of, God what is it? What is it that's more than the pain?

"It's your will, Charlotte. Your will is broken."

Charlotte looked at me with wide eyes, her face replete with relief. I shouldn't have made it that easy for her. I should have led her to it but let her find it on her own. She would have. And then it would have been more hers than mine. And, the truth is, it was mine. My childhood assault had felt that same way. I believe this is true for anyone who is attacked physically. I was not at my best that day she told me about her talk with Jenny. I was impatient, even at this most profound moment for Charlotte Kramer. My mind was not on Charlotte and Jenny but rather on my wife and my son.

Yes! She said, *Yes. Your will is broken.*

I sighed with frustration at my incompetence. I know better than this. Still, there was value in her having the answer, no matter how sloppily we had managed to come across it.

That's why you feel like an animal. You have no power, your voice is not heard, your body is not your own. Yes, that's what it is! Like you can't believe you have lost your power over your own body, over your movements and your . . . your integrity . . . your physical integrity. We do this to animals, don't we? We take wild horses and we ride them into submission. But they, they get over it, don't they? They sit in their stalls and eat their dried hay and shit at their own feet and savor the stroke of a brush held by the very creature who broke their spirit.

"Yes," I said. "Some animals can thrive in a submissive environment. Others do not. Humans do not. History shows this, doesn't it? War? Rebellion? What did you do then? Did you touch her scar?"

Charlotte shook her head. *No. I hugged her and I told her that it wasn't going to be like that ever again. That she had to think of it like a wave in the ocean that takes you by surprise and tumbles you to shore. Have you ever felt that? My kids love to ride the waves at the beach. And even after they get tumbled and their bathing suits get filled with sand and they even get scraped up sometimes, they still go back because it's fun to catch one and feel that you're on top of that power and not beneath it. And then you and the wave just ride safely to shore. I couldn't think of a better analogy. I don't think she understood completely. But it was a start.*

"I think that's an excellent start. I imagine the difference between a wave and a rapist is that the wave has power whether it tumbles you or carries you to shore. You've simply gotten in its way. The rapist has power only when he's hurting his victim. Rape is not sex. But that was still a good start."

I know they are different, obviously. But the mechanical part of it is the same. Everyone uses that expression to describe what you just did—about the power and all that. I don't know. Call it what you want—rape, sex, whatever—there is penetration by one person of another.

"Yes. That is true. Maybe we are just saying the same thing with different words. The important part is that you spoke to your daughter about this."

It was the first time I've felt reconnected to her since the rape. Maybe even long before it. I did, I felt this connection, this bond which I couldn't share with her, but it was there for me. I know it's different, what happened with me the first time. But some of it, that moment that she described to you, of being an animal and having someone, like you said, take your will from you in that way. That part, that one part felt very similar.

"So you realize what that means, don't you?"

I'm not sure.

"Well, you've told me that you remember *wanting* to have sex with your mother's husband. That can't be true if you had that feeling, that same feeling Jenny had. Maybe you didn't physically resist him. And maybe he would have stopped if you'd asked him. But you did not want it to happen. Your will was broken by a need for love that should have been filled by your mother."

She was silent then. She was not ready to accept this. To let herself off the hook. She had become so accustomed to living her double life. Bad Charlotte was a part of her and bad Charlotte wanted to stay.

"And how was Tom with everything?"

My question was devious, unethical. It may seem benign to you, but I was now also living a double life. The doctor trying to help this family. And the father trying to protect his own.

I don't really know. I don't know what he's feeling anymore. He fell asleep in bed with his computer on his lap. I don't know why I did this, but I removed the computer, and I took off my clothes and then I pulled down the comforter. Tom woke up. He looked at me almost with shock. We haven't had sex for almost a year. The one time we tried after the rape, I could tell it felt wrong to him. Like he couldn't enjoy himself until Jenny was okay and her attacker was behind bars. I didn't really want to either. I just thought it was time. But last night I didn't care. I climbed on top of him and we had sex. I don't know if he enjoyed it. I don't care about that either. He didn't seem to like it, but he did nothing to stop me. It's like everything else in our marriage. He just crumbled. I feel like shit. I don't know why I did it. Do you think I was trying to do that same thing to him? To take his will?

"No, I don't."

Then what?

"I think you wanted to feel the wave take you safely to shore."

This session came the day after I promised Tom I would try to find a memory of a blue sweatshirt. And the day after my wife found the blue sweatshirt on the floor of my son's closet.

But I have gotten ahead again. Let's go back to the afternoon following my meeting with the Kramers, the meeting when I told them about Jenny's recalled memory.

I was deeply satisfied as I drove home. Jenny and I had recovered the memory, and now I had shared the news with her parents. I was hopeful that more memories would come. More and more until she remembered every detail of that night—the moment when she first felt his hand on her body; the moment when she realized he was going to hurt her; the instinct to fight; screaming for help, still hopeful, still not believing this was happening; then the cool air on her skin as her clothing was ripped off; the memory she recalled—the penetration, the stealing of her innocence and her will and her humanity. What else was in there waiting to be found? Pain; acceptance; the stick scratching her skin, reaching the nerves under the first layer and the nerves of each layer after that which sent more pain signals to her brain. Agony. Despair. Ruin. I have been doing this long enough to know.

It was early afternoon. The Kramers had been my last appointment. I try not to schedule patients after Jenny or her parents in case we need to go longer. I do the same with Sean. Their sessions are unpredictable, as you have seen. On this day, I was looking forward to sharing with my wife the tremendous news about the bleach and the memory recall it had provoked. I had not told her yet, because I had not decided whether it was appropriate. I decided I would do so as I drove home. I simply could not keep this to myself for one more day.

"Julie?" I called out from the kitchen. The lights were on. Her car was in the garage. There was no answer.

"Honey?" I called out again. This time I heard her. She yelled to me from upstairs.

Alan! Alan! her voice sounded surprised and relieved and panicked all at once. She had not been expecting me, but was now in immediate need of my assistance.

Of course, I set down my briefcase and keys and hurried up the stairs.

"Julie? Where are you?"

Here! I'm here!

I followed her voice to our bedroom.

It would be too easy to say, simply, that I saw her sitting on our bed with the blue sweatshirt, her face contorted by fear, and that I knew our son was in trouble. I do not know if you have experienced something like this. Most of us have, to varying degrees. It is not at all dissimilar from what Jenny described, the slow putting together of facts and then the horrific realization of what is happening. You have a moment of mental rebellion, where your brain rejects the information that is coming in. It is too toxic, a virus, and it is going to require the massive realignment of emotions and attachments that give you pleasure or maybe just peace of mind. It is going to wreak havoc.

The information entered my brain. The sweatshirt. My wife's fear about our son being at that party. Her fear infecting me, making me call that lawyer. Then it was real, this risk to our own family from that night. The new facts entered my brain, and within seconds the rebellion was lost and the realignment was in place. They were painful seconds. Like a tooth being pulled.

I found this in his closet.

She got up and walked to where I was standing. She got close to me and pressed the sweatshirt into my chest.

The lawyer called this morning. He told me one of the other boys had his interview today and they asked him about a blue sweatshirt with a red bird. He told me that Jason would be asked this same question and did I know how he would answer. I bought him a hoodie for his birthday that year, remember?

I did not remember. It had not been important to me then.

We got it on our trip to Atlanta. That conference you had, remember? We had to go to that Hawks game and we got him this. The red bird—it's a hawk! Look.

She held up the sweatshirt. There was a red hawk on the front and the back. The name of the team was in white, but the letters were small. On the back was just a hawk. I took hold of her arms and looked at her sternly.

"What did you tell him?"

I told him the truth. That Jason had a blue hoodie with a red hawk on it.

"Oh, Jesus!" I let go of her arms and turned away, thinking, thinking.

Did you know about this? Did you know they were looking for a boy in a blue sweatshirt? Did she remember? You would tell me, wouldn't you?

"I didn't know about the sweatshirt."

Yes, I know. The lies continued.

She blabbered on and on. *What was I supposed to do? He's our lawyer! We can't have Jason lie. What if someone remembers? He wore that thing all spring. If he lies and they find out he lied, he'll look guilty.*

"Of what?" I asked. "No one would believe Jason raped Jenny Kramer."

Think about it, Alan! He's a swimmer. He shaves his legs and arms. . . . Maybe he shaves everything. . . . What if he does? What if they ask him and he has to admit he shaves everywhere?

I waved her off. "The whole goddamned team shaves! Half of them were at that party. That doesn't mean anything!"

But now this! She held out the blue sweatshirt. *When I got off the phone, I ran upstairs and started going through his things. I couldn't remember him wearing that sweatshirt since that spring. It wasn't there anywhere. Not in the laundry, or his drawers. Then I just started tearing apart his room. I started to think, maybe it's gone. Maybe he'd lost it, and maybe he'd lost it before the party! Then he couldn't have been wearing it that night. And then . . . God! I started digging through all the crap on the floor of his closet. And there was this plastic bag and it had the sweatshirt!*

"Why was it in the bag? Was that all there was?" I was shifting then to damage control.

There were some sweatpants and socks and a pair of boxers. Sometimes he does that when he changes at the pool. He puts his school clothes in a bag, and then he changes into whatever he's wearing to go out after.

"Where are they? Where's the rest of it?"

I followed her into the laundry room, where she'd placed the rest of the clothing into the machine. She hadn't started it yet.

I didn't know what to do. If I should wash everything or throw it out. It all smells like the pool.

She handed me the sweatshirt then, and I pressed it to my nose without thinking. It smelled of the pool where Jason spends most of his free time. It smelled of chlorine. You can already see where this is going.

I leaned against the wall and closed my eyes. I reasoned with myself why I should tell her, though the real reason had nothing to do with reason. It was my purely selfish desire not to be alone with my agony.

"Jenny Kramer had a recall yesterday. A memory from the night of the rape."

Julie looked at me warily.

"It was the bleach, Julie. He smelled of bleach."

Her eyes grew wide then as her hand drew slowly through the air to cover her mouth. *That's three things. Three things they could use against him!*

"There were a lot of swimmers at that party. Half the team, you said."

We both looked at the sweatshirt.

"He didn't do it," I said.

I know that.

"Do you? Do you know that the way I do? I know it! In my bones and in my heart. This man was a sociopath. Do you understand?"

Of course I do!

"He held her face into the ground. He gripped her neck and defiled her over and over for an hour!"

I know . . . I know.

"And then he took a stick, a sharp stick, and whittled away at her, at her flesh until he was all the way through her skin, every layer of skin!"

Okay! Just stop! Stop it. I know what he did to that poor girl!

"Then you can't possibly be worried that our son did this."

She took a long breath then and waited for me to calm down. I was indignant, and it was wrong of me to direct it at her. It didn't matter what we thought, what we knew about our son. The world would accuse him, would doubt him. The world would want to believe. Tom Kramer would want to believe. Charlotte would want to believe. Jenny would want to believe. A thought rushed in, and I was too overwhelmed to stop it from coming back out.

"They won't let me treat her anymore. If this goes any further. I'll be out of the case. I won't be able to help her get her memory back."

Julie looked at me with contempt. *That's what you're thinking? Our son could be accused of a brutal rape. His life could be ruined, and that's what you're thinking?*

"He didn't do it."

It doesn't matter, Alan. You know what will happen. The case will never get solved, and the suspicion will hang over him for the rest of his life!

She was right on all fronts. I don't know why my mind went to the case and to treating Jenny. My selfishness was more powerful than I had imagined.

"You're right. I'm sorry."

What do we do?

I didn't have all the answers.

"Call the lawyer back. Tell him you were wrong. The sweatshirt was white with the red hawk. Anything. Just tell him you were wrong and that you're so relieved. I don't trust him. He could help his other clients by throwing Jason under the bus. It's too great a conflict now. We'll talk to Jason ourselves. We'll come up with an answer that will work. Not a lie, but some kind of answer."

Julie agreed. She asked me what then? Surely someone would remember the sweatshirt. And now with the chlorine and the shaving—those would go together, wouldn't they? Parsons and Tom Kramer would be on that trail, on the trail of a swimmer. It made perfect sense. Every kid on the team who'd been at the party would be scrambling to get out of the way of that train.

As I've said, I didn't have all the answers.

But I would.

Chapter Nineteen

Remembering these days and recounting them is extremely difficult. They were fraught with emotion. Fear, mostly. They are not well organized in my mind.

I saw Jenny on a Wednesday. She recalled that one memory. She remembered the bleach. The next day I saw the Kramers together to discuss this finding. Cruz Demarco had already admitted being at the party and said he'd seen a boy with a blue hoodie with a red bird on it walking into the woods. I have discussed this as well. Tom made me promise I would work on recovering a memory about the blue hoodie now that we'd found one memory of that night. The Kramers went home that afternoon. Thursday afternoon. Tom spent the rest of the day on the computer, searching for blue hoodies with red birds. Charlotte began to see the connection between her experience with her stepfather and what happened to her daughter. She reexperienced that night on the sofa through Jenny's one recalled memory, and she held her daughter in her arms and tried to give her comfort and hope.

Then she gave some to herself by making love to her husband. I went home to my wife and the blue hoodie with the red hawk.

The next day, Friday, Charlotte came for her session. Tom would come in later that day. I have already told you some of it, how she spoke about her talk with Jenny and how I did her the disservice of feeding her conclusions. Now you understand why I was so incompetent.

After seeing Charlotte at eight thirty that Friday, I had been a bundle of nerves. Two patients came and went, and I faked interest in their problems. It was a morning of frivolity. Mrs. C was having a dispute with her neighbor over a fence. She was chronically depressed, but this was what she wanted to discuss. The neighbor. The fence. Mr. P had insomnia again. He didn't want to take Ambien. I spent the hour addressing his moronic concerns. Do you or don't you want to sleep? That's what I wanted to say to him. But I did not. I exercised miraculous self-control, waiting for my wife to call.

She called at eleven fifteen. I took the call even though Mr. P was in my office. I told him it was a patient emergency. Lies, lies, lies.

I told the lawyer the sweatshirt was dark purple and that it had red letters, not a red bird. I did what you said. I told him I was so relieved.

"Did he believe you?"

I think so. He seemed to. He said they were interviewing three more kids today and that Jason wasn't on the list yet. He spoke directly to Detective Parsons.

"Did he say how much time we have?"

He said it would be at least a week. But I think if we tell them he has a swim meet next Saturday and final exams that maybe we can push it back even more.

"Okay, sweetheart. That's good."

She paused. I could hear her sighing. She was tired from worrying all night. *You'll talk to him tonight?*

"Yes. As soon as I get home. Make sure he doesn't go out, okay?"

I will. And the clothes?

"What clothes?"

The clothes . . . the . . . oh. Okay.

"You see?"

Yes. I'll go through the photos on the computer. You'll get his phone?

"Yes. Tonight when we speak. And the social media. I'll have him check everything."

Okay. I love you.

"And I love you. Good-bye."

This was all I had at the moment. Get rid of the clothes, that damn blue sweatshirt. Get rid of all pictures of Jason in the sweatshirt. He would have to be informed and then, based on what had happened that night, he would have to have a story. The world is not a just place. I have already said this many times. I am reminded of it every week when I go to Somers. I am reminded of it when I think about my patient, Glenn Shelby. I believe I've also mentioned that Shelby would eventually commit suicide.

That is not to say there is never justice, or fairness, or righteousness. It is to say, rather, that you cannot count on such things and so you must protect yourself any way you can. I knew I would have to sit with my son and open his eyes. I would have to explain to him that he does not remember what he wore to that party and that he was not near the woods and that he did not see the blue car or Cruz Demarco. I would have to explain to him that he doesn't remember what happened to his blue sweatshirt, or if he ever had one. He has dozens of sweatshirts. I would have to explain that these small transgressions against the law and his own integrity were necessary for his survival in this unjust world. I told myself this was a good thing. It was giving me a chance to educate my son before something bad happened. I had started to calm down. Jason did not commit this crime, and now he would not be falsely accused by some low-life drug dealer.

My next call was to Detective Parsons. It was not prudent. I was not in the best state of mind. But I had access to the detective, to information, with an ongoing cover story, and I could not stop myself. Knowing about the inner workings of the mind, even one's own, does not imbue the power to control it.

This call is what sent me over the edge.

Hey, Alan. Good to hear from you. Anything else on your end? Does she remember the blue hoodie?

"I haven't seen her since the last session. That was Wednesday. She's coming in this afternoon. I imagine Tom has told you about the last session?"

She had some kind of a flashback. She smelled bleach.

"It wasn't a flashback. It was a memory. An actual memory of the actual event."

Okay. Whatever you want to call it. It's helpful. Too bad she didn't see a face. She didn't, right? So I was thinking we should be looking at the swim team again. A lot of swimmers were at the party that night. I got one of my men reading through the interviews from last year. I'm still waiting on a roster from the school—

"Good, very good. But we need to be very careful here. I would really like to do some more work with her before jumping to conclusions. Memories tend to be clustered together, each piece from one event. Like the chapters of a book. It is possible the bleach smell was from chapter four—in the bathroom, perhaps—and the rape in chapter ten. If I can just get the other chapters, we might be able to put them in the right order and—"

Do whatever you need to do, Alan. There's no harm in circling back with the swim team and anyone who interacted with them that night. Go at this from two sides, right? I don't like it. Believe me. I'm not winning any popularity contests in Fairview by looking at our own kids. But I have to do my job.

"Yes. Of course." My heart was in my throat. I almost started to tell him about Jason—not the sweatshirt, but that Jason was on the swim team and had been to the party. I did not know Parsons last year. When Jason was interviewed, I had been with him but it was a young female officer who spoke to us. It had been in our home. It had been very informal. She didn't take more than one line of notes, because Jason had not seen anything helpful. I fully expected Parsons to be surprised by this disclosure. The longer I withheld it, the more surprising it would be. And at some point, surprise becomes suspicion.

But then Parsons spoke. *Listen. Tom said he's coming to see you today. Maybe you can be the one to break the news to him. It's about Demarco.*

"What is it?"

He made bail. But that's not it. We pressed hard on that kid. John Vincent—you know, the kid who bought the drugs from him outside the school. Threatened to put some charges together. His lawyer brought us a statement. Clears Demarco of the rape. Puts him somewhere else with John Vincent.

"Somewhere else? How is that possible? He told you he saw the man with the blue hoodie go into the woods around nine. And the neighbor's kid saw his car, his empty car around eight forty-five. And what about that boy? Did you ask him about the man with the hoodie? Demarco is making all this up. Don't you see?" I have to admit that at this point, I had foolishly thought I saw a way out. I was quickly corrected.

Yeah, yeah . . . course we did. He didn't see any kid walking into the woods. But listen. Demarco was at the back door of the house around eight thirty, talking to some kids. I've got two who admit they were offered weed. I'm sure the little pricks bought the weed, but whatever. We have independent corroborating stories putting Demarco at the house at eight thirty. John Vincent claims he met Demarco back at his car at nine fifteen and drove with him to Cranston to buy coke. I think Vincent might be dealing for Demarco. We should have picked him up that day outside the school. Bet he had more in that bag than a couple of joints.

"Wait. So what are you saying?"

I'm saying Demarco must have made it back to his car around nine—after Teddy Duncan passed by and right when he saw the kid with the blue hoodie go into the woods. Then, a few minutes later, as they had planned, John Vincent comes down from the house and gets in the car. They go to buy the coke in Cranston. They're gone for an hour.

"That . . . that's just a story. Sounds very convenient to me. They fit everything into the facts they were given. Think about it! You can't believe anything either of them is saying."

Nah—listen. The Vincent kid said they stopped for gas and cigarettes. He used his debit card. We have the bank record—the ten bucks charged at 9:37 the night of the rape. And we got the security tape. Shows the Civic, Demarco, and Vincent at the gas station. They were six miles from those woods. Demarco didn't want to tell us about driving some teenager to buy coke. That's another felony charge. Child endangerment. We got him on it now, though. The DA might give Vincent a walk for testifying. Demarco's gonna do some time.

"Just not for the rape."

No—not for the rape. But we've got the hoodie, right? And now we've got the bleach and the memories that are coming back. I'm disappointed, too. Believe me. I thought finding that Civic was the end of this.

"Yes. Tom did as well."

Looks like it's just the beginning all over again. Gonna take a hard look at the swim team. Jesus Christ. I never thought one of our kids could have done this. The brutality. The carving. Shit. I want to find this guy, I do. I just don't want to find him here. And it's not looking like she'll remember a face, right? It's all gonna be circumstantial.

I was on the verge of having an anxiety attack. It was not the right state of mind in which to make any decisions about anything. I talked myself down from telling Parsons about Jason. Thankfully, I had the self-discipline to say nothing else except an appropriate good-bye. I hung up the phone and pulled open my desk drawer. I took out one half milligram of lorazepam, very mild, and swallowed it. I needed to be calm so I could think.

I had two chances walking through my door later that day—Tom and then Jenny. I let the pill kick in; then I calmed myself with slow, steady breathing. I stared at an object, the sticker on the tulip plant. It was the first thing that came to mind. Then I made a mental assessment of everything I had to work with.

First was Tom. We had made significant progress in the three months we'd had together. You already know about the issue he had with his ego and how that affected his marriage and his job, and how it stemmed from his childhood. I have described as well my plan for his treatment. Surprisingly, he had already begun to channel some of his anger toward his parents. He had been remembering some of the things they said to him when he was just a boy. How his father would always say, "How do *you* feel about how you did?" and how his mother would say, "Not everyone is good at everything," and, "We have to accept who we are and learn to love ourselves, even with our limitations." And yet neither of them had ever accepted their own shortcomings. When his father was passed over not once, but three times, for Department Chair, they would speak harshly about the committee members, even mocking them personally—a bad hairpiece, or foul breath, or crooked teeth, or an ugly wife. And his mother had harsh words for her tennis partners—they were lazy, fat, and always stupid. Everyone was stupid compared to them. Tom had been recalling all sorts of bad behavior by his parents that contradicted their words and the highbrow philosophy they touted.

Fuck them, Tom had even said one day about three weeks ago. *Seriously. Fuck them. You have kids, Alan. Would you ever tell them they were limited in their abilities? Isn't there a better way to direct a kid toward a successful life? I always felt like whatever I achieved— grades, salaries, promotions, even my wife and children—was a mistake. Like I had somehow fooled everyone into thinking I was worthy of what they'd given me. I still feel that way.*

Tom felt undeserving of his beautiful wife. He felt undeserving of his beautiful children. And he felt undeserving of his success, no matter how small it may seem to you. Tom made enough to live in Fairview and belong to a country club. He had savings for college educations and a full head of hair and a fit body. He was well liked and healthy. And he loved cars, the cars he sold and the cars he drove. He looked forward to going to work every day. At least until the rape of his daughter.

Finally, I thought he was ready to hear what needed to be said.

"Tom," I said in our session last week. "Let me ask you a question." *Okay . . .*

"Do you feel you deserved Jenny's rape?"

What kind of question is that? Tom was shocked. "Horrified" might be too strong a word, but it was close.

"You don't deserve her, or Lucas or Charlotte. You don't deserve your job. So maybe this is the universe getting even with you for taking all these things that you don't deserve. Maybe you're the reason this happened."

My God! What a cruel thing to say! How could you say that to me?

"Tom—you know that is not what I think. But did any of that resonate with you?"

Of course it did. I was not distracted back then, what was it? Eight days ago? My skills had not yet been compromised by the vulnerability of my own family. Tom sat back in the chair and let the thought sink into his bones. His eyes grew wide and then his face crumbled the way it always did. Red splotches, then a few tears with loud sobs. Tom cried almost every time we met.

So that is where Tom and I were in his personal journey. Tom felt guilty. Some of it was normal—the guilt of not having protected his little girl. But more of it was abstract—the guilt of feeling he had caused it. It is not rational. Dismiss it if you must, if you do not believe in the subconscious mind. I don't have the time or inclination to educate you or convince you. There is too much ground to cover now.

Guilt is powerful, and in the evil, maniacal state of mind I was in that Friday afternoon, I knew I would be able to use it somehow.

I was about to turn my thoughts to Jenny, but the time had passed too quickly. Tom was arriving for this new session, this new day, and I had in my mind everything we had discussed since his therapy began—the things I have just described to you. I heard the outer door to my office. It was time for our session. I was disheartened that I had not come up with a plan to save my son. But Tom was about to change all that.

Chapter Twenty

Tom was visibly agitated. He had not slept well. His mind was obsessed with the blue sweatshirt; his ego conflicted from his wife's sudden sexual advances. And his heart was breaking from his daughter in her room down the hall, the memory of being violated now set free to torture all of them.

He sat down on the edge of the sofa, legs spread, hands on jumpy knees. His shoulders were up by his ears, and he took short breaths in, then huffed them out.

I was slightly sedated.

"You don't look well today. Did something happen?" I asked.

No. Nothing. That's the problem.

"I see."

Do you? Do you see? I feel like I'm the only one who gives a shit about finding my daughter's rapist. I was up half the night, looking through pictures from Fairview. Searching clothing catalogs . . .

"For the blue sweatshirt with the red bird?"

Yes. Yes! What do you think? My God, don't you understand that this is the key to finding this monster?

"You seem very frustrated."

Tom started to calm down. He apologized for his outburst.

"Did you find anything useful in your search?" I already knew the answer from Charlotte.

Do you have any idea how many blue sweatshirts there are? And the red bird—it could be anything. A cardinal. Air force wings. A hawk . . .

"But nothing in Fairview?" I stopped him when I heard that word: "hawk." "No sports teams or clubs . . . nothing like that in town?"

Nothing. And no pictures of anyone wearing one. I went through all the school pictures on the Web site, looked at hundreds of articles from the Weekly Advertiser *. . . but there are hundreds more. Why aren't the police doing this? It's too much for one person, with work and the kids and Charlotte . . . it's too much!*

The tears came early in this session, and I did what I always do. I let them come. Tom slumped back against the cushions. His knees pressed together and his hands rose to cover his face. He felt ashamed when he cried. Yes—this, too, goes back to his parents. They didn't know they were supposed to let children feel things. And cry. Those parenting books wouldn't come out until the 1980s.

"Tom . . . what will happen if this man is not found?"

I had been using the word "man" with everyone since I found my wife in our bed clutching Jason's sweatshirt. "Man"—not "boy" or "kid" or even "guy." The word "man" provoked images of someone older than my son.

Tom shook his head. *That's not an option. It's just not.*

"Okay." I passed Tom a box of tissues.

I've been reading about rape recovery—not by doctors, but victims. No offense—I mean, I don't discount what you've done for us.

But my daughter's voice was stolen by those damned drugs. She can't tell us what she needs to feel better, so I've been trying to understand.

"That's fine. It's good to educate yourself."

What they go through, the feeling of being overpowered and then . . . I still can't say it. . . .

"Penetrated. Forcibly penetrated."

Yes. That stays with them. Some of them describe it as taking their dignity. That's the one that's been in my head since you told us about the session. About the memory. How she said she felt like an animal, like he was riding her, breaking her like an animal.

Tom had stopped crying. I've said this before, but it felt as though he'd run out of tears, out of water. It is certainly not because he had stopped feeling his despair.

And this is the thing. I don't leave here and forget what we talk about. I don't listen to Charlotte and then dismiss what she says. I get that justice isn't some magic bullet to fix Jenny. I really do. But these women, almost all of them describe the healing that comes from seeing their attackers punished. Some of them talk about it being an eye for an eye—you know, knowing that this fucker is going to feel what they felt a hundred times over in prison. They don't say it like that, and I'm sorry about my language. . . .

"It's all right. Say what you want in here. That's the point, Tom."

I mean, they don't actually say it makes them feel better to know their rapist is going to be raped in prison. But he will lose his rights and his freedom and his dignity. And when he comes out, he'll forever be labeled for what he did. His life will never be the same. Their lives will never be the same. They're in their own kind of prison. That's what they say. That it feels like prison to be inside their own heads. I guess you hear all of that from your patients.

"I do."

I guess I needed to hear it myself, from the victims. Others talk about being heard, about the world hearing what happened and believing them because in the moment when it's happening, their voices are powerless. Their will is not respected. When the rapist goes to jail, they feel like they have some power back. It seems to help some more than others. But not one said it didn't help at all. So, yes, you have the skills to help Jenny get her memory back so she can, what is it . . .

"Attach her emotions to the right set of facts."

Right—so she can start to process them and put them in the right places. So she doesn't feel like she wants to die again. Not ever again. That can never happen. Never.

"I'm hopeful about that, Tom. Doesn't she seem better to you?"

I don't know. Sometimes. She seems better when she comes home from the group. I was wrong about that. I was worried about her going there and being with all those other people.

"And now?"

Now I can see that she needs to hear their stories. The same way I needed to hear them from the books. She almost seems alive again, you know? In her eyes. I can see a glimmer of life.

I hid my worry very well. The sedative helped with that. I have not had the time to tell you about that life in Jenny's eyes. About how it had everything to do with a married Navy SEAL.

That's what you can do for her. But what about me? I'm her father. I have to do something. And what I can do is help find her attacker and see him punished. Even if that gives her only a small amount of closure or peace or whatever you want to call it. At least it will be something I did.

"Have you given any thought to what we've been discussing? About your feelings of not deserving her? About your guilt?"

Of course! That's not something a person forgets. I don't know. I do feel guilty that I didn't protect her. But the rest of it, about the universe punishing me . . . mostly I feel powerless.

"Explain that to me."

Tom rolled his eyes. He made a face of exasperation. *I don't know. Charlotte wanted to make love last night. I don't know why. But I felt like it had nothing to do with me. And then at work, there's this secretary at the Jag dealership. The one out on Route 26.*

"I know the one." I did not know where this was going. But I knew Tom had not slept with a young secretary. If I had been wrong about that, I would have handed in my license.

I got a call from a client. This guy has bought four cars from me in the past few years. He's not a guy you say no to. I was heading home and he called and he said he wanted to test a new F-Type convertible. I'd closed up and left for the day. It was almost dark, so it must have been after eight. My numbers were due the next day, so I was the last one out. But I turned around for this guy. I got back to the showroom in twenty minutes. The client was still ten minutes out. I went inside and I heard this sound. It was unmistakable, you know. People screwing. I should have made some loud noise, turned on the lights. Pretended I didn't hear anything and given them a chance to sneak out or get dressed. Whatever.

"But you didn't. I understand. It's human nature to want to know."

Well, I'm not proud of it. But I did it anyway. I walked quietly into the showroom. I stood against the wall. And then I saw them. There was light coming through the window. From the streetlamps. Through the glass. Shining right on them.

Tom shuddered at the memory of what he saw. I gave him a moment to let it pass.

It was my boss—the owner. Bob Sullivan. He was with Lila—this young woman. A girl, really. She's twenty years old, for God's sake! He's fifty-three. And I don't know why, but I find this the most disturbing part—he plays golf every weekend with her father. They've been friends for decades. Raised those kids in the same town, at the same club. He had her bent over the hood of a silver XK. Her skirt was hiked up to her waist and he had his hands pinning her down. One on her shoulder and one on the back of her head. It was disturbing, really. He was doing her from behind and she was pretending to like it. Moaning and whatnot. But I could see her face. I could see how every time he thrust into her, he pushed her into the metal hood of that car, using her face and her chest to brace himself. I could see her wince every time he did that. God—you must think I watched them for a long time. Honestly, it was a few seconds. But it was long enough. I don't think I'll forget that image for a long time. He knew that girl when she was really just a child. Pigtails and Barbie dolls. But now that she has a woman's body, he can bend her over a car.

This is where everything stopped. My heart. My soul. My professional integrity. The only thing moving was my mind, and it was moving fast.

"So what did you do?"

I went back outside. Back to my car. I'd pulled in from the back entrance, but this time I drove around to the front and drove right in so my headlights were shining into the showroom.

"To give them time to escape."

Exactly. I did what I should have done the first time. I jangled my keys at the door. I turned on the lights and coughed. Bob came out of the showroom, his face all flushed. I felt like punching him.

"And what, he made excuses for being there so late?"

Of course. And I pretended to buy them. Didn't even give it a thought. I lied more easily than I thought I could. He didn't question it. We talked about pricing for the client coming in, how much of a discount I could offer him. I'm sure Lila snuck out the other side door. I didn't see her leave.

"When was this?"

Tom shrugged. *Last Tuesday.*

"Did you talk about it with anyone? With Charlotte?"

No. No one. And I would prefer to keep it between us. This is my job. My career. I run all the showrooms. I'm Bob's second-in-command. No way I'm going to jeopardize that.

"Not even for this young girl? Is that why you feel powerless? Why you told me this story?"

Tom considered this. *Yes, I think so. I feel—no, I am powerless. She's an adult. Young, but still an adult. She probably thinks she can get something from him. I know she needs money. Maybe she's thinking she'll get a nice bonus in her next paycheck. Her father had some rough times and she wants to go to college. What am I supposed to do? Threaten to tell his wife? It's none of my business.*

"And if you didn't work for Bob Sullivan? If you had just been a customer, for example?"

I guess then . . . well, I don't know. Maybe I would feel the same way. Maybe I wouldn't.

"But you would have a choice. The decision would be yours to make and not dictated by your employment?"

Yes. That's it. That's exactly it.

I nodded. I was pleased with myself for saying what I would have said under normal circumstances.

Still, I was a child with a box of matches.

"Tom," I said. "I just have to make sure. You said he was holding her shoulder with one hand and the back of her head with the other. And you saw her face."

Yes. Well, I said his hand was in her hair, didn't I? He was touching or maybe pulling her hair, but not in a forceful way. . . .

"And you are certain that it was consensual?"

Yes! My God. After everything that's happened . . . I would have thrown him right through that window if I thought it wasn't consensual. Why are you asking that?

I took a breath then to slow my mind and think about my plan. I had not told Tom every detail about Jenny's recalled memory—about the placement of her attacker's hands, one on her shoulder and one around the back of her neck. I considered telling him now, but no—it was not the right time. This is not uncommon when people fornicate in this manner. Men like to pull hair, or run their fingers through it. And they need to brace themselves against something. It is not uncommon at all. And yet in this situation, it was so useful. So very, very useful. I was about to burst wide open.

"I'm sorry, Tom. I just wanted to make sure. This incident should not in any way integrate into our work and your emotional pain from what happened to Jenny. You are right—this woman is an adult. It sounds like she knew what she was doing, that she has her reasons, no matter how sad they are. And that Bob thought she was enjoying the experience."

Tom seemed slightly unsure now of his impressions. I did not say anything more. We moved on to discuss Charlotte and the work I would be doing with Jenny, issues with his parents again, more stories of woe from his childhood. I let him wallow as I thought ruthlessly about my next move. My work with Tom was done. For now.

Chapter Twenty-one

I had one and a half hours after Tom left before I would see Jenny. I had not seen her since we recovered that one memory, that one piece of the puzzle—the anchor piece that I believed would lead us to the other pieces until we had the whole story perfectly reassembled. Remembered.

But I was not thinking about Jenny then.

Bob Sullivan. That's who was on my mind. It did not surprise me that he was sleeping with other women. Charlotte and I had discussed their "love" affair, and Charlotte truly believed that he loved her. That she was the only one. That he was tortured by his love for her. But I did not believe it. Not for one moment. His ego was as large as the billboards out on the highway. Men like that didn't love one woman.

We have not returned to this topic since I told you about that night in the parking lot when Charlotte was still covered in her daughter's blood. There is more to tell. Three months had passed—three months of therapy and three months of weekly encounters between Bob

and Charlotte. We had discussed it again that very morning, right
after she told me she'd had sex with her husband.

"How are things with Bob?"

We had come to discuss her affair with the same acceptance and
nonchalance as her tennis game. This was intentional on my part.
Her affair was anything but normal. But she had to come to this conclusion on her own. And she did not need my opinion of her behavior
to muddy the waters. I had maintained meticulous neutrality.

Oh, I don't know. She said this with a heavy sigh. *It's been different since that afternoon—you know, when we found Jenny in the
pool house. We meet at this house on the west side of Cranston. A
friend of his asked him to house-sit while he's traveling in Europe. I
go only when the cleaning lady comes. That's on Mondays. I don't
leave Jenny alone in the house. Not for more than an hour, maybe—
if I need to go to the grocery store or dry cleaners. I don't see friends.
I don't play tennis. When I get in my car and pull out of the driveway, all I can think about is Jenny lying on that floor. . . .*

Charlotte did her reset: The long breath. Closed eyes, just for a
second. A slight shudder to chase away the demons.

*So on Mondays when the cleaning lady comes, I drive forty min-
utes to see Bob for one hour. We don't really talk anymore. We say
hello. He asks about Jenny. I give him an update. I ask how he is. I
ask about the boys. Then we have sex.*

"You say that with less of something. Enthusiasm? Interest?"

*I feel less of something. In fact, last week I actually felt irritated.
He was taking longer than usual. I pretended to have an orgasm so
we could be done. I don't know why, but I just didn't like the feel of
his hands on me that day. It's been like that more and more since
that night when I met him in the parking lot. That horrible night. It
feels like it's dying a slow death.*

"Do you think it's because of you or him?"

She shook her head from side to side. *I really don't know. I mean,*
he says the same things to me. And he does the same things to me.
He still sends me text messages.

"The suggestive ones?"

They're more than suggestive. Some of them I delete immediately.
They're pornographic. Pictures of his erection. Descriptions of things
he wants to do.

Charlotte seemed disgusted as she spoke about it. In the past, she
had been embarrassed. And aroused.

He always says he loves me. But it's not the same.

"That must be very difficult. Bob has been an important piece
of your framework."

He made me feel whole. Like we talked about. He knows about
my past and he still loves me. He still wants me.

"So what's changed? Why isn't that working its magic anymore?"

Charlotte shrugged. She didn't know. I looked at her and sighed
myself. She asked if I was upset with her, and I assured her I was
not. I said I was just very tired. I never share my personal feelings
with my clients, but I was growing impatient—remember, I had not
yet taken the lorazepam. I had been hobbling myself together for the
better part of our session.

I left Charlotte to consider why things with Bob had changed.
Of course, I knew the answer. Bob had not muttered those four little
words that night by the Dumpsters at the Home Depot. He did not
say, "It's not your fault." The supply of acceptance and forgiveness
had been interrupted, and she now had an inkling of the truth—that
all this time, as Bob held her and told her that he loved her, even
though she had slept with her mother's husband, even though she
had been sent away to live with her aunt, he was lying. Bob was a
liar who wanted to fuck her. He was masterful. Cunning. I have to
admit that a small part of me was impressed by him. He knew

somehow what would appeal to her, that bad Charlotte would feed on his acceptance like the starving child she was and that she would open her legs and not care about her own satisfaction as long as he brought the food. But now his words were empty. The food he was serving her was rancid, and she was having trouble swallowing it down.

I wondered what he was feeding Lila at the Jag showroom. What did she need so desperately that she would bend over a silver XK and let him shove her face into its hood while he rode her like an animal? Money, perhaps, as Tom said. Or maybe she needed her daddy's love. It could have been a million things. And Bob, that sly dog, had figured it out. Yes. I was impressed.

By the time Tom left my office later that day, my thoughts were in a frenzy. I kept thinking over and over—*This is too good to be true.* It was. It was too perfect.

You probably cannot picture this, but I actually got up and paced the room, back and forth like some primal beast. I had seen Charlotte. Then I had seen two other patients. Then I'd seen Tom and learned about Bob and that little slut at the Jag showroom. I hope you're following along. This day, this Friday, was absolutely pivotal. I had become monomaniacal in my mission to save my son from accusation. My wife was right. The accusation alone would change his life forever. Social media would leave its nasty indelible footprint. I also have to admit—to you and not my wife, because it would continue to upset her—that the consequence of not being able to treat Jenny also weighed heavily upon me. No parents in their right mind would allow that to continue under such a cloud of suspicion. And I needed to finish my work with her. I am a selfish bastard, aren't I? God, how I was coming undone that day!

But I was not too undone to continue with my fledgling plan.

Jenny arrived just after four in the afternoon. Three Kramers in one day. I was immersed in their stories, and it was helping me immensely to piece together the details. I heard them arrive in the waiting room. Charlotte always brought Jenny. Lucas was with them as well. It didn't matter. They would leave as soon as I opened the door, and I would be alone with Jenny for an hour. More, if I needed it.

I finished the work I had been doing on my computer. Then I opened the door.

I'm starting to feel like I live here, Charlotte joked. She seemed sad. I imagine she had started to figure out why Bob had lost his magic.

I smiled but said nothing. Jenny walked past me and sat down on the sofa.

"I'll be right back, Jenny. I just want to talk to your mom for a moment."

Jenny said, *Fine.* She pulled out her phone like every teenager. It's not possible for them to sit in the silence. Of course, the room was not silent today.

I closed the door, leaving Jenny inside. Alone. I spoke to Charlotte about the schedule and pretended to need an update on Jenny since that morning. She didn't think twice about it. She pulled out her phone and checked some dates and times. I reminded her that I go to Somers on Tuesdays.

"Hello, Lucas," I said. I shook his hand and met his eyes. I had not been seeing him as a patient, and he still looked at me the way children look at doctors. They are right to be apprehensive. Doctors mean something is wrong with you, or might be wrong with you. Doctors do things to you that sometimes hurt or make you uncomfortable. I did not take offense.

All of this took not more than three minutes. But that was all I needed. I said good-bye and then entered my office.

My computer was on, playing a looped commercial from Bob

Sullivan's dealerships. It was all Bob, his voice, over and over. Jenny wasn't bothered by it one way or another. She smiled at me when I passed by and walked to my desk.

"I'm sorry. I didn't realize I'd left this on."

It's fine, she said.

I turned off the commercial, then walked to the chair across from the sofa and took my seat. "I like to watch the news sometimes. But I hate those commercials. I know your dad works there. I think I just hate commercials, period."

She smiled and I settled into my chair. I was pleased with myself for completing this part of the plan, the mission. But then I saw her face. Her eyes. I lost my breath.

I have described my impressions of Jenny before, how I had been confused by the girl I saw the months between the rape and suicide attempt. How she did not present as a trauma victim. Certainly not a rape victim. And then, when the truth came out about her receiving the treatment, it all made sense to me. I think I even said that I felt relieved to know I wasn't losing my professional mind. After I began my work with her, and if I'm being honest, after she met Sean Logan, she changed again. As her father said, the life was back in her eyes. The last time I'd seen her, that Wednesday, we had the breakthrough, a light piercing the blackout. The memory. I had seen the panic rip through her as she relived that one moment. I had seen a glimmer of pain and shock and horror. But then it all collapsed into exhaustion. When she left, it was hard to detect anything. Two days had passed. Two days of living with the memory.

I tried to smile politely as I studied her face. I could see it then. For the first time. I could see the rape in her eyes, running alongside the life.

"How have things been since Wednesday?" I managed to say.

Oh, what a horrible person I am! I could not believe what I had done. I could not believe that I had set in motion the most devious betrayal. I had opened up this path back to that night. The patient was on the table and I was about to infect her with the germs of a lie. I had the chance to give it all back to her, the truth in all its purity. But instead, I was going to go in with my evil plan and corrupt it to my own end. To save my son. To save my family. I told myself I could do just this little bit but keep the rest, find the rest, intact. But how could that be? This one corruption would be the end of the truth. The germs would cause an infection that would feed on the healthy flesh until it was all dead. The truth, dead. My despair was profound. The irony staring me in the face. If I pulled back now, my son would be questioned and I would be taken from my work. To save my son, I would have to defile my work. Do you see? Do you?

Jenny started to talk then, about the memory and how it had become clearer and clearer. The hand on her back. The hand on the back of her neck. The smell of the bleach. His penis entering her and the shock that followed as he pushed harder and harder, tearing her inside. The violation. The pain. The animal broken. Its body and its spirit. Broken. It was perfect, the way this memory was coming into focus. I am not sick to think this. But it was perfect because it was real. It had been there all this time, carefully preserved, and now it had found its way back. Not only as a series of facts, but in the past two days it had connected to the feelings it created. They were no longer floating inside her, the ghosts that Sean Logan had described. They had found their home, and now they could be recognized and, finally, processed. It was working! Jenny cried. She sobbed. *I hate him!* She screamed in my office. *I hate him!*

"Yes!" I said. I wanted to cry myself. I was overwhelmed by the power of what we had unleashed inside her.

Why did he do this to me?

"Because he is nothing without the power he took from you. He is nothing, and you are everything. Can you feel that? How desperate he is to take your power? How hungry? He is the animal, Jenny. Not you. He has no soul."

So he took mine. He stole mine.

"He tried to. But he took only a small piece."

I want it back! Do you hear me? I want it back!

Oh, how her strength moved me that day! I nodded my head and said the only words that came to my mind.

"I know."

I let her sit with this for a moment. And I allowed myself to enjoy that moment. To savor it. And then I swallowed every ounce of integrity I had left and pressed ahead with my plan.

"I want to focus on sound today. Maybe on a voice."

She agreed. She trusted me completely. I had in my mind the events of that afternoon in the pool house. I did not have the investigator's tape by then, but I had Charlotte's recollection. She had told me what was said. How Bob had repeated over and over the same exclamatory expression. *Oh dear Lord!*

"There are some things that might have been said. Things people say when they are highly emotional. I imagine this creature, this animal, was in a heightened emotional state. I'm going to say some of them to you. You need to close your eyes and just let the words float in like we did with the smells. Don't force them. Just see if any of them resonate."

Jenny opened her bag and took out the props. She sat with them as she always did and then nodded and closed her eyes. I did not put on the music. I did not let her smell the bleach. I did not want her to go back to the night in the woods, but instead to that afternoon in the pool house.

Now we would see. We would put to the test the theories and studies about memory. Jenny had been unconscious as Bob Sullivan stood over her, wrapping her wrists, trying to save her life. Would his voice be in there somewhere? Would his words be lingering, waiting to be pulled from the stacks of files? Could I pull them out and refile them, not with that afternoon in the pool house, but from that night in the woods?

Jenny closed her eyes.

"Are you ready" I asked.

She nodded. I took a breath and shook my head with disgust at myself and what I was about to do. Then I started to say the words.

"Oh my God. . . . My God . . . Yes . . . Do you like that? . . . Yes . . . Oh my God . . . Mmmm. . . . Uhhhhh . . . yes!. . . . Oh my God . . . Good God. . . . Good Lord. . . . Dear Lord . . . Oh dear Lord, dear Lord, dear Lord . . ."

Chapter Twenty-two

Jenny did not falsely remember Bob Sullivan's voice from the night of the rape. Did you think it would be that easy? That session was just the beginning. It was a little seed, planted in the fertile soil. It would take more than just our sessions. More than the gimmick of playing Bob's commercials right before our sessions. If this work were that simple, any moron could do it. It is not simple. Nor was my plan. But nothing more could be done until Monday.

I went home that night hopeful. And destroyed.

My son was waiting for me. He was annoyed at having been detained on a Friday night by his mother.

"Hi," I said. He was in the family room playing on the Xbox. My wife remained in the kitchen after saying a nervous hello and kissing me on the cheek.

I stood in the doorway and did not go further. His back was to me and he could not hear anything with his headphones blaring. Soldiers were killing combatants in an urban village. My son was using a knife to cut their throats. He was screaming at his friends who were playing the game with him through the Internet. They were playful screams, followed by laughter. A combatant came up from behind and stabbed my son. He yelled, then laughed very hard. He told his friend, *You're a fucking idiot. Where were you? What? Stuck at the bridge. Dude, you have to get on the bus to get over the bridge. You killed me, dude. What the fuck. Hahaha.*

It had been less than two days since I learned that my son had a blue sweatshirt with a red bird. Since I realized that it must have been he who was going into the woods the night of the party. My wife and I had discussed what we would do to keep him safe.

I have always been fascinated by the bond between parent and child. I'm sure you have gleaned this already. It is in us. It is why we are here. To fornicate, to make babies, and then to die protecting them. In that respect, we are animals. And yet, we also have morality, and that is what distinguishes us from animals. I don't care what anyone says about animals. They do not have morals. Any animal behavior that mimics morality is nothing more than a coincidence. They are driven by the need to survive and this need, this raw instinct, sometimes causes them to act in a "moral" way. When they protect a vulnerable member of their tribe. When they band together in a herd to keep a lion from picking them off, one at a time. When they accept members from another tribe or herd into their own. All of that is about self-preservation. Something is gained by the herd. There are just as many behaviors that are immoral. Male pigs who kill their own offspring so the mothers will stop lactating and become fertile again. Old rhinos who are shunned by the herd because they are of no use being alive. Female dogs who literally eat their defective newborn pups. On and on I could go.

I see it at the prison, where the forces of socialization are stripped away. I see it with the Axis II disorders, people who lack empathy. Sociopaths. We are not far from the animals. The very thing that distinguishes us is fragile. But it is real.

I have been observing my wife and have come to the conclusion that she has not ruled out the possibility that our son raped Jenny Kramer. It has been difficult to accept this because I know he is innocent and am disturbed by her ambivalence. It is not that she does not love him. If I investigated, I know what I would uncover. She cannot explain his presence in the woods or the shaving or the bleach. I admit these are difficult hurdles to overcome. And so she has gone down a less strenuous mental path, the path of justification. Perhaps he was high on drugs. Perhaps it was a "date rape" gone wrong. Perhaps one of his friends followed him and was also involved, and maybe it was the friend who was so violent. Surely our son could not have done what they are saying. But the girl doesn't remember, does she? The "facts" of the rape are still just speculation. Anyone could poke holes in the story they had created.

She had spoken of the now infamous date rapes down in the southern part of the state. We both remembered when that teenage boy was on trial. We both remembered hearing the evidence at the trial, how the victims were persecuted, their stories broken down and torn apart. He had known them all from school. They had gone places with him willingly. He went to jail anyway, but there was always doubt. His loving parents had spent a fortune defending him. There was no question we would do the same for our son.

When the teenage rapist came up for parole years later, we watched the hearing on cable. He presented as such a nice man, repentant, remorseful. Rehabilitated. Then his victims spoke. For the first time, they told their stories without the interruption of clever defense attorneys. Julie and I were shocked at what we heard. They were horrible stories of violence, rape, sodomy, verbal obscenities, and strangulation. The press had not relayed the facts truthfully those many years before. It had all been spun to create an interesting he said–she said controversy. Parole was denied. The nice young man was transformed. He became belligerent. My wife said she could suddenly see the "crazy" in his eyes. I was disappointed in myself that I had not detected his Axis II condition. I would see that today, having worked at Somers these past few years.

My point is this: Julie had brought this up because she wanted to make sure I would protect our son the way that this family had protected theirs. She wanted to make sure I would do that even if we came to believe he had raped my patient. Even if he turned out to be a sociopath. She was reassured by my conviction. And I was disturbed by her assumptions.

I used to wonder about that family. I used to wonder if they knew he was guilty and didn't care. Or if they clung to every piece of conflicting evidence, convinced themselves the victims were just regretful sluts, so they could believe in his innocence and justify their actions. I admit as well, to acknowledging to myself, in a somewhat whimsical manner, that I would be extremely adept at justifications, given my deep arsenal of psychological knowledge. I did not have to answer those questions or put my theory about myself to the test. I did not share my wife's ambivalence toward our son.

I walked in front of the television and blocked his view. He tried to operate around me, looking left, then right, his fingers clicking away on the remote. Finally he looked at my face and knew the time had come for the talk his mother had told him was coming—the reason he was not out already on this weekend night.

I gotta go, he said to his friends. He clicked more buttons, then put down the remote. His avatar disappeared. I turned off the television.

I won't bore you with the details of what each of us said. I will simply say that I told him about Cruz Demarco. The man in the blue Civic. I told him that he saw a person in a blue hoodie with a red bird go into the woods right at the time of the rape. I laid out the facts that would make him a suspect if they were ever known. The shaving. The bleach. The sweatshirt. It was the last one we could do something about.

I could see him processing the information. I could see his mother's brain and not mine inside his skull.

"Do you see what I'm saying? They will question you again."

I know that. They're bringing in the whole swim team.

"Let's get one thing straight," I said. "I know you didn't do anything to hurt Jenny Kramer."

I didn't! I could hear the fear in his voice.

"I know. But you can see how this will look. They will ask you if you shaved—not just your legs, but everywhere. And they will ask about the sweatshirt."

He didn't say anything then, and that's when I knew. He had shaved everywhere. He had worn that sweatshirt to the party.

"Jason. You couldn't possibly remember that far back, could you?"

He looked at me strangely, but then he started to understand. I gave him my speech about the world being unfair. I told him the things that would be used against him, and I could see that he knew what had to be done. We discussed morality and the very few times it was acceptable to cross the line, to be an animal. Self-preservation was one of them.

"You are innocent and you deserve to be treated as an innocent. That's the bottom line."

Okay, Dad.

"Now. I just want to know one thing about that night so we can make sure we have thought of everything. I need to know what you were doing in those woods."

My son lied. He looked me square in the eye as he did it. He thought he could deceive me. I am underestimated in my own home.

I wasn't near the woods. I never left the house.

"Jason. Please. You were seen."

I wasn't there! I swear!

"And there's not one person except that drug dealer who will say otherwise?"

No! I swear!

"And the sweatshirt. Why was it on the floor of your closet?"

I don't know. My room's a mess. I throw stuff in the closet when I get home sometimes.

I was again struck by the power of my bond to this weak, mediocre liar. I was disgusted by him in that moment. And yet I still persisted in my plan to protect him at all cost. At very dear cost. I could feel self-loathing creep into my bones. And I could not bear to think about the effort it would require to forgive myself one day. So I did not.

We agreed on what had to be done. He went to his room to delete any photos of himself in that sweatshirt that might be on any social media anywhere. He seemed to understand the boundaries I had set. The limits on my willingness to lie for him and cover for him. The fact that I was doing this only because I believed him to be innocent of the rape. I did not tell him it would not have mattered. Or that his mother did not share my conviction.

He left an hour later to meet his friends. I don't know what came over me, but I had a large glass of scotch and then I took my wife upstairs and fucked her like Bob Sullivan fucked that secretary.

We did not linger in bed. My wife kissed me and smiled, then got up to shower. Blood was surging through my veins and I pleaded with it to bring me the thought that I knew was hiding inside me. Torturing me. Fucking my wife like an animal had not chased it away.

I closed my eyes and let it emerge from the shadows. All this time I had been worried about my son being in those woods because he might be accused of being the rapist.

My son was in those woods. My son was in those woods with the rapist.

I let out a loud gasp.

Dear God, I thought.

My son could have been the victim.

Chapter Twenty-three

The weekend was awkward and emotionally painful. My wife cried several times, mostly in the bathroom with the water running. She would come out with a red face, red eyes. My son was unusually quiet and spent most of his time training at the pool and then going out with his friends. He did not want to be around us.

As for me, I wrangled my fear and put it in a box on a shelf the way my wife does. My son had not been raped, and it was a waste of my mental resources to dwell on what might have been. I focused my concern on what was still posing a threat to him.

The time I had to reset my brain was productive. When Sean Logan arrived Monday for his session, I had concocted another aspect of my plan.

Sean had been stuck at that red door. In spite of our dedication to the process, no more memories had been recovered. I had begun to move from frustration to acceptance. Sean had been just off from the center of the blast. It was his colleague, Hector Valancia, who had taken it straight on. The investigative report put him standing over it, like maybe he was looking down at an IED. Still, Sean had lost consciousness. It is quite possible the memories from the time around the blast never got filed at all.

He came in with a smile on his face, and he seemed uncharacteristically relaxed.

"How are you? How was your weekend?" I asked.

Sean sat down and patted his knees. *Pretty good, Doc. Pretty solid.*

"That's good to hear. Anything in particular?"

I dunno. The weather's starting to turn.

"Yes. The snow is finally all gone, isn't it? Took a while this year."

Sure did. Got to sixty degrees on Saturday. Sun was shining. Took my kid to a Bluefish game. Might as well have been the World Series, he was so excited.

"That sounds really nice. And Tammy?"

You know. She's hanging in there.

"Any outbursts?"

Nope. Not a one. Guess the meds are finally doing their job.

"It's not just the medication, Sean. You've been on the same regimen for over a year. It's the work you're doing."

Sean was the most humble, modest man I have ever known. In spite of our stalled progress recovering his memories, he had been fighting like hell to control his behavior, to recognize his emotions, his "ghosts," and order them to retreat before he punched more walls in his home. He had never hit his wife or his son. He would put a bullet in his own head before doing that. Still, it was terrifying to be around him when he lost control. When the ghosts won the fight.

He shrugged and looked down at the carpet.

"You need to own your success, Sean. What do you think has been helping you?"

I knew the answer. I was curious as to whether he would say it out loud.

I dunno.

"Can you describe one thing, maybe how you felt with your son at the baseball game? In the past, you were just going through the motions. Pretending to enjoy him so he wouldn't feel rejected. Did it feel like that on Saturday?"

No. Not at all. There was this moment. Our team had bases loaded. I nudged him and said, "This is it, big guy! The bases are loaded!" And he got all wide eyed . . . stood up and grabbed the rail and started bouncing up and down. He started saying, "Oh boy! Oh boy!" And I was like, "Yeah, buddy! This is it, right?" He didn't really know what that meant. I don't think he understands anything that's going on, really. But then he looked at me and he was still so overflowing with joy and he . . . he just couldn't contain himself, like he was about to explode with joy . . . Sean's voice started to tremble.

"It's all right, Sean." I said.

And with that permission, he teared up a little. Just a little, mind you. *Uhhhh, Doc, I'm sorry. It's just . . . it just overwhelmed me. I can still feel it.*

"That's really good, Sean. It's good to feel things. I know we spend a lot of time trying not to feel things—the things that don't belong inside you. But this does. This overwhelming joy belongs very much."

Aw, man. Damn. I guess.

"What did Philip do then, after jumping up and down with joy?"

Sean grinned from ear to ear. *He looked at me and he said . . . Aw, man . . . hold on a second. . . . Okay . . . he said . . . "Daddy! I just love you!"*

A few more tears fell. I handed him a tissue. It was so beautiful.

Even after my twisted weekend, the corruption of my very soul, I was still moved by the sight of this enormous, powerful man completely decimated by the love of his child.

"Sean," I said. "What you're feeling right now. This is good! This is love. You felt, and you still feel, love for your son. What else?"

I'm grateful, you know? Just so fucking grateful. This little guy, this little life living in this crazy-ass world, and somehow I managed to fill him with joy. Just by driving an hour to Bridgeport and buying him a hot dog.

"Ah, but it wasn't just that! Don't you see? He felt your love for him and your desire to be with him, and that's what filled him with joy! That connection. In this crazy-ass world, there is a big strong man who loves him, and so he knows he'll be safe. He knows he'll have a home—not walls and windows, but a home in another person's heart. That is what it means to be human!"

Sean looked at me strangely, and I realized I had become far more emotional than I normally allow. I took a breath to contain myself. My nerves were frayed and now my guts were spilling out all over the room.

"The feelings you just had when you recalled this memory—do you see how our emotions and memories are connected?" I shifted gears quickly and with admirable precision.

Oh yeah. I'm sorry I lost it. Shit. I never cry, Doc. Never.

"And can you imagine just having that powerful feeling and not knowing why?"

Sean laughed. *Yeah. I'd probably think I was in love with you or something, right, Doc?*

I joined him in his laugh. "Indeed. Or a stranger on the street, perhaps. That would be very awkward."

Yeah, I get it. I wouldn't mind if this were one of the ghosts. This ghost could stick around.

"We could all use a little more spontaneous joy, I suppose. Do you want to work more on the memory recall?"

Yeah. Let's do it.

I got up and walked to my desk to grab my laptop. We always worked with the simulation playing. "Okay. Can I ask you first . . . are you coming to group this week?"

I watched his face carefully. Group was where he saw Jenny. Neither of them had missed a session in the months since she joined.

Sure, yeah.

He was conspicuously nonchalant.

I had suspected they were growing closer. Not to disregard my efficacy, but there had been a drastic change in both their moods that did not correlate with the progress, or lack thereof, of the memory work. I had asked Jenny about him. Too often, I feared. She had started to wonder if what they were doing was wrong. I could hear the hesitation in her voice.

It wasn't wrong. How could it be when it was helping them both? But they had progressed from texting and Skype to coffee and long walks. Sean was working odd jobs. Jenny was not in school. She rode her bike to town, and they were meeting there, in Fairview, then driving to places where they wouldn't be recognized. Charlotte thought she was shopping or meeting friends. She was eager to see Jenny leave the house. She'd told me that Jenny seemed happy, truly happy, when she was going to town, so she never worried about her then. She was always back home in a couple of hours.

Jenny had confided these secret meetings to me, and I felt obligated to keep her confidence. Still, Sean was twenty-five. He was married. Jenny was sixteen. It was one of those dilemmas that sits in the back of your mind, like a small crack in the ceiling. You forget about it in the midst of everything else going on. But once in a while, your eye catches it and you think, has it gotten worse? Is it time to fix it? I would not let their relationship become sexual. I would not let the ceiling collapse entirely. But then, we never know when the crack will finally give way, do we? We can't see behind the plaster.

Sean was feeling love for his son *because of* his connection with Jenny. Jenny and Sean shared something unique, an understanding, that went beyond the empathy that I and the other people in their lives could provide. And within this understanding came a connection. And that connection gave Jenny a home, a safe place to be. And it gave Sean power.

When Sean called Jenny in the middle of the night, his rage tearing through him, his hand in a fist, she knew what he was feeling. She didn't have to say anything to him. She just had to listen. Sean did the same for her. Before she recalled that one small memory of her rape, she had told me what it was like to be with him.

I think about it for hours. I close my eyes and I picture us sitting at the diner or walking by the lake. I can see his face and I go through everything I want to tell him. Like I'm rehearsing for a play or something. I can't think about the homework I have to do for the tutor or my mother's schedule or anything at all. I imagine that I'm taking all the bad feelings and putting them in a garbage bag, like a giant black plastic bag. One by one, the burning in my stomach, the pounding in my chest, the fear of everything and nothing, that feeling that nothing is what it seems, the disorientation—everything we talk about in here and everything that made me so crazy I tried to kill myself—I start shoving it all into a bag. And then I carry that bag on the back of my bike and then I see his car and he gets out and then right away, in a second, he takes the bag and puts it in his trunk and then it's just gone the whole time we're together. It's really, really gone! And whatever happens, whether we just talk about stupid stuff or I cry the whole time or he goes off on things that made him angry that week—it doesn't matter at all, because the bag of garbage is locked in his trunk.

"And what happens when you go back to town and he parks his car and you get out and unlock your bike? Does he give you back the garbage bag?" I asked her. I usually know the answers to my questions. This time I did not.

He doesn't give it back to me. He would never do that. But there's always more garbage.

"I'm sorry, Jenny. That must be very hard to know it's not gone forever when he drives away with it."

But the thing is, I know that in a week or ten days or whatever it is, I can give him the bag and for that small amount of time, I'll be free of it. So when it comes, I just imagine I'm putting it in the bag. And then more comes, and I put that in the bag. I just fill that bag up and then put it on my bike and carry it to him.

I cannot hold the bag for Jenny. Nor can her parents or her friends or the other members of the group. Only Sean. Can you imagine having that power?

Sean does not give his garbage bag to Jenny. I have not asked him about this, or about Jenny at all, because this decent man does not need one more ounce of guilt. But I know. Sean would not take any pleasure in passing along his burdens. His pleasure, his joy, lies within the power he has to hold hers. He takes her garbage bag and she gives him purpose, a reason to get up every day. A reason to keep fighting. A reason to live.

Yes, Sean loved his son. I did not know yet whether he loved his wife or just felt obligated to her. They had never shared one peaceful day. Regardless, he loved Philip, and his love was set free by what he had with Jenny. She had found a wormhole through his guilt and around the ghosts. They could not touch the power she gave him. And that power was like an invisible force field around his love, protecting it, making it feel safe to come out of hiding.

I feel frustrated. I am mixing so many metaphors. How I struggle to explain things to you.

Can we at least agree that they shared something very special?

The trouble is this: He is a man and she is a woman—young, yes, but still a woman. And when there is a connection this strong, it wants to go to the ends of the earth. And the ends of the earth for a man and woman involves sex. Not sometimes. Not maybe. *Always.*

I sat down at the table between myself and Sean. I was moving slowly because the phone call came five minutes later than I had requested earlier that morning.

"Oh, I'm so sorry, Sean. I have to take this. Do you mind waiting?"

It's all good, Doc, he said.

I took my cell phone in the small chamber between my office and the bathroom. I closed the door, not all the way.

"Detective Parsons. Thank you for calling back," I said. I stood very close to the opening in the door. I did not lower my voice.

No problem. You said you had something for me to look into? Has something happened with Jenny? Another memory?

"Something like that. Listen, though. This cannot go further than you and me, do you understand? When I tell you, you will for sure."

You definitely have my attention, Alan. What is it?

My heart was pounding wildly. I felt corrupted. I had been so filled with goodness that morning with Sean. Hearing about his moment with Philip. Sharing his tears. It felt pure and sacred. And now I was about to continue down my evil path.

Sean was light. I was the darkness. He was good. I was evil. He was clean. And I was filthy.

I swallowed down my bitter pill and carried on. The child with the box of matches. A match now lit.

Alan—you there? Who's the person you want me to look into?

Then I said it. I just said it. And I said it loud enough for Sean to hear me.

"Bob Sullivan."

Chapter Twenty-four

The next day was Tuesday, and I went up to Somers as I always do. I felt relief to be with the criminals, to be yelled at, disrespected, and deceived. My relief concerned me. Were my own crimes so despicable, I now felt deserving of this mistreatment? Was I now destined for a life of martyrdom to pay the debts of my transgressions? I would sooner join poor Glenn Shelby in the grave than live that way.

It was an easy day for Somers. Or maybe it was just easy in comparison to the week I'd had back in Fairview. My usual drug seekers came to abuse my patience. The truly deserving inmates were neither healed nor appreciative of the small comfort my prescriptions afforded them. The staff reminded me how miserable life can be when you aren't careful to pave the right path for your life—to build yourself a good house. Still, there was nothing about the day that upset me.

I have said very little about my own family, my parents and my sister. It does not seem relevant to the story, and yet much of what I have explained to you involves childhood mishaps and dysfunction.

Perhaps to understand why I did the things I did, you should have some more pieces to my own puzzle.

You already know that my parents were lovely, generous people. I see them once a year in the summer. Julie is very good about this. They are a plane ride away, so it requires planning and effort. They are older now and do not like to travel, so the onus is on us to make the journey. My sister is ten years younger, and we have little in common. She is a history professor in London. She never married but seems quite happy with her life. She sends us a card every Christmas with a picture of her and her two Labs.

That seems enough for now. I hope I have satisfied you that my motivations to help my son were driven by the selfish but normal instincts of a parent to protect a child and not anything more devious or corrupt than that. I feel the need to justify myself, and my actions. That is a manifestation of my guilt. I tell my patients that nothing good can come from guilt. It leads us down paths where we do not belong if we are to move forward. It is, by its very nature, a backward-looking emotion. See how it has already taken me from the task at hand?

These were challenging days, and I knew enough to recognize the help I needed to give myself. They say doctors make the worst patients. That is because we exercise such incredible power. The power to heal if we are competent. And the power to hurt if we are not. To throw ourselves in with the lot over whom we exercise that power is a humbling endeavor. Too humbling for some. It requires a very robust ego to maintain the degree of confidence we must have to wield our power. There cannot be hesitation or doubt, or we would never be able to function, to do our jobs. Imagine a knife in your hand, a scalpel; soft flesh beneath the blade. The movement of your hand will determine the very life of the patient on your table. Or, in my case, a pen in hand, words to be written that will send chemicals into the patient's body, altering the mind. The mind, that controls the body. Admitting weakness. Accepting help. It feels like a slippery slope to a doctor's demise.

I have not taken much medication in my life, and I did not intend to start. I limited myself to the small doses of lorazepam. I sat with my anxiety the way Jenny had to sit with hers, and Sean with his. I told myself I was building my empathy, that this would make me a better therapist. But I was not so foolish that I failed to recognize the difference. Jenny could afford to cry all day, or put her feelings in the garbage bag and give them to Sean. And Sean had the luxury of walls to pound and miles of road to run. He had Jenny to feed his sense of purpose. I had no such luxuries. I had to show up for work. I had to see my patients. I had to smile at my wife and watch my son's swim meets. I had to be supportive but strict with his behavior. And I had to implement my plan with moderation. Precision.

The rest of the week passed. I saw Tom on Friday. He was growing more angry at Detective Parsons for not finding the boy with the blue hoodie. I saw Charlotte on Thursday. She had another unsatisfying encounter with Bob, another fight with Tom, but her focus was on her new bond with her daughter. She told me that Jenny had been upset about something after the group session Wednesday night. She asked me if anything had happened, and I lied to her. I worked with Jenny on voices, on the words *Dear Lord, oh dear Lord.* And I worked with Sean on the red door. Both of them had been distracted. Both of them had concealed something from me. After the group met Wednesday night, they talked for a long time in the hallway. Charlotte was waiting outside in the car. The other patients walked past them. It ended with a long hug, which I observed undetected.

I would not learn about the things that happened away from my office until the following week. But, of course, everything that happened had been my doing.

It was Charlotte who first gave me the information. She called me the following Monday and asked to come in. She rushed past me as I closed the door to my office. She did not wait for me to sit down before she started to cry and talk all at once.

It's bad! It's so bad!

"Take a breath, Charlotte. Close your eyes. We have time for you to say everything, to tell me everything, so just . . . take one moment to gather yourself."

Okay, okay . . .

She did as I asked. And I waited, giddy with anticipation. Jason was scheduled to have his interview the following week. Parsons was now aware that my son was on the swim team. That he had been at the party. But I will get to that. I had begun to think, to worry, that nothing I did had taken hold. That the match I'd lit and thrown to the ground simply went out without catching fire to anything. I had little time. Was I wrong? Was there fire? Charlotte opened her eyes, the tears under control. And she answered my question.

This is all going wrong. Your work with Jenny, these memories she's recovering, they're all muddled together now, mixed up, and she thinks . . . Oh God . . . has she told you? She said she hasn't told anyone, but it must have happened in here . . . it must have!

"Charlotte," I said, "slow down. Tell me what Jenny said, and then I can tell you what I know about it."

Her mind was running wild. I could see it in her eyes. I imagined she had been up most of the night with her spinning thoughts, and now they were just a tangled web of loose wires.

She thinks it's Bob. Jenny thinks Bob raped her! Can you imagine?

"I see." I had practiced the tone of my reaction for days. I know I got it just right, because Charlotte remained focused on the crisis. "How did that happen?"

You tell me! She said you were working on voices, words. She said she remembers Bob's voice. She played some of his car ads on

YouTube for me. And she's met him dozens of times at the dealer-ships and in town. He's Tom's boss, for God's sake!

"Did she say when this happened? It's true we've been working on words and voices, but she hasn't had any recalls in our sessions. I thought it was going to be a dead end."

Charlotte was holding herself with both arms, rocking back and forth on the sofa. She shook her head from side to side. All very com-mon mannerisms for acute anxiety.

She said it had just come to her. She was really quiet at dinner last night. Then she went to her room and I could hear Bob's voice in those ads. I went in and asked her what she was doing, and when she turned from the computer, her face was soaked with tears. She looked like she did that day she remembered the moment of the rape.

"So she has remembered something and it feels real to her?"

Of course she remembers something! But she's remembering all wrong! She's remembering his voice from that afternoon in the pool house . . . when Bob helped save her life! But she's placed it with the night of the rape! She thinks she heard his voice while she was being raped, not while she was being saved! Don't you see! It's all mixed up!

I rubbed my chin with my hand. I squinted my eyes and looked away. I was surprised and concerned, and in the appropriate doses.

"That is very possible. I had not considered that she would have a memory of that afternoon after she lost consciousness. But it is actu-ally quite possible. People hear things while in comas. They form memories. It all depends on what the brain is doing while it's uncon-scious. There are many factors involved."

I paused and pretended to consider a course of action. Charlotte watched me carefully, as though I were a life raft floating nearby. Would the current bring it to her? Or would it carry it away and leave her to drown?

"Well," I said, "I have to ask you the one thing you don't want me to ask. Because while it is possible that her memory of his voice is misplaced, we have to at least rule out—"

Absolutely not! She interrupted me quickly and decisively. *There is no chance Bob Sullivan raped my daughter.*

"All right," I said. "Then we will sort this out. She should not have been listening to his voice on those ads with this idea in her head. She knows better than to work on her memory recall outside this office."

Oh, you have no idea! I went on the browser history. She's been doing this for days—searching for his ads, listening to them over and over. She even asked Lucas some questions about Bob, whether he ever felt uncomfortable around him. As if he would do something to a ten-year-old boy! She Googled Bob and his family, has them on her alerts. . . . It's in her head and now she's convinced herself it's a memory.

"When did it start?"

Wednesday. After the group session. That's the first time she looked it up on the computer. I don't know . . . maybe there's more on her phone, but I don't want to punish her for this or make her think she did something wrong.

Yes. Wednesday after group. Sean had told her about what he overheard in my office. That was the long conversation. That was the hug. I asked Charlotte about the rest of the week, about her behavior. Jenny had been to town twice since the group session. She had a lot of garbage to give to Sean. And a lot of secrets she'd been keeping from me.

Can you fix this before it goes any further? Before she tells Tom? My God—can you imagine?

"What do you think will happen?"

Are you kidding me? Tom will confront Bob. And then Bob will have no choice but to tell him.

"About the affair? About why his voice is in Jenny's head?"

Yes! Yes!

I nodded with empathy and conviction. "I can understand why this is so upsetting. Have you told Bob?"

Absolutely not. He would tell Tom. He'd get so far out in front of this . . . you have no idea. He's running for office, for Christ's sake!

"Well, then he wouldn't want the affair to be public, would he?"

It's better than a rape accusation.

"Yes, but there is no accusation yet. I'm seeing Jenny later today. I'll speak to her about this, about how she has likely corrupted her memory recall by listening to those ads. I can't make her promise not to tell her father. But I can ask her to use discretion and to give us more time to try to find the real memories from that night."

Charlotte sighed heavily. *Thank you! Oh . . . thank you thank you.*

"But, Charlotte, you have to know one thing. I'm not going to tell Jenny that she's wrong. I don't know that for sure. I mean, I certainly respect your opinion. But it would be unethical for me to discount her memory entirely without absolutely knowing. What I will try to do, is see if I can help her find the misconnection—in other words, track this voice memory back to a place that isn't the rape. I doubt she'll place it anywhere, because of the circumstances. This is very problematic, indeed. And I'm walking a fine line. I have to maintain the integrity of the treatment."

As long as you get her to realize this voice memory she has is not from the rape. Remind her how many times she's met Bob and heard his commercials. Maybe she heard it in the car driving to the party? Who knows? Something. Anything! I can't have Bob accused of rape! And I can't tell my husband what I've been doing. I just can't. Not with everything going on. He'll break. Or he'll leave me. And I'll be the one who did it.

What a horrible dilemma for Charlotte. She had been making such progress on this front. We had started discussing her dissatisfaction with Bob, and she had been toying with the idea of ending things with him. I had not yet introduced the rest of my plan for her—to tell Tom about her childhood, to integrate the two Charlottes. To eradicate bad Charlotte once and for all. I knew Tom could handle the truth. In fact, knocking Charlotte off her pedestal, seeing her as the beautiful but flawed woman she really was, would give him back a piece of his manhood. There was so much work to be done. And now this terrible interruption.

Charlotte left. I considered the fire that had indeed started to burn from my little match. Sean had told Jenny about Bob being a suspect. Jenny had obsessed about Bob and immersed herself in his image and his voice until she created a false memory. Just like those subjects in the shopping mall experiment who had never really been lost. I felt like a character in a novel, the brilliant but evil professor. Dr. Frankenstein. I felt slightly pleased with myself. I had succeeded in creating a straw man to deflect the attention from my son. I could imagine it all playing out, and I drifted away in a fantasy: Bob would never be charged, but his notoriety, the race for the state legislature— all of it would lead to a media feeding frenzy. And when he was vindicated, there would be hell to pay. Lawsuits would be filed. Parsons would be reprimanded. The investigation would come to a screeching halt. No more questioning of innocent boys. No more "witch" hunts for blue sweatshirts.

When I was done with this disgusting self-indulgence, I lied to myself about what this would mean for Jenny and for Sean and for my work with them. I told myself that they would continue on with the treatment. I turned my fantasy to miraculous moments in my office. Sean jumping up from the sofa, screaming out into the universe, *I remember! I know what happened at the red door!* Then going home to his wife and his son and living in peace. And for Jenny, I could barely let myself think it. It was like dreaming that I'd cured cancer or brokered world peace. It was too much to allow into my fantasy. I let it come as a flash, and nothing more. I did not dwell in the elation of giving her back that night, that worst nightmare.

I keep returning to the same thought as I reflected on that week. The child with the matches, thinking he was old enough to handle it. I lit the match and let it fly. My fire had started. I could not possibly have predicted the strong wind that would blow in, giving it life, and a power I would not be able to contain.

Chapter Twenty-five

When I saw Jenny later that day, I kept my promise to Charlotte. I did not need to be the advocate anymore. I needed to do what I would have done had I been a disinterested party.

Jenny knew her mother had told me about her memory. About Bob Sullivan. I asked her point-blank how this idea got into her head in the first place.

I don't want to tell you.

I respected her honesty. And I was grateful for it. What would I have said if she had told me the truth? That Sean had told her what he'd heard in my office? I had only two options to explain why I was discussing Bob Sullivan with Detective Parsons. One was to let Sullivan off the hook. *Sean misunderstood. . . . Sean heard incorrectly. . . .* The second was to offer an explanation as to why I suspected him, which did not exist. Jenny spared me with her refusal to come clean.

"Okay. I won't make you tell me."

I couldn't anyway. I made a promise.

"Your mother feels, and I can't disagree with her, that it is some-what unlikely that this memory is accurate. First—because you came across it on your own with your own kind of immersion ther-apy. And second because Bob Sullivan is an unlikely suspect. He's running for office. He has a lot to lose. He's been married for over thirty years with no scandals, nothing in his closet of this nature. And he's your father's boss, so there would be a high probability of you recognizing him."

So what? Most women are raped by someone they know. Half the women in group were raped by someone they know.

Jenny's voice was different on that Monday. She was speaking to me not like I was the one person who could save her, but rather like I was an outsider who didn't understand. I didn't like it. I wanted to change it. I could not lose what we had worked so hard to create.

"You know what? You're right. I'm going to be totally honest with you. The work we're doing here is very controversial. Remember how I told you about the false memory people? How they think recalling memories can be corrupted by suggestion? And how false memories can then be formed? Like the people who were told they were lost in the mall."

Yeah.

"So, now we have a situation where suggestions have been brought into this process. You don't have to tell me now, but at least concede that a suggestion entered and that you have bolstered that by im-mersing yourself in that suggestion."

Jenny slumped down in the cushions. I could see she was con-flicted.

"My fear is that if we move too quickly with this new theory, and it turns out to be a false memory, then nothing you ever remember again will be given any credibility. And even you will have trouble believing. So let's try to weed out the suggestions, do our work quietly, and make absolutely sure about this before telling anyone else."

Like the police?

"Yes."

And even my dad?

"I can't tell you what to do with any of this. What do you think your father will do if you tell him?"

I think he'll call the police. Or worse.

"Worse?"

He's really angry.

"That's understandable. That's his job—as your father."

I guess. But he's more angry than I am.

"Actually, you don't seem angry at all today."

Jenny shrugged. *I feel tired. I feel like my brain hurts. I remember hearing his voice, and now my mom, and you, are telling me it's just a mix-up. It's like someone's telling me to solve a math problem I don't understand, and I keep trying but I just can't do it. I just want to quit.*

This alarmed me more than I can express.

"How did you feel before you told your mom? When you had this memory come back, the memory of Bob's voice?"

I don't know. I felt excited like I had solved the problem. I told Sean right away. I cried a little. I stared at pictures of Mr. Sullivan, watched videos. I thought about his stupid sons and how ashamed they would be of him. I thought about my dad and how he would want to kill him.

"But wait . . . don't you remember? Last week, when you smelled the bleach and you recalled that moment in the woods. You were distraught and despairing. You asked me why he had taken a piece of your soul. And now—when you looked at pictures of this man you think did that to you, you didn't feel any of those things?"

Jenny looked defeated. I opened my mouth to speak again, to tell her why this was so—Bob Sullivan did not rape her. She did not remember him raping her. There were no emotions attached to his voice, or even worse, positive emotions from being saved. I had the power to explain this, and yet I could not because I needed her to stay with the theory, with the false memory, even as I pretended to convince her not to. I closed my mouth and swallowed the words. The truth.

I just want it to be over.

She said this again through sniffles and tears. I wanted to shake her until she snapped out of it. What was it? Was it Sean? Was he distracting her? Had they been intimate? It didn't make any sense to me. She had only one small memory of the rape, and she knew how much it had helped her. She had told me what a relief it was. She'd talked about it in group last week, before Sean told her about Bob Sullivan, before she'd taken this turn of indifference. More memories would bring only more closure, more relief from the ghosts that roamed inside. There was more work to be done!

I felt angry then. How many times have I said this to you? This was a difficult time for me. I was angry at Jenny for wanting to give up. Angry at Sean for allowing their friendship to distract her. And angry at my son for putting me in this position, where I had to compromise my work with Jenny to save his sorry ass.

I held myself together. Jenny and I went back to that night in the woods. This time, we used the bleach and the music and I did not say the words. I did not play Bob Sullivan's commercial. I wanted things to be the way they were. I wanted another moment of pure success to happen in this office. I wanted the magic of that moment to return.

It did not. Jenny was blocked, detached. I could not do this alone. When she left, I sat at my desk and wallowed in my misery.

It was then, right then at that moment of despair, that Detective Parsons called with the wind that would ignite my little fire.

Chapter Twenty-six

Parsons was upset. I could hear it in his voice. He had not believed Bob Sullivan could be a viable suspect. He had not wanted to. I couldn't blame him. This case was never going to have a "smoking gun." Any investigation into any suspect would require a leap of faith followed by professional exposure. It was one thing when the exposure involved a man like Cruz Demarco, or even the boys who were at the party. But Bob Sullivan was Fairview's finest. And he wielded significant power throughout the middle part of the state. Parsons and his whole investigation would be under a microscope.

There was also the issue of my son and his name being on the list of boys to be interviewed. I had timed this meticulously.

"It has occurred to me that you should have my son on your list," I said. I'd made the call the past Friday afternoon. "I'm sorry I didn't think of this sooner, but he is on the swim team and he was at the party."

Parsons, as expected, had not looked at his list for the following week. *Really?* He said. *Let me see. . . . Oh yeah. We have him. He's scheduled for next Thursday. We're having to make appointments because everyone wants to come with a lawyer.*

"I'm sure. My wife does as well, I'm afraid. I have no problem with any of this. You should absolutely cross every t and dot every i. I want nothing less for the Kramers."

Parsons was quiet for a moment. He was thinking. *I suppose they know your son . . . uh, Jason, was there? The Kramers, I mean?*

"Well, I don't really know. I try to keep my professional life separate from my personal affairs. I suppose I should tell them, or at least Tom. I'll take care of that right away."

That had been the end of it. My wife called the station and got the appointment moved again to the following week. I mentioned the interview in passing to Tom at one of our sessions. I waited until he was worked up about the police being incompetent for not finding the blue sweatshirt.

We were now past that. We were on to Bob Sullivan. I had managed to kick the can down the road. But the road was not endless.

Alan, we did some checking into Sullivan. Do you have anything else on your end?

"Well, actually, I do, but it's really quite uncertain. I don't want to jump the gun."

Look . . . I need whatever you have. Fuck . . . this thing is spinning out of control.

"What's happened? What did you find?"

Sometimes life just hands you a gift. You don't know when it's going to happen. You can't count on it. But when it happens, you come very close to believing there's a god.

Uh . . . man. I don't even want to say it. I have your word it will remain between us until I have enough to question him?

"Of course."

Okay. Spring 1982. Fort Lauderdale. There's a file that made it to Skidmore, where Sullivan went to college. Nothing came of it. No charges. Nothing like that. But it involves a sexual incident. The victim was a sixteen-year-old. Local girl out with her friends, looking to party with college kids on their spring break. Sounds like it might have been a case of morning-after regret. There's a photo . . . tight little tube top, miniskirt, black eyeliner . . . you get the picture, right?

"Yes."

Sullivan's parents got him a lawyer. Charges were dropped on condition his college was informed. It's nothing. And between you and me, if Tom Kramer wasn't such a loose cannon, this file would be in the shredder. This is the kind of thing that ruins a man's life. And it's apples and oranges.

Oh, what a gift, this wind!

"Well . . . I can see your dilemma. How can I help you?"

Parsons sighed. I could hear his exasperation with me. *I need to know why you set me out on this path. I need to know what Jenny Kramer remembers. I can't go at this guy with a thirty-three-year-old allegation that never even led to charges. It'll seem like a persecution.*

"But isn't it your job to follow every lead, even if it takes you to a man like Bob Sullivan? Maybe there's more to find. He obviously has some appetites. Possibly control issues. He's an aggressive man. You can tell that from his success, his ambitions."

You want me to go at him with that? Seriously? Well, it makes sense that you would brutally rape a local teenager—after all, you're ambitious and successful—

"Detective," I interrupted him, "let me ask you this: Wasn't the first thing you did on this case to look for anyone in and around Fairview with a sex offense? That and the blue Civic? If this college record had been an actual charge, wouldn't you have at least asked him politely for an alibi so you could rule him out? Surely he would understand that, and gladly provide one. You've done more than that with half the teenage boys in this town, haven't you?"

It's not the same. The boys were at the party. We already knew that. How am I gonna explain my reasons for digging up his records? He'll hire his own investigators. A team of lawyers. This whole thing will be out of my hands then. And over what?

"But he's running for office. I'm shocked the press haven't already found it. Let him believe someone handed it to you."

I don't know. Seems like a stretch. It's the state legislature. His opponent is an eighty-year-old probate judge with a couple of nickels to rub together. No . . . even if I don't tell him why I need the alibi, I gotta have something. Don't tell me what it is. Just tell me there's something if I need it. Tell me you didn't send me on this goose chase without a really good reason.

I pretended to mull this over. I sighed. I hemmed and hawed. Parsons was very nervous.

"There is something. It's not reliable. It would get torn apart in court. But it certainly is enough."

I don't think this is what Parsons wanted to hear. I think he wanted a reason to close the door on Bob Sullivan. Parsons's zeal for this case came and went with the turn of the spotlight. When it was shining outside of Fairview, he was a tiger on the hunt. I think about him in that car, dying to pounce on Cruz Demarco. When Demarco came up with an alibi, Parsons went back at the swim team and the search for the blue sweatshirt, but with far less ambition. He did not even know the names of the boys on the list. He had been surprised to hear about Jason. What kind of detective work is that? I did not know why this was. Perhaps he didn't want to muddy his own pond. For weeks, he'd been doing what he had to do to keep Tom Kramer satisfied— and no more. Although Tom never was satisfied.

Parsons hung up. It was only a matter of days before Bob would be interviewed, before he would know he was in the mix somehow. He would then go to Charlotte, and she would tell him about the recovered memory of his voice and how Jenny had mixed it up in her head. What then? That was the question. Where would the wind blow next? What else would the fire burn? Bob's marriage? His run for office? Charlotte?

I went home after that call. I could not concentrate. I could not listen to anyone else's problems. I took more lorazepam. The dose was small. It was barely enough to smooth the edges of my anxiety.

My excitement at the gift, the wind and the fire it fed, was fleeting, and I realized that a great darkness was covering my sky. I don't know how else to explain this to you. Some of you will understand. Those of you who come to my office and sit on my sofa and tell me the things you have done that cannot be undone, or the things that have been done to you. All of life is just a state of mind, isn't it? We are all just walking slowly to our graves, trying not to think about it, trying to find meaning, to pass the time pleasantly. Look around you. Everyone you can see will be dead in one hundred years: You. Your spouse. Your child. Your friends. The people who love you. The people who hate you. Terrorists in the Middle East. The politicians raising your taxes and making bad policies. The teacher who gave your son a bad grade. The couple who didn't invite you to a dinner.

I have gone down this mental path when things have upset me. I find it puts life in perspective. It can be a good thing, to remember that there is very little that truly matters. A bad grade. A dumb politician. A social slight.

Unfortunately, there are things that do matter. Things that can ruin what little time we have here. Things that cannot be done over or remedied. These are the things that we regret. And regret is more devious than guilt. It is more corrosive than envy. And it is more powerful than fear.

Why did I take my eyes off the swimming pool? Why did I take my eyes off the road? Why did I cheat on my wife? Why did I steal from my clients?

People fight every day to control their regret, to keep it from stealing their happiness. Sometimes they fight just to function, to work and drive their kids to school and make dinner without jumping off a bridge. It is painful. Brutally painful. The skillful ones manage to outmaneuver it. Then they go to sleep and it finds its way back to the throne. Morning comes and they awake again as slaves to this ruthless dictator.

I pulled into my driveway, a slave to my own regret. I could already see how irreparable my actions were. I felt stained by the kind of stain that never comes out. The kind of stain that would make you throw the thing out. Red wine on a white tablecloth. Blood on Charlotte's blouse. I thought about Bob Sullivan. A cheater. A liar. But an innocent man. I thought about Sean Logan. A hero. A tortured soul. And now the anger at Bob Sullivan was festering within him. I thought about Jenny, I thought about her blood spilled on that bathroom floor and how I was so close to giving her back her memory, and with it her very life. These things I had done, I might as well have slammed into these innocents with my car while my eyes were looking away. Maybe it's worse than that. This was no accident. This was me driving down the road, my son on one side and these innocents on the other—and no room to pass safely between them

My wife was in the kitchen, making a snack for my son. I could hear that fucking game on in the TV room, my son's laughter, gunfire, explosions. More laughter.

What's wrong with you? What's happened? my wife asked me.

I did not know this at the time, but I had been crying. Fury at having to save him this way and fear that escaped from the box on the shelf seeped from my eyes. There were a lot of tears that day.

I walked past her to the TV room. I did not stop to turn off the game. I grabbed my son by both arms and pulled him to his feet.

Dad—he started to say.

I took the remote from his hands, and I threw it at the TV. I shattered the screen. My wife screamed and ran in from the kitchen. She had the plate of food in her hands.

Alan!

Holding my son's arms, I shook him, hard. "You tell me right now! Why were you in those woods? What were you doing in those woods!"

I wasn't! I told you!

I shook him again and again. My wife set down the plate and rushed to my side, grabbing hold of my arms, trying to pull me away from our child.

"Do you know what you've done? Do you know what might have happened? Tell me! Why were you there? Why were you in those woods?"

Julie stared at him, waiting for an answer. The more time that passed, the more she had come to wonder whether he had raped Jenny Kramer. I could see it in her eyes, the sadness that had crept in.

I saw his phone sitting on the couch. I grabbed it. I knew the password because my wife had told me. I also knew from my wife about the porn she'd found on his computer. I opened the home screen and checked the browser history.

What are you doing! Stop that! Jason screamed. He lunged for the phone, but I was faster. His arm swept through the air, missing me completely.

I let an image load, some porn star's hairless pussy with a giant cock about to enter. The picture started to move into video. The image of people fornicating on the screen. The sound of people fornicating on the audio. My wife gasped, her hand drawing to her mouth.

Mom . . . Our son turned to her for help. She looked at him and then to me. My emotions had infected her.

"This is how you're building your house? This is what you want the police to see if they get your phone? You want one more thing that makes you look like a rapist?"

Jesus, Dad! Everybody looks at this stuff. It's just regular stuff! It doesn't make me a rapist!

"Regular stuff?" I said, shoving the phone up close to his face. "There is nothing regular about this. Nothing!"

Julie pleaded with him. *Jason, please! We still love you. We'll still help you. But we have to know. Tell us! Please, just tell us!*

My son's face was bright red, and I knew we had turned him. I knew he was breaking. And for a moment, I actually thought it was possible that he had done those terrible things to my sweet Jenny. Oh, the places the mind can go! We are so fragile. So very, very fragile.

Okay! He screamed at us, pulling his arms from my grasp. *Just let me go!*

We stood there in the center of that room. Julie and I holding our breath with anticipation. Jason gathering his courage. I turned off the phone and tossed it onto the sofa.

I was there, okay! I was fucking there! Are you happy now? Are you happy I'm going to jail?

Julie gasped. *What did you do? My God, what?*

"Jason . . ." I said, almost in a whisper. My mind was out of control.

Jason started to cry. I told you there were a lot of tears that day. He sat on the couch and hung his head into his hands.

I went to find that guy. The guy in the blue Civic.

"Cruz Demarco?" I asked. "The drug dealer?"

I had a hundred dollars. And I went to find him.

"Where did you get a hundred dollars?"

I took it. From a wallet in the kitchen. I don't know whose it was— it was just there and it had all this money in it.

"So you thought you'd steal the money and buy drugs?"

There was this girl. She asked if I had anything. I knew the guy was out there. Kids were coming in and out, whispering about it. He had all kinds of stuff.

"And you thought if you bought these drugs, then what? She would go out with you?"

I looked at my wife. She was almost laughing. I wiped my face and tried not to smile. Relief had swept through us both.

"What happened next? How did you get from the road to the woods?"

I just . . . I got close to the car and I got scared. So I pretended I was just walking by. . . . I went to the other side of the car, the side next to the woods, and as soon as there was a clearing, I went near the woods just to the line of trees, then came back to the house. I put the money back. I told the girl the guy had left.

"So you were never in the woods?" My head was spinning then. It is one thing to ask the question. It is quite another to know the answer is coming. This is the reason many questions remain unasked. Sometimes it is easier not knowing.

No!

The word echoed, bouncing against the walls of my heart. Thank God! Oh, sweet Jesus, thank you!

My wife couldn't speak without revealing her joy, pure joy that her wonderful son was still wonderful.

"This is not who you are," I said sternly. I don't know how, but I managed to conceal myself. My head was spinning.

"Stealing money and even thinking about buying drugs!"

Jason slumped back into the couch. He really had no idea about anything.

"Why don't you go to your room. Take the Xbox with you. I'm sorry I broke the TV."

Am I grounded?

"Yes. Until next weekend."

Jason got up, unplugged the Xbox, and grabbed all the wires and controllers and games. He skulked away to the stairs and then up to his room.

Julie fell into my arms and we both laughed. The fear was gone. The box on the shelf empty. It did not lift the darkness. It did not clean the stain. But I was resigned to live dirty, under this shadow for the flawed but wonderful creature we had created.

Chapter Twenty-seven

I went forth with conviction. With purpose. It is not that I needed proof that my son had not raped Jenny. It was that I needed to see his innocence, his goodness again. He had been lying to us about that night, and now he had confessed. And in his confession, the way it was told, the words and tone and expression, was the innocence.

This is my son. My child. He is my legacy in this world. He is an extension of me. I came to see their pursuit of him as a pursuit of myself. I felt it inside my gut like nothing I had ever felt before. It was primal. I went forth like a lion protecting his cub.

I did not let go of my own desires. With my head clear, I constructed more of my plan. I believed I had found a way to not only keep my son from being dragged into the investigation, but get Jenny back on track, too. I became two men. The first was the doctor curing his patients. The second was the puppeteer, holding his wooden sticks, making his subjects dance to the tune of his will.

I saw Charlotte two days later. She was irate. *You told the police! About Bob and the voice. You told them!*

"Calm down, Charlotte. I didn't say anything to them about Jenny's memory. Why don't you tell me what's happened."

Charlotte found her composure and studied my face. I told you, I was steadfast in my conviction. A rock. The doubt and anger she'd been carrying for over sixteen hours were gone in a second. My power seemed to have no end.

He asked to see me. Bob. I met him at the house, but he didn't touch me. Not even a kiss hello. He was upset. Worried. So of course, I asked him what was wrong. I tried to hide my fears. I pretended that I didn't know anything. I don't know ... I think he believed me.

"I'm sure he did. It was the truth, after all. You could not have known what had him so upset."

I suppose. It felt like a lie. I felt guilty pretending.

"Did you tell him?"

No. I let him tell me. Detective Parsons paid him a casual visit. Bob said he was nice as could be, and very apologetic. He said he'd gotten a hold of some record from a million years ago. College. Bob went to Skidmore.

"College?" I asked.

Yeah. He said some girl he was with on spring break lied about her age and then cried to her friends the next day. They told their parents and their parents told the girl's parents and the police had to get involved because the girl was underage. Nothing happened from it. Bob said he was worried it might be found. You know, because of the election, he said he thought it wouldn't happen until years from now, when he runs for a national office. I guess it's always been in the back of his mind that someone might dig it up.

"And what does that have to do with the matter at hand? With Jenny?"

Obviously, it's a sexual offense or complaint or whatever. Detective Parsons said he had to just do a quick follow-up to cover his bases and then he could close the file.

"So he wanted an alibi?"

Yeah.

"And did Bob have one to provide?"

He said he couldn't remember. He said he would call back after checking his wife's calendar and speaking with her. So Parsons left and Bob said he did that—called his wife. She reminded him they were at a club function. The spring wine-tasting dinner. I had wanted to go to that, but we had dinner plans instead.

"I remember. You said you quarreled with Tom in the car over that."

Yes. Anyway, Bob called Parsons back and told him.

"I see. So that's that. He has an alibi?" In all honesty, I had not considered this possibility. I don't know why, but I had assumed Bob would say he was with his wife somewhere and then they would not be able to prove it or disprove it. A wife was never a good alibi. But a club dinner would have a record. And many witnesses. Still, I did not lose my focus.

"I do think it's odd that he didn't remember where he was. I think everyone in this town remembers where they were that night. The news of the assault was shocking to us all."

Christ! I don't know what to think. I really don't.

"About what? This should be good news."

It would be if Bob had been at that dinner. Or if he had said he was somewhere else.

"Wait. Are you saying he wasn't there? How do you know that?"

Because I know. She was there, his wife. Fran. Uh . . . this is humiliating. My friend from the club who went to the dinner was filling me in on the gossip. It was weeks later. She was trying to get my mind off Jenny. Bob never showed up. Fran sat with my friend and her husband and made excuses for his not being with her. If it had been anyone else, I wouldn't have cared or remembered. But it was Bob, and I hadn't seen him, you know really seen him, since that night. I got this ache in my gut. I was worried that he was see-ing another woman.

And the wind kept blowing.

"I see. Did you tell Bob you knew this?"

Of course. I mean, I didn't tell him that I was worried. But I reminded him that Fran had been alone that night and had sat with my friend. He looked surprised, like he really didn't remember where he was. Like you said—that's strange, right?

"It is to me. But you never know. Did he have any other explana-tion for where he was?"

No. In fact, he just kept telling me I was wrong, that Fran had already confirmed he was with her. Parsons believed it. Case closed.

"Then you should feel relieved."

But Charlotte was not relieved. I could not be entirely sure whether she was starting to doubt her own lover's innocence with regard to the rape of her daughter. Or whether she was feeding her suspicions that he had been with another woman that night. I watched her body, her face, the way her knee bounced beneath the leg that was folded on top of it, causing her foot to dance in the air. She was not horrified. She was anxious. I concluded her distress was from the latter.

He stopped talking then. He reached for my waist. We had sex. We left. I went home to my family and pretended to be good Charlotte.

"You are just *Charlotte.* You are winning this battle. Can't you feel it?" The doctor had returned. Charlotte had adopted my lan-guage, the "good Charlotte" and "bad Charlotte" paradigms that I knew would begin to resonate within her. She had been feeling less attached to bad Charlotte and less deserving of good Charlotte. My hope, my dream for her, was that she would let go of both of them.

I know I have used many metaphors. Pick the one you like best— the roller coaster barreling down the hill, the cars heading for a collision, the strands of sugar winding their way into a perfect cone—the end of the story. This is the part where everything accelerated.

Charlotte and I worked on her internal struggles. The doctor was brilliant that day. The timing, the words, the way he led her to the truth within herself. She left feeling sick inside, disgusted by her behavior. Bad Charlotte was losing ground. I worked on dismantling good Charlotte. We talked about her connection with Jenny, how good Charlotte, perfect Charlotte, would never have been able to understand her daughter's pain, how she'd felt that night when her will was taken from her. She understood. The thoughts were in her head, and they were starting to take hold.

Before she left, she told me this one last thing:

Oh . . . I almost forgot. When you see Tom this week, just be prepared. He found a picture in the yearbook—a kid with that sweatshirt. You can't see his face, because it's from behind and he's standing in a crowd, I think it was at a football game. He's obsessed with it now. I don't know how he found it, honestly. He must have gone over every picture with a magnifying glass.

"I'm sure he'll tell me all about it. Has he given the yearbook to Detective Parsons?"

Called him at six in the morning. Can you imagine? He's out of control. I'm so tired of it.

I smiled. Charlotte left. I was perfectly calm.

"Detective Parsons?" I had him on the phone the moment I heard the door close.

I will not recount the conversation. Let's just say that I betrayed my patient's confidence and suggested Parsons confirm Bob's alibi with the country club. He did not press me for details. Nor was he pleased that the case was not closed. Between my call and Tom with that cursed sweatshirt, I'm sure Detective Parsons was having a very bad day. That was not my concern.

Have you ever seen one of those acrobats who can walk a tightrope while spinning plates on two sticks?

Sean Logan came in later that afternoon. He was agitated.

"Has something happened? You seem upset."

Nah. I'm all good, Doc. His tone was sarcastic.

"Sean. I know this is crossing some boundaries. And boundaries are important in the work we're doing. But I feel I would be negligent if I did not address the things of which I am aware and which I believe have been bothering you for several days."

Sean looked at me with the face of an irreverent teenager. Then he shrugged. Even just one day earlier, this would have made me feel sick. Physically sick. Seeing my patient, my beautiful wounded soldier, without his smile and his humor and his affection for me, well, it would have hurt me deeply. But today I was the rock. And I knew he would come back to me.

"Sean—I know you are very close with Jenny. I also know that she is in a bad place right now because of something she has remembered. Or thinks she remembered. And because she's frustrated that I am worried about that memory being real."

Sean started to heave in and out. He was still so quick to anger, all that guilt, the ghosts, roaming inside him.

Doc, I gotta tell you. I don't know why this fucking monster isn't behind bars. I don't see how you can sit there, knowing what you know and what you're not telling me you know with all your fancy bullshit talk, and not have that man arrested and locked away with the rest of the scum on this planet. Is there anything inside you besides this bullshit? Is there one fucking emotion about what this poor kid went through?

I sat back in my chair, my heart beating just a bit faster. His anger was finding something to attach to, something not innocent like his wife and young son. Something that would not cause him to move heaven and earth to contain it.

"I do have emotions, Sean. I work very hard to keep them from interfering with my work, with my patients. With you. With Jenny."

I let out a sigh and looked away. A pained expression washed across my face, the kind I have seen so many times, it is now second nature to me.

"And I have Jenny's best interests at heart. In my heart," I said through my pained face. "This memory and the person in the memory who is being investigated—I won't say more than that, because it's not my place—but my job is to make damned sure it gets done correctly. He's not going anywhere. There's no harm in taking the time to do things correctly so that if, and it is still a big 'if,' he does turn out to be the perpetrator, then he will not walk away on bad evidence."

Sean looked up at me again, this time with a softer expression.

"You know how easy it would be to corrupt your memories of that dreadful day in Iraq, right? Think about how careful we are when we reconstruct the events, the surroundings. When your brain starts to pull out the file—that process is so precarious. So vulnerable. I fear Jenny's memory has been corrupted that way."

She doesn't think so. She's pretty certain.

"And yet when she thinks about this person, have you noticed? There is no fear or rage or sadness. There's just a bland, flat intellectual response."

Sean considered this. He knew I was right. I could see it. He exhaled loudly. His body relaxed against the cushions. *Fuck.*

"You want it to be this man, don't you?"

*Fuck yeah! She needs this to be over. You know that. She needs
to move on. To live in the future.*

"She needs to remember. That's the only way the ghosts will leave.
And so do you. Should we get to work?"

I worked with Sean for two hours. We went back to the desert. We
went back to the mission, the radio calls as his comrades were murdered one by one on the streets of that village. Valancia at his side.
Seeing the red door, the locals who had not fled to safety. Women
and children. An old man. His anger was deeper than usual. Jenny
was in his head. And worse—she was in his heart. I believed he was
calmer when he left. I believed I knew the extent of his anger and the
power he had to control it. He was not a violent man by nature. But
as much as I never forget he was a soldier, I somehow managed not
to remember.

Chapter Twenty-eight

Somers, the winter before Jenny's rape, was not the last time and place I saw Glenn Shelby before he died. My parents raised me to be generous. They raised me to be charitable. And they raised me to help those in need.

I mention this now because I went to see Glenn that evening after my session with Sean. He had been on my mind since he left the prison, well over a year before. So much about him had found its way into my conscience, and it had become acute to the point of distraction. I located him quite easily through his parole officer. He was working from his studio apartment, doing data inputting for some sleazy Web marketing firm—the kind that captures your data and sends you crap you then have to delete. His aunt in Boston got him the job. She had also kept the apartment for him in Cranston for many years, paid the rent and utilities. The money came from the small estate of his dead parents. His aunt was an elderly woman, and she had little interest in him other than her duties as trustee, for which I imagine she received a token salary. I do not think she knew of his latest imprisonment, though she was aware of his other transgressions against the law. He had two priors for stalking.

Before this job, which kept him at home day and night, Glenn had been employed by a property maintenance company. As was the case in any situation that required social interaction, Glenn was let go within a few months. This had left him bitter. He liked the soil, the smell of the grass, and mostly the interaction with other people. Every new person was a chance for intimacy. Unfortunately, he had pushed too far with one of the clients, a buttoned-up suburban mother whose politeness had been misinterpreted as genuine interest in Glenn and his life philosophies.

Glenn Shelby was a pitiful creature. I have already told you two things. First, he was a master at teasing stories from his targets, personal stories that are usually revealed only to close friends and lovers. It has always bothered me that some of his stories came from our sessions, came from me. And second, that he is the one patient I could not save.

I went to his apartment that night. It was very troubling to be there with him, if I must admit it. The apartment was in a complex that is arranged like a motel, with the front door opening to the outside, the way a house does. But inside, it was just one room. The cars were all parked outside. They were mostly shitty cars, old and uncared for. There was a swimming pool in the center of a courtyard, which was plagued by the indifference of the residents and, in all honesty, reminded me of an open cesspool. It was a mere step up from a homeless shelter. Many of the residents were criminals or, like Glenn, surviving on the goodwill of relatives. They had told Glenn their stories, and Glenn had told me during our sessions at Somers. I remembered them well.

He came to the door in neat khakis and a button-down shirt, like he was about to leave for an office job. The smell from inside was quite strong, a concoction of cleaning products and curry. The company Glenn worked for employed a disproportionate number of Indians, actually in India—no surprise to anyone who has recently called a customer support line. They were frequently on training calls together, or coordinating their data entry, virtual coworkers. Their culture had rubbed off on Glenn, and he apparently had an obsession with Indian takeout.

Glenn was shaking, though he wore an indignant smile. *Well, well, well. Look who's here.*

"Hello, Glenn. May I come in?"

He stepped aside and showed me to a small sofa in the corner of the room.

"How have you been?" I asked him as I sat down.

The apartment was meticulously tidy. Dishes were neatly stored in glass cabinets. Papers sat in small piles on the kitchen table, each one the same distance from the next. Each one lined up at the top and bottom. Small porcelain knickknacks adorned his dresser. Obsessive cleanliness is a stereotype of patients with this degree of psychosis. Ironically, so is filth.

Glenn shrugged. He sat down adjacent to me on a wood chair, crossing his legs before finally coming to look at me. *I'm quite well, Alan.*

"I hope it's okay that I came to see you. It's not normal for doctors to do this, but I have been worried about you for a long time."

Glenn sat back. The indignation began to give way to his profound need to reconnect with me. It was remarkable how quickly this happened. *I was wondering how long it would take for you to find me.*

I smiled at him. His eyes grew wide, and I was suddenly back in time to our sessions at Somers. Sessions I had to terminate because of the boundaries he would not respect. And the boundaries I had foolishly allowed to be crossed in my efforts to help him.

"Glenn, I should have come sooner. I know that. I was informed that you stopped seeing Dr. Westcott. I ran into him at the prison last week, and he told me things didn't go well once you got out. Do you want to tell me what happened?" All of that was true. Once boundaries have been breached, they cannot be rebuilt. They are not walls made of plaster or brick. They exist in the mind, like words that cannot be unsaid. I had asked that Glenn be reassigned to another volunteer therapist, Dr. Daniel Westcott, and upon Glenn's release, Westcott had agreed to continue his therapy. It was more supervision than treatment, making sure he was not allowing himself to become too obsessed with someone. Making sure he didn't lose control again.

Glenn looked at the floor and shrugged. *It wasn't the same.*

"What do you mean? He's an excellent doctor. And his practice is right here, in Cranston."

You know the answer, Alan.

I felt a shudder travel down my spine; my hair stood on edge. In the months that followed the transfer of Glenn's treatment from me to Dr. Westcott, I began receiving letters from Glenn at my home. I do not know how he obtained my address or knew the names of my wife and children. I informed Dr. Westcott and the prison officials. Glenn was made to stop, and I believed that perhaps I had dodged a bullet.

Patients with borderline personality disorder are far more likely to form unhealthy attachments to their therapists than other patients. There are numbers for the increased likelihood as high as 40 percent. The numbers don't matter so much as the certainty that it is true. Part of our training is to maintain strict boundaries. But as I have already confessed, my training proved inadequate when I first encountered Glenn Shelby. Boundaries were crossed, an obsessive attachment was formed, and a period of stalking followed—one that was, mercifully, snuffed out by the fear of solitary confinement and possibly new charges that would have kept Glenn in prison.

As an aside, this is a perfect case study to disprove the notion that no patient with an Axis II disorder can be effectively treated. The milder forms are in fact treatable, using the very basic techniques of carrots and sticks. These patients can and do curb their behavior to get rewards and avoid punishment.

They can be treated. But they cannot be cured. Once the carrots and sticks are removed, their behavior invariably returns. I never received another letter from Glenn, even after he was released from prison. But I had come to learn that the letters were not the end of his efforts to feel close to me. I came to see him this day to make it stop.

Our conversation continued for about an hour. Then I left and went home.

One week later, Glenn was found hanging from his ceiling.

When I heard the news, I would remember the things in his apartment I saw that day—things that caught my eye for one reason or another but did not give rise to any concern. They were entirely benign. The jump rope in the corner of the room, coiled up like a snake. The step stool in the kitchen. And the metal pull-up bar that had been installed into the ceiling near the bathroom door. The ceilings were quite high—eight feet, perhaps. I can close my eyes even now and picture him swinging from it, the white stool lying on its side just past the reach of his toes. The rope tied nice and short so his feet would not reach the floor. Naked except for a pair of blue briefs. I do not like to dwell on this. Perhaps I do because it was not just an average failure, the way that most people experience failure in their professions. My failure, this failure, ended with the horrific image I have just placed into your head, the same image I live with every day. It is always there, reminding me that even I cannot cure every patient.

I left Glenn alive, shaking but otherwise functional. I drove back to the office, saw another patient, then went home to my family.

The next day I got a call from Detective Parsons. It was a call I had been expecting. Remember, I was functioning at my very best again, clearheaded, precise. I could see the future. I could see it because I was controlling it. My puppets on their strings. The sticks in my hand.

You were right, Alan. About the alibi. It's all fucking crap!

"I'm sorry. I really am." I was not.

How did you know? Are you gonna tell me? What else are you hiding?

"I can't tell you. I've explained about—"

Yeah, your sacred patient confidentiality. Honest to God, Alan. Sometimes I think you're screwing with my head.

"It's quite normal to want to shoot the messenger. I'm not offended. Nor did I create that assault record from Florida or lie about an alibi. All of this is real. I had no part in its making."

Parsons sighed loudly. *I know that. I'm sorry. I'm just not looking forward to this shit show. I can feel a bad ending. One way or another. I feel it in my gut. He's gonna have a whole team of people crawling up my ass.*

"And yet it has to have one, doesn't it? It has to end," I said calmly. "Have you asked Sullivan and his wife about it?"

They claim it's an honest mistake. But the bills from the club don't lie. There's one charge from the wine dinner. The tab was signed by the wife, Fran. Sullivan has no alibi.

"I see."

And he has that record in Florida. The world is gonna eat this up. He'll have to come out swinging.

"I imagine that's true," I said. I did not challenge him on his conclusion about Bob's innocence. It didn't matter what Parsons thought. What mattered was the fear in his voice. This was the sort of "fucking crap" that ruined a man's career.

"What happens next?"

He already hired a lawyer. Some shark from Hartford. Karl Shuman. Got those gangbangers off back in the late '90s.

"I remember that case."

Made a name for himself. Now he just handles anyone who can afford him. And now we can't go near Bob unless we formally detain him. Bring him in for questioning. That's when the press will know. That's when this whole thing blows up.

"I am sorry you have to deal with this. I wish I could help you more."

Alan, please, can't you just say whether this will stand up or not? Give me a little wink or a nod. Anything? I gotta make a decision here.

"The truth is, Detective, that it wouldn't matter if I gave you a wink or a nod. Nothing that has happened in this office would ever be admissible. That's the trouble with this treatment all these victims are getting. Even after a memory is recovered, there's just too much uncertainty for the law to give it any weight. I've read the cases, the decisions. These patients get beat up on the stand, and the court has to allow it."

Parsons was silent for a moment. He did not want to hang up the phone in the same state of mental chaos he'd been in when he dialed my number. He was in a box, and there was no way out. If he did nothing and the press found out there was enough to move forward, he would be called out as a panderer to the rich and powerful.

But if he dragged Fairview's golden child through the mud for no reason, there would be lawsuits and private investigators. With lawsuits came dismissals. With the PIs would come close scrutiny of his efforts to solve the case, of which he seemed increasingly fearful. He was damned if he did and damned if he didn't. The only way out was if Bob Sullivan was guilty. And he was not.

Poor Detective Parsons.

Chapter Twenty-nine

The seeds of doubt grow like weeds when given enough sun. Enough water. Enough nurturing.

Charlotte sat in my office at her next visit with her doubt about Bob sprouting from her pores. She had not seen him again, but he had called her to tell her about the problem with the alibi and his new lawyer. He would not come off his story that he was at that dinner. And yet there were no more flirtatious text messages. No more pictures of his erect penis. He was being careful like a guilty person is careful.

"I'm sorry things with Bob are troubling you. Sorry because I can see you're anxious about it."

I am. It's very troubling. I mean, what is he hiding? I even asked him, I said, "Just tell me where you were that night. If you were with another woman, then I'll deal with it." He just kept saying he was at the club and everyone was persecuting him because of his run for the seat and his money and blah blah blah. He was overselling it, you know?

"Yes. It sounds very strange, and I can see why you are concerned." I let that sit for a moment. "How has Jenny been since the group session?"

The same. She was doing so well before she remembered the voice. And now she just seems to have given up. It's like she doesn't believe in the therapy anymore and is just resigned to being in constant pain. God, it's so hard to watch. And worry—all over again.

"I see. I thought maybe the session would have changed that. There was a somewhat graphic disclosure by one of my other patients. Another rape victim. I was going to stop it because I am always very cognizant of Jenny's age. But I let it go. It was not that disturbing in and of itself. But it was of the moment of first penetration, and that is the one memory Jenny has regained of that night."

Charlotte's eyes got wide and she sat up on the edge of the sofa. *I didn't realize she'd told you in that much detail.*

"Well, of course. What did you think happened in that session?"

I don't know. I guess I thought she just remembered it and told you she remembered it. I haven't wanted to ask her the details. But I did not realize she told you. . . . It just seems . . . so personal. Not that it's wrong. Oh, I don't know what I'm saying!

"No—it's fine. It is strange to think that your daughter described this act to me, a man, in such a sterile environment."

Charlotte stared at the sticker on the plant. Her face was scrunched up like she was thinking. And pained by her thoughts.

"Would you like to know what she said? Would it help you to share this knowledge?"

Maybe. Yes. Actually, I would like to know. Everything that was said. Everything.

This was all too easy.

I told Charlotte about an act of penetration. The act I described was not the rape of Jenny, although it was not far off. Rather, it was

Bob Sullivan fucking his teenage secretary in the showroom. The rear entry. The hand braced on her shoulder. Her face pressed to the ground. The hand on the top of her head, fingers intertwined with her luscious hair. The powerful thrusting, back and forth like an animal.

Charlotte sat back and folded her arms. And on her face, I could see that I was right, that Bob Sullivan had fucked her exactly the same way. And that now she was wondering where he really was that night.

Five days later, the sprouts would bloom.

But let's not jump ahead.

We were all very concerned about Jenny and the abrupt cessation in the progress we were making. I took the chance that I had done enough to fuel my little fire—that there was now enough smoke for my son to slip quietly out of sight. I decided to return to my selfish desires to save my patient.

"How have you been?" I asked Jenny at her next session. "Still feeling like you can't solve that stubborn math problem? That you want to give up?"

Jenny shrugged.

"You seem sad today."

Tears came. I handed her some tissues.

"Is it the memory? The one we recovered?"

No. I feel better about that. It really is like you said. Even though I hate the images that come into my mind—I mean my skin actually crawls when I remember his hands and . . . everything else. But it's like I have those moments when my skin crawls and when I want to scream and cry and curl up and die even, and then they go away. When I think about other things, or do other things, the feelings go with them.

"Yes!" I was beyond excited. "The feelings have found their home. They have attached to the memory and can stop haunting your mind in search of it. That's exactly how trauma recovery is supposed to work. And over time, as you let those feelings come out, and let the images come out, they'll start to recede and fade. They'll come out and see that you are safe and that they do not need to provoke you."

Jenny nodded. But then she sighed.

"So what is it, then?"

I don't feel right talking about it.

Then I knew. "Sean?" I asked.

Her face gave her away.

"You can tell me. Sean knows we speak about your relationship. And he speaks about it to me as well."

Really?

"Yes."

Okay. I don't know. I feel like I'm bad for him. Like I'm making him feel bad.

"In what way?"

He's just so angry. He really thinks Mr. Sullivan raped me, and he . . .

"He what?"

He's just really angry. When we meet now, I feel like I can't talk to him about anything, because he just goes back to Mr. Sullivan and the fact that he hasn't been arrested and that he'll never get punished, because I was given the treatment so my remembering his voice won't even matter.

"I see. And do you still feel that the voice you remember is from that night in the woods?"

It's the same as before. My brain thinks so. But I don't really feel weird around him or anything. I should, right? I saw him at my dad's work last week, and I got nervous because of the memory but I didn't feel anything else.

"Do you think Sean knows they've questioned him?"

What?

"Your mother didn't tell you? Oh—maybe she's afraid of your dad finding out."

Oh my God! That explains why he walked the other way when I saw him! Jenny hung her head in her hands like she was ashamed. *Oh my God!*

"It's fine. Really. He's not being questioned because of anything that happened in here. He did something in his past. And then he lied about where he was that night. The police know nothing about our work. About your memories. I promise."

It's happening, isn't it? There's going to be a trial and everyone will see how messed up I am in my head! And Sean . . . Oh my God!

"What are you afraid of for Sean?"

He just . . . He's just so angry. He said he . . .

"What did he say, Jenny?"

I shouldn't tell you.

"It's okay. Do you trust me?"

Yes . . . it's just . . . he's, like, my best friend. Sometimes I think he's my only friend.

"Then help me help him. Tell me what he said."

Jenny looked at me then, like a little mouse trying to not be heard even as she opened her mouth and let out the words. *He said he wanted to kill him.*

"Well," I said dismissively, "people say that all the time, don't they? Just this morning, I yelled at my dog and said something like that. 'I'm going to kill that dog!' Right? People say it, but they don't really mean it. It's an expression."

No. You don't understand. He said that he pictures Mr. Sullivan like one of the terrorists he was sent in to kill. He says he feels that way about him, like he has to die for what he's done and so he doesn't do it again. And then he said . . . he said he pictures Mr. Sullivan holding that stick and carving my skin with it. He just, like, sits there and lets himself imagine it, like an obsession. He said he has a gun. Said he knows how to fire it with his left arm. Like he's been practicing.

"Really? When did he get this gun?"

I don't know. He just said he would kill Bob Sullivan if he wasn't brought to justice. He said he had a gun now and he would just do it. I told him I would rather die myself than see him get in trouble like that. And he just . . . he just held me really tight and . . .

Jenny was crying again. Oh, my twisted emotions! Crying was what she needed to do. She needed to keep feeling anything and everything. Can you see how this works? The feelings had found one memory and attached to it. Now we could use them to lead us to the others; we could follow them back to where that memory was hiding and see what else was hiding there. It was just a theory. But I believed in it.

And yet, the agony for my poor soldier! The fact that this was weighing so heavily upon him broke my heart. He was identifying these facts with what had happened the night he lost his arm. The terrorist behind the red door, needing to be brought to justice. To be killed. I was suddenly anxious to get him in for a session.

And then there were other concerns.

"Jenny," I said in a steady voice, "when you say he held you, what do you mean?"

He just holds me sometimes. It's not like anything bad. He says I'm like his sister, but also like one of his soldiers, you know, the ones who are under him. The rookies. He says he will die protecting me. Fighting for me.

"I see. That's a relief, actually. I was afraid that your friendship might become something else, and that would not be good for either of you."

But I still love him. He's the only thing I look forward to now.

"Well, we are going to change that." I leaned forward and took hold of her hands in mine. "We are going to finish what we started. You will remember everything from that night. We will put all the ghosts back to bed, and then you will get on with your life. Do you hear me?"

Jenny looked at me, a little surprised. I had never touched her before, or spoken to her with any emotion. I had not lost control. Rather, I was giving her a small dose of what she got from Sean.

"Do you hear me?"

Yes.

"Do you believe me?"

I don't know. I'm scared to hope for that. I'm scared to find it. I feel like I'm poison, and if I can just keep myself away from people, I won't hurt anyone.

"No, Jenny," I said. "You are not the poison. You are the cure."

Chapter Thirty

I would not see Sean again before this story ends. I had not real-ized this at the time. Too many spinning plates. Too many puppets to manage.

Detective Parsons reluctantly pursuing the lead on Bob Sullivan. Bob lying about his alibi to Parsons and Charlotte. Charlotte begin-ning to think he was guilty. Bob's wife covering for him. The law-yer protecting him. Jenny and I resuming our work to keep her from slipping away from us. And Sean seeing Bob carving his sweet Jenny with a stick while he viciously rapes her. That leaves Tom. And my son.

First things first. I had become very intolerant of Tom and his ob-session with the blue sweatshirt. I had not come to disdain or dislike the man. Quite the contrary. I looked at him like a petulant child, my petulant child, who would not obey my instructions.

I just don't understand why they don't have every forensic guy looking into this picture! Tom was holding the photo of my son from a yearbook. You could not see his face.

"This is from a lacrosse game? At the school?"

Yes! The spring Jenny was raped.

"And what do you think they will be able to tell with more forensics? This is a medium-sized teenage boy, nondescript body, a Fairview High School cap. I'm sure you've looked at it with a magnifying glass. Every inch, right?"

Tom stared at the photo. *Yes. I have. I just . . . Look, I can identify one of the girls standing behind him, and one of the boys next to her. If they showed this to everyone who went to that game, surely someone would remember!*

"Maybe. I'm sure that's the problem. They're talking to all the kids at the party again. Maybe they're afraid to have this thing start looking like a witch hunt. They don't have to come in for questioning, you know. Under the law. Right now, it's all voluntary. That could change if people got the wrong sense of what this has become."

Really. And what has it become?

"Well, we've talked about your guilt. About your parents and how they affected your self-esteem. Your sense of self. Your 'id,' if you will. Tom, these things will not be changed simply by finding the man who raped your daughter."

Jesus Christ! Are we really going to talk about my id when we have this lead? Can't I just find this fucker, and then, I promise you, I'll come back in and disparage my poor parents until I can stand up to my wife and my boss and anyone else you want me to. How's that?

Two words popped into my head then. Oh shit.

"Okay," I said. "Maybe you need to see this through. Maybe our work has to stop for now. But consider this before we do: This photo—all it shows is a boy with a sweatshirt. You can hardly see what the shape is on the sweatshirt from the angle it's at. And the only reason you're concerned with the sweatshirt is because of something a drug dealer said to reduce his sentence. Do you see my concern?"

Frankly, no. Not at all.

I leaned forward, elbows on my knees, hands clasped together and head hung to my chest. I could feel Tom's eyes upon me, waiting for the words that I looked so pained to find. This technique is extremely effective. When I lifted my head, I wore the face of conviction.

"Over the past few months, we have dug very deep and stirred many feelings about your childhood. And in doing so, you have courageously faced your anger at your parents—and there is anger, Tom. It doesn't matter how lovely they are, how supportive of your family. You parent your children in a way that is in complete defiance of everything they did with you and your sister. And that tells me that you know, in your heart, that they caused you harm. Emotional harm. You feel unworthy of everything in your life that's good, like you've stolen it. And you have a subconscious belief that the bad things that come your way do so as retribution for your theft. You have guilt for that, Tom. Anger and guilt."

Tom was following along, and I was gently leading him to the path I needed him to follow.

I was so fucking sick of that blue sweatshirt.

"Where has that anger gone? Where has the guilt gone?" I took the picture from his hand. "Here, Tom! Here!" I waved the picture. "It's all here—directed at some kid wearing a sweatshirt. You're not seeing the big picture—for yourself or for the investigation."

You are weary of my descriptions about my patients crying. But I assure you, I have been very judicious in this regard. Every patient I see cries at almost every session. Do the math on that.

Tom cried. If it annoys you, don't worry. We are moving on and moving quickly.

I held Tom's hand and then I gave him a gentle push down the path.

"Tom. Have you considered that the police have other leads? And that maybe they're not including you, because of this blind rage you have at the moment? Maybe it's all under control and you can just hand them the reins and let them do their job. That would be a relief, wouldn't it?"

Tom looked at me with a new fire in his eyes. *Would they do that? Would they not include me? I've been part of this investigation for over a year. Since it happened!*

I shrugged. "I don't know, Tom. It's just a possibility I would like you to consider. I was hoping it would put your mind at ease. Let you lay down your sword and shield and rest for a while."

I have to go, Alan. I'm sorry. I know I'm being a bad patient. I will deal with these things you raise. Just not now. Not now!

We both stood up. I extended my hand, and when he gave me his, I cupped my other one around it. "Tom. Please. Consider what I've said. Lay down your weapons. Let the professionals do their work."

But Tom was already gone.

Now for my son.

The interview could not be put off any longer without raising suspicion. Attorney Brandino went with him. I did as well. I told my wife to stay home because she did not have the ability to hide her emotions. Two young male cops asked the questions. They were tired of all this, of Tom Kramer, of the daily calls to small-town districts, asking about old rape files, sitting on hold with the phone pinned between their ears and necks, giving them cramps and headaches and keeping them from their tweets and Snapchats and Facebook updates. This was their town as well, so in addition to the boredom, they were reluctant to ruffle feathers. It is not fun to go through one's day being scowled at.

Questions were asked. Answers were given.

What time did you arrive at the party? What time did you leave? Were you with anyone? Did you exit the house at any time? Was anyone with you? Did you see Jenny Kramer? Was anyone with her? Et cetera, et cetera . . . Do you own a blue sweatshirt with red symbols or letters?

Jason held up well. His guilt came across as teenage fear. He reminded me of a boy meeting a girl's father for the first time on prom night. Was he a good kid? Yes. Did he want to have sex with the man's daughter? Yes. Would he? Probably not. It's an accepted deception. It has been many words since I told you what I think about honesty, about the need for lying in the human relationship. If that boy told that father that he had pictured his daughter naked, imagined her breasts in his palms, his tongue in her mouth, his hands reaching up her dress, and that he imagined all of this while masturbating just an hour before this civilized introduction—well, you can imagine how many kids would show up at the prom. I have been crude. But I wanted my point to be made.

I don't think so, Jason said about the sweatshirt, squirming a bit. *I mean, I don't have one now. I don't remember having one before.*

This was the brilliant part. He executed it perfectly.

Did you leave the party at any time to go outside?

Jason paused before answering. He looked at his lawyer, who nodded and patted his hand. He looked at me. I did the same. I may even have said, "Go ahead, son. Tell the truth."

Jason sighed. Now, mind you, none of this was acting on his part. He is not a good liar. He is a good boy. A wonderful boy. My boy.

I went out for a few minutes. I was looking for that man. The one in the blue Honda.

The cops got a little more interested then, but their interest was, of course, being misdirected. No one else had admitted to doing anything wrong, because nothing could be proved. Cruz Demarco made over a grand that night, and yet, somehow, only John Vincent had admitted to buying anything. This interview was like finding a small nugget of gold in the pan.

I see. One of the cops said, *So you were going to buy drugs?*

Jason nodded sheepishly.

And did you?

No. I saw the car and I got scared so I walked right by it and then turned around and walked on the other side back to the house so he wouldn't see me.

What time was this?

I don't know. It was before nine thirty. After eight. I'm not sure.

Did you see anyone else?

No. But people were coming in and out from the street all night, looking for that guy. Everyone was talking about it. I think he came to the house, to the back, also.

Attorney Brandino jumped in. *Are we done? As you can see, my client has been very forthcoming and honest. It was not in his interest to tell you of his intention to buy drugs. I hope you can give him some credit for that.*

Yes. Credit. But it was done not for any "credit," whatever the hell that meant, but to explain his nervous disposition, his squirming in his seat when he was asked about the sweatshirt. You see?

There was more to the interview. But it was of no consequence. The lie about the sweatshirt and my son's poor performance in telling it had been perfectly deflected.

When we got home, my wife was in the kitchen, having a glass of wine. It was just early afternoon, but she had been a ball of nerves.

"Sweetheart, I could have given you something. Now you'll have a headache."

She ignored me, rushing to our son and pulling him into her arms. *Are you all right? Oh, my poor boy!*

Jason let her squeeze him for a moment before pulling away. *I'm fine. Can I go?*

We let him leave. The new TV went on. Then the violent video game. I didn't care.

Julie looked at me with the questions bleeding from her skin. I did not make her suffer.

"It's fine," I said.

She fell into my arms. *Promise?*

"Yes. I promise." And I meant it more than I have ever meant anything.

If we can't protect our own children, we are wretched.

Chapter Thirty-one

Can you imagine what was going through the mind of Bob Sullivan when he saw the fear in full bloom on Charlotte's face?

They met at the house on the outskirts of Cranston five days after I saw Charlotte. She had been remembering Bob's hand on her shoulder, the other one in her hair, sometimes pressing against the back of her head as his hips pushed into her thighs. The deep penetration, the moans he made each time. And sometimes when she did this, she imagined Jenny in his grasp instead. She did not tell me this. I think it would have been far too personal. But I knew just the same.

I couldn't even look at him. I felt like I was in an alternate universe, where everything was the same, but not the way I thought. Does that make sense? I imagine it happens all the time, right? When people learn their spouse is having an affair or stole money? God—I just realized that Tom will look at me like that one day, won't he? If he finds out about what I've done? When he has to accept that good Charlotte doesn't exist.

"Let's not dwell on good Charlotte today. Let's focus on what happened with Bob. This is very important. Very traumatic, even though
you may not realize it yet. You loved Bob, or at least the man you
thought he was. And you believed he loved you as well, that he really
loved you, all of you with all the secrets of the past."

*I don't even know how I feel, Alan. Truly. So, let me just tell you
what happened. Tell me what you think, all right?*

I nodded. "Of course."

*I did not bring up the wine dinner again. He had been so insis-
tent that I was wrong the last time, and I really wanted to know
how I would feel being with him. If I could live with the lie and all
the uncertainty or not.*

"Charlotte," I said. "You haven't started to wonder if Bob was the
one, you know, who did those things to Jenny. Have you? Or is this
about wondering where he was that night, and whether it was another
woman?"

No! I mean, I could never believe that about Bob. She lied well.
*But I knew he remembered where he was that night. That was the
problem. Why wouldn't he tell me?*

"All right. Continue, then."

*So he poured me a drink, which I sometimes accept if it's not too
early. He poured one for himself as well. It was good to have things
in our hands, since neither of us seemed eager to touch the other. I
asked if everything had been resolved. And he said it had not—that
the issue with the wine dinner had gotten out of control. He said he'd
had to hire a lawyer, and that they, he and his lawyer, were refus-
ing to answer any more questions. I guess he doesn't have to, right?*

"That's right. He doesn't. It sounds as though he's calling their
bluff."

Yeah. That's what he said as well. That the only thing they could do next would be to get a warrant, and that would require going public. His lawyer made it clear that he would immediately sue them. The loss to his business, to the election, his reputation, and his family . . . Well, they're betting the higher-ups won't go for it. I mean, really—what do they have? An ancient college record. And a misunderstanding over a dinner that happened over a year ago? They won't get a warrant, right?

"I don't know, Charlotte. But it sounds as though he was still worried. Or did he seem confident?"

No—he was not confident at all. He was angry. He said things like, "How can this be happening? To me, of all people? How could anyone think that I would rape a young girl? I'm worth over twenty million dollars! I'm about to become a state representative! I've met the fucking president!" Then he said he felt like his head was going to explode, or something like that, something very dramatic. All of this was just one huge insult to his ego.

"That's not very attractive, I have to say. Could he not understand their position? That they did have an obligation to follow through?"

I told you—it made me see him in a different way. I couldn't just put it out of my mind, have sex, go home. . . . I just couldn't this time. I said what I was thinking, which was what you said just now. That they had to cover their bases and make sure. I told him he needed to tell them where he was that night and then it would all just go away. I told him I didn't understand why he wouldn't do that.

"How did he take that?"

Not well. He got furious with me. He threw his glass across the room, and his face got very hot, you know, red and wide-eyed, frantic. He got very close to me, and he took my arms, and he looked at me, studying me. And he asked me straight out if I thought he had raped my daughter.

Charlotte gasped then, her hand drawing up to her mouth. She shook her head slowly, her eyes on that sticker.

I said I did not. I said I knew he would never do anything like that. But then why, why would he not say where he was? And then there was Jenny and the voice in her head. I don't know. I think he just didn't believe me.

She was lost then, in her memories of that meeting. I let her stay there for a moment, long enough for the memories to mix with more of the doubt. You know why, don't you? So they would return to their files just slightly altered, decorated perhaps with the doubts about Bob.

"Charlotte, how did it end? How did you leave things?"

Ohhh. Well, it wasn't good. He said "fuck you," and then he left.

"'Fuck you'? That's all he said?"

Uh-huh. After three years together, after all those professions of love and tender moments making love. After all those times he looked lovingly into my eyes—how is that possible? How is it we can do those things, things that feel permanent, like even if the relationship ended, those feelings would still be there? It makes me not believe in anything, in any feeling, in any profession, in any love at all. It's all just bullshit. Just hormones and lust and needs and filling people's gaps, the holes in their souls. We all just use each other, don't we? Nothing is what it seems.

"Well, that is a lot to discuss, Charlotte. You are right. People do that to each other. But sometimes it becomes more than that. Sometimes the weaker loves, the lust-driven loves, the filling holes, turn into more. And sometimes those momentary connections, the ones that catch us off guard like a cold wind coming around the corner of a building, sometimes those stay put and then become an anchor for a more permanent connection. That is what most people in stable relationships describe. It's the connection, and the need for that

connection. And from there, like anything we need, we take care of
it with kindness and caretaking—acts of love. But that is really too
much for one day, isn't it? Tell me how you feel now, after Bob said
'fuck you' and left?"

I feel disoriented. I feel like I'm lost in my own life.

"That's perfect, Charlotte."

Perfect? It's miserable.

"Let me ask you this: If Bob called you and said he was sorry,
would you go to him? Would you make love to him again?"

*I would want to. But I couldn't. How could I possibly do that af-
ter all of this? After I saw the person he is, the lying, the cruelty, the
way he dances in and out of affection and aggression. But I would
want to. It feels very hard to know that it's gone. It was the thing
that made my life possible.*

"I know. It will be hard to quit Bob. Just do one thing for me?
Don't find a replacement. Just sit with the discomfort. Be lost for a
while and see how long you can stand the pain. It's my guess that it
will pass. Like when you stub your toe on the edge of the sofa."

Charlotte agreed. She had given up her one cigarette, at least
for now. And I was so very proud of her! Yes, I had been monomaniacal about saving my son. And yes, I had also wanted to finish
my work with Jenny. I had not considered Tom or Charlotte. There
was no room for them. But that does not mean I no longer cared. I
was deeply invested in both of them. As Jenny would say, they were
a math problem I knew I could solve, and solve easily. How could I
not want to do that? I am a doctor. It is my calling to heal and to
cure.

I had not considered the possible synergies embedded within my
plan, but I could see them now. It might have taken years for Charlotte to quit Bob. Years! And by then, it may have been too late. I felt

deeply satisfied for Charlotte, and at the risk of sounding egotistical, I was very pleased with myself. Charlotte was going to be all right. I could see it. The quitting was the hardest part.

Bob would not fare quite so well.

Chapter Thirty-two

Fran Sullivan is a woman after my own heart. That is such an odd expression, but we all understand its meaning, don't we? She was not a good person. Nor was she a kind person. But she took care of her own.

Fran and Bob had met in high school. She was one of those people who likes to indulge, and so she does not exercise or watch her diet or inhibit her cravings in any way. She wears what she likes. Sleeveless dresses in the summer that highlight the flesh under her arms. They swing like elephant tusks as she marches down the street with her brood of men—her three sons and her rich husband. In the winter, she pulls out her furs, coats made of dead baby animals, which repulse most people these days. Her hair is big, her makeup bold. You can smell her perfume blocks away. I imagine she was no more attractive when they met as she was now, but I can also see why Bob married her. She was a valuable member of the team.

I have never met Fran Sullivan in person. Our paths do not cross socially. But she is a large personality in a small town. It is impossible not to notice her.

It is said by many that Fran Sullivan made her husband what he is today. I believe this to be true. I believe that she saw in him a large ego with a huge appetite and that she knew she could use this hunger to her advantage. They had grown up together in Cranston. Lower middle class. Sick of the struggle. Sick of the wealth just miles down the road that was out of their reach. Fran did not attend college. Fran worked as a secretary, helping Bob pay for Skidmore. Bob got a job in a car dealership. He came home every night with his stories about stolen commissions, ass-kissing, backstabbing—they were gladiators in the Colosseum, these salesmen. They are notorious, aren't they? Car salesmen? Fran had a brilliant mind, a cunning mind, and no conscience whatsoever. In every battle, Bob Sullivan was the last man standing.

Of course, this is all speculation on my part. But I cannot be far off.

Fran also knew that with a large, hungry ego came the need for other women. Younger women, prettier women, more successful women. Think famous sports celebrity with low-life strippers. Why does a man risk everything just to have one more woman tell him how much she loves his big, hard cock? Fran understood men and their egos.

And so when she decided it was time for Bob to run for office— the first office in a line of offices she dreamed would march them right into Washington one day—she hired the private investigator to document his dalliances.

This is how she explained it to Charlotte:

She said it was worth the risk. Having those tapes and photos. She knew she could pay the PI as much as he would be offered by any media outlet. She had already bought his loyalty with years of

solid income. She kept them all. Each tape, each photo of her hus-
band with other women. She said they were her insurance policy for
two possible storms. The first against any allegations of force. I guess
she didn't want a repeat of what happened when he was on spring
break. Can you imagine? She was home working her ass off, and
he went on spring break in Florida. Anyway, the second storm was
if he ever tried to leave her.

Bob had affairs with dozens of women over the years. There were
tapes and photos of them. Some were one-night stands. Some were
strippers. Others were staples, like Charlotte. The investigator
planted recording devices in the locations where Bob was a regular. The showrooms. Lovers' bedrooms. The friend's place in
Cranston. The Kramers' pool house. He also kept a device in Bob's
briefcase. Most of them were voice activated. Some he could get
only when he was in radio range, and so he followed Bob any evening he was working late or attending a sales dinner. He gave
the recordings and hard copies of the photos to Fran, who kept
them in a safe deposit box. A spare key was held by her sister in
Hartford.

Fran followed Charlotte to the grocery store two days after Bob
said "fuck you" and left. She waited in her car until Charlotte came
out with her bags.

I was putting the bags into the trunk when I heard her say my
name. I turned around, and my heart nearly stooped. She had this
big smile on her face. It was so big and sweet that it was terrifying. I
said hello, how are you, what a surprise, and all of that. I've known
her for years. Obviously, we've had many social functions and work
parties. We even played golf at the company's annual outing. She
helped me with the bags, and then she just walked to the passenger
side of my car and got in.

"You must have been very scared."

You have no idea! She didn't say anything. She just sat there, staring at me until, finally, she pulled out a small tape player. Then she let it play. It was Bob . . .

Charlotte broke down, remembering that moment.

"Wait, stop. . . ." [female voice, worried]

"What?" [male voice, alarmed]

"The bathroom door . . . It's closed, but under the door . . . I think the light's on." [female voice, whispering]

[rustling, then silence]

[loud female scream]

"Oh dear Lord! Dear Lord!" [male voice, terrified]

[female screams]

"Help her! My baby! My baby girl!"

"Is she alive? Oh shit! Shit!"

"Grab a towel! Wrap her wrists, tight!"

"My baby!"

"Wrap them! Tight! Oh dear Lord! There's so much blood. . . ."

"I feel a pulse! Jenny! Jenny, can you hear me! Hand me those towels! Oh dear Lord, dear Lord, dear Lord!"

"Jenny!" [desperate female voice]

"Call 911! Jenny! Jenny, wake up!" [male voice]

"Where's my phone!" [female voice, shuffling]

"On the floor! Go!" [male voice]

[footsteps, shuffling, female voice speaking to 911, giving address, hysterical]

"You have to go! Right now! Go!" [female voice]

"No! I can't! Dear Lord!"

I stared at that machine, listening to the recording of that horrible day. My baby! All that blood!

"My God. She was recording you," I said. I am not easily surprised. This one did it.

For years. She had dozens of tapes. That's what she told me. And then she pulled out a second tape and she played that one.

"Where are your parents?" [male voice, sexy tone]

"They're out." [female voice, flirtatious]

"Mmmm." [male voice, a heavy moan]

[rustling, kissing sounds]

"I'm gonna fuck you so hard while your mommy and daddy are away." [male voice, aggressive].

"Oh no. But I'm a good girl. I can't." [female voice]

"You didn't hear me, did you? I'm going to fuck you right now. I'm going to bend you over and pull off your little pink panties." [male voice]

[female gasp]

"No, stop, don't . . [female voice]

It was disgusting. That man is a disgusting pig.

"Who was this woman he was with?"

One of the girls from his dealership. Lila something. She's twenty years old! That makes her nineteen at the time. And he's known her family for years. He plays golf with her father!

"And why did Fran Sullivan want you to hear this tape—out of all of them?"

Because this was recorded the night of the wine dinner at the club.

I had suspected as much—that Bob was with another woman that night. But I had not counted on there being hard evidence. I had counted on Bob not wanting to disclose his whereabouts and the woman being equally reticent. I had counted on more time.

This is where he was that night. He wasn't raping my daughter. He was raping someone else's.

"But you said it was all role play on the tape."

She's a child. He's fifty-three years old. Call it whatever you want.

"I see. I'm very sorry, Charlotte. He certainly has turned out to be a horrible human being. I still don't understand why she played those tapes for you."

Blackmail. Plain and simple. She said she was bringing the one tape from that night to the police, Detective Parsons. The lawyer is going to ask for a confidentiality agreement before they hand it over. It clears Bob, and she wants to do it quickly and quietly. She still thinks she can keep this from the public eye. She said something like, "I imagine you will hear about this from the detective, one way or another. And I imagine it would make you feel scorned. Bob did sell you a bag of goods, didn't he? Love, right? Might feel good to expose him? Humiliate him? Destroy his career?" Then she said, "You do your part and let this go. And in exchange, I will do mine and keep the tapes of you with my husband to myself."

"I see. So Tom won't find out."

Yes. She said one last thing. "We are in the same boat now, aren't we? If these ridiculous allegations about your daughter continue, all of this will come out. All of it."

"So what will you do?"

Charlotte looked at me with that momentary but brilliant melding together of defeat and blind courage. It happens when there is nothing left to lose.

I'm going to tell Tom myself. Tonight. I won't let Fran Sullivan tell me what to do. She can go straight to hell. You were right. I need to sit with the pain. I need to live through it. That's what I've been trying to do since I saw Bob. Since he said "fuck you" and left.

"I'm very proud of you, Charlotte. That takes a lot of courage."

There are two things I can tell you now: First, Charlotte had been lying to me when she said she had been working on her feelings about giving up Bob. Second, Charlotte would not have the chance to tell Tom that night. Tom would not be home.

Parsons called me shortly after Charlotte left. It seemed Fran Sullivan wasn't messing around.

Sullivan's cleared. I thought you should know. Whatever led you to believe that he might have been involved, well, it's a mistake.

"Really? What happened?"

I can't disclose the details. But I can tell you that he gave us an alibi. It ain't pretty, but it checks out.

Parsons met with Fran Sullivan and the lawyer. She did not play the tape for him, but rather told him what was on it and encouraged him to speak with the young woman. Of course, Parsons wound up at her parents' house. They were told about the incident only after forcing their daughter to explain the presence of the police at their door. Their longtime friend, the father's weekend golf buddy, fucking their daughter for over a year. The father was so distraught, it took Parsons an hour to calm him down. I would learn all of this later.

"I see. Well, that must be a relief," I said to Parsons.

I guess. But let's just say this is one messed-up world.

"So where does that leave you?"

Well . . . it leaves me where I was before. With Tom Kramer crawling up my ass, no answers, no suspects. Just one blue sweatshirt and one photo from a yearbook. Oh—but there was one thing. . . .

"What's that?" I have to admit that I was not truly listening at this point. Time was running out on the Bob Sullivan ruse, and without a media frenzy, lawsuits, and the other goodies that would have made everyone close up shop and go home. I was not looking forward to plan B.

There is a case from Oregon—one of those phone calls my guys have been making, you know, to the local precincts around the country? Well, this old-timer remembered a report about a kid with the same kind of scratch on his back. A straight line, deep carving right above the pelvis. It was a long time back, but he said he would try to find the file in storage. Doesn't remember any rape involved, but it might be something.

"I see. Well, it sounds like a stretch, doesn't it? I mean, this was a rape primarily. Not an assault with the rape as some sort of incidental. And it's the other side of the country. Don't you agree?"

Alan, I'm gonna finish every last lead on this case.

Yes, well. We shall see about that.

Chapter Thirty-three

This is what happened the night of the collision. The night the roller coaster came screaming down the hill. The night the cotton candy was almost complete. There will still be a few strands left to wind after I tell you.

This is what happened the night Bob Sullivan died.

Charlotte had lied to me. I know why and it is not important. She was not able to go home and sit with her pain after she quit Bob. She had his words in her head. "Fuck you." She had the strong suspicion that he had raped her daughter in her head. That was my doing, but also a consequence of the shock that comes when you learn the truth about your lover. When "I love you" becomes "fuck you," the mind mitigates the pain by casting the lover as the most despicable villain. None of this could be swallowed down. That pill had been too bitter, and she'd found herself choking on it that night.

She cannot claim innocence. Just like me with my box of matches, Charlotte knew Tom was at the end of his wits about finding Jenny's rapist. She knew that he did not sleep. She knew that he could barely manage to eat. That he had stopped doing anything enjoyable, of feeling anything joyous. Even with Lucas and Jenny. It was all an act, a ruse. His halfhearted cheers at a lacrosse game. His smiles when he greeted them in the morning. He was in a state of acute discomfort.

It had been my plan for him that if he could survive this discomfort, he could come out the other side a changed man. A man accepting of the demons that lived inside him. That is the process. That is the road to being well. It was the same road for Charlotte, now that she had given up Bob. But Charlotte had revenge at her fingertips, and she had chosen to employ it.

She left my office and went home that day. This was before she knew Bob was innocent. Before Fran Sullivan sat in her car and played those foul tapes for her. She was angry at Bob and, more important, had been wondering if he had raped Jenny. She waited until the kids went to bed. And then she told him.

I couldn't believe what I was hearing. That Bob Sullivan, my boss, a friend to my family all these years, was a suspect in my daughter's rape. You had put the idea about a new suspect in my head, Alan. It made sense that a new suspect was the reason they weren't interested in the photograph from the yearbook. I tried to find out from Parsons, but he wouldn't tell me. But Charlotte did. She told me about the girl years ago. And about his missing alibi, his lie to the police. But it was the part about Jenny hearing his voice—that's what made me believe. I could have killed him that night. I sat in bed fantasizing about killing him. About taking a baseball bat from the garage and crushing his skull.

I went to Jenny's room after she was asleep. I went on her phone and I read her messages, texts to and from that soldier she's been friends with. The one from the group who had this dreadful treatment in Iraq. And I saw it. The words. "I think it was him . . . I hear his voice in my head." There are dozens of texts from the past two weeks. No one told me. I guess now I know why. Still, everyone knew except me, didn't they? You, Jenny, Parsons, Charlotte. Everyone but me.

Tom sat with his anger the whole next day. But that was all he could take.

I knew he would be at the Jag showroom that night with a client. I ate dinner with the family. I ate my entire plate. Steak. Potatoes. Green beans. I ate everything, and I was hungry for more. It was the first time I'd had an appetite since my daughter was violated. I told them I had to finish some paperwork at the showroom. I kissed my wife on the lips, a long kiss. Long enough to surprise her. I kissed my children on their heads. I hugged them tight. I knew it was the last time I would see them like this, in our home. I walked down the stairs, as clearheaded as I've ever been. I got the bat. I put it in my car. And I drove.

Tom was not the only man on the road that night.

I had not seen Sean Logan since he told me how he felt about Bob Sullivan. How he, too, believed that Bob had raped Jenny and how he had come to view him with the same hatred he held for the enemies in Iraq. Bob was the terrorist. Jenny was Valancia, the rookie he was supposed to protect. He had been so very frustrated by our lack of progress. We were stuck at that red door, and he needed to know—did he cause the death of his colleague, the man in his care? That torment was now directed at Bob Sullivan.

I see it now. How I had taken that rage and placed it on another man, another situation that I could do over again. I couldn't protect Valancia. But I could protect Jenny. I had been feeling better. You remember, how I was able to feel love for my child because of the power I had to help Jenny? You made me understand that. But that power, it was ignited by the thing with Sullivan. The thought had been building in me for days. This power had exploded. I didn't come to our sessions, because I knew you would see it in my eyes and try to stop me. The only thing I wanted to stop was the agony—Jenny's and mine. One way or another, it had to stop. I loaded my gun. I left a note for my wife in the bottom of a drawer. I figured she would find it eventually, but not that night. I spent the day looking for him, following him, until it was dark. I watched the showroom for hours, waiting.

Tom stopped his car a few blocks from the showroom.

My heart was beating wildly. I thought it would burst—or it would bust out of my chest. I was hyperventilating. Air was coming in, but I couldn't feel it. I was suffocating on my own breath. Thoughts were jumping out at me. Do it! Voices screaming. Images of my baby girl in those woods. Images of Bob fucking that young girl on the car. Everything was melding together. But I didn't move. I heard my parents talking about me. My wife chiming right along. "He won't do it. He doesn't have the courage. . . . Not everyone can be a soldier. . . . We all have to accept our limitations. . . ."

Sean watched the client leave. When his car was out of sight, the headlights fading away, Sean got out of the car, released the safety on the gun, and began walking with conviction toward the showroom.

I had the first vision when my feet hit the ground. It was clear as day. That street. An old man with a pipe. Three kids with a ball, still now as they stare at me. The street is frozen. No one moves. No one runs. I saw them. And not just from the things you read to me. I saw new things, different things from that day. From that street with the red door. I stopped walking and shook it off. I looked at the lights in the showroom. I made my plan for an ambush. I saw a way in. A door on the side that was cocked open. Maybe from a mechanic earlier. I focused on the mission.

Sean was having a recall. The emotions, the gun in his hand, the focus on the mission, the intent to kill—these were the things we could not simulate in our sessions. And now that they had arisen, they were leading him back to the memories from that day, that last mission.

As Sean continued to walk, Tom tried to drive. He put the car in gear and pulled back onto the street. He made it another block, then stopped again.

I can't describe the anger I felt then. Hearing my parents disparaging me. Calling me a coward because I was freezing up. I was about to kill a man! I think that is worthy of some trepidation, some consideration. I would be leaving my children. There would be no source of income. They would be fatherless. And for what? Jenny would still be a victim. Killing her attacker would not change that. She would still be without her memory and her ability to heal. Killing Sullivan would not bring them back. And then I considered the justice I had been so obsessed with. The stories of other victims and how justice had helped them heal. And how Jenny would never have justice any other way. We had taken that from her. I stared at the dashboard and calmed my nerves.

Sean walked, step by step, toward the open door. And as he did, the memories, little flashes, kept coming.

I thought I was losing my mind. I couldn't focus on the mission. I had to keep stopping, shaking off the flashes like little gnats. I would not fail this time. I lifted a foot, moved it, placed it back on the ground. There was Valancia suddenly in front of me where my foot was. I took another step and looked behind, but he wasn't there, he was in front, he had moved ahead of me! I saw Sullivan's shadow through the window. I picked up the other foot and dragged it forward. "What the fuck, man!" Those were my words. "It's no good. It's no good!" My words! Valancia had pushed ahead of me. He had tears streaming down his face, carving through the dust on his skin. It was fear. He had been so ravaged by fear. Fuck! He was gonna do it! "I'm not afraid!" I think that's what he said! That's what I remembered as I was walking to kill Bob Sullivan! I remembered!

A car drove wildly past Tom as he sat parked on the side of the road. He would remember it later, though he paid no attention at the time.

What does it mean to be a man? What does it mean to be strong? Those were the questions in my head. Was I stronger if I swallowed this anger and followed the rules? Or was I stronger if I made things right for my daughter? Can you believe that? At forty-five years of age, I still didn't know. I had no idea what it was to be a man.

Sean fell to his knees. It was not voluntary. His emotions had taken the wheel.

That stupid little fuck. I felt the pavement against my kneecaps. I set my gun down at my feet and held my head in my hands. I closed my eyes. I wanted it all to come. Everything, once and for all. He turned his face away and started to run like a bat out of hell for that red door. I reached for his arm, but he slipped out of my grasp. The people all stood still. They knew what was happening. They knew what was at that door. I ran after him. "It's no good, rookie! Stand down!" I'm almost there. Almost to the door. And that's where it all stopped.

Sean cried out into the night. I have wondered if Bob Sullivan heard his cry, if it alarmed him at all. That's one question we will never have answered.

I opened my eyes. I grabbed the gun and I ran back to my car. I drove home to my family. I couldn't do it. Just like I couldn't lead Valancia to his death. Don't you see, Doc? I didn't do it. He wasn't following me into some suicide mission. I was following him. I was following him!

Tom pulled back onto the road. He had made his decision. He did not stop again. I imagine Sean passed right by him.

I thought I would at least go there and confront him, make him confess. I could at least do that. It was a compromise. That's what I told myself. I got to the showroom. The lights were on in the back office. I left the bat in the car. I did not trust myself. Maybe I'm an idiot. Maybe I didn't have it in me. And maybe I didn't want to find out. I unlocked the door and went inside. I had the words in my head that I would say, and I was mumbling them to myself as I walked into the showroom. That's when I heard the sound. It was a man crying.

I stepped around the corner, the same way I had done that night Bob was with Lila. Only what I saw on this night . . . good Lord.

The car that had sped past Tom belonged to the father of the girl Bob Sullivan had been with the night Jenny Kramer was raped. Lila from the showroom. Her father played golf with Bob. That was the man Tom found crying on the showroom floor, next to the bloodied body of Bob Sullivan.

He had a crowbar in his hand. Bob was lying on the hood of the silver XK, blood pouring from his skull. "My baby girl!" the man cried. I ran to Bob, pulled him to the floor, felt for a pulse. It was weak but it was there. Still, the wound to his head—I could see brain matter oozing out. I was in such a state of shock, I can't even describe it. It was surreal. I managed to get my phone and call 911. I told them where we were, that a man had been struck. That he was dead.

"Tom," I said. "Why did you tell them that if he had a pulse?"

I'm not proud of this. Or maybe I am. I still don't know. But I did not do a thing to save Bob Sullivan. I laid him on the ground and I let him bleed to death. I sat beside this man, this father. He kept saying over and over how Bob had raped his little girl, and I had no idea who he was at the time. The alibi had not come out. But those words, it was like this man was me, the other me who wanted to kill Bob Sullivan. Who wanted justice. I put my arms around this man and I held him, rocking him back and forth as he cried in despair. I can't explain it but to say that he was crying my tears. And that I was feeling his justice.

And there it is. That is the collision. Wasn't it something? But that is not the end of the story.

Chapter Thirty-four

I have no remorse over the role I played in the death of Bob Sullivan. It was coming, you see? He had a liking for other people's wives and daughters. There were more of them on the tapes. They were all disclosed, eventually, in the trial of the murderer, the distraught father who took a crowbar to poor Bob's head. Even the tapes with Charlotte.

The content was sealed by agreement. No one had any interest in destroying Fairview, which is what would have happened. This is a small town. I have said this before, but it is worth saying again here. No one wanted to have to make choices about their marriages, their friends, their kids' teacher at the school, their daughter, their mother. There was not enough space in this town for the kind of anger that would have been generated. So, only the dates and ages of the women were submitted into evidence. The tapes were eventually returned to Fran Sullivan, who, I imagine, keeps them in a nice safe place in her new home down in Miami. Of course, she could not stay in Fairview. She still had to raise her boys. The dealerships were sold (two of

them to Tom Kramer), and the Sullivan family started over some-
place far away.

Charlotte did eventually tell Tom about her affair. She told him
the day after he let the man die.

*I couldn't let him wallow in that guilt. It was still so raw, the im-
age of his wound, his brain matter spilling out, all the blood. And
that man just crying on the floor. Tom was shaken by what he almost did and horrified by what he actually did do. I was the one
who drove him to it, to put the bat in his car and drive to the showroom. I had to make it right.*

Charlotte didn't say it, but I could tell Tom's courage and, in the
end, his ability to contain his rage had caused her to see him in a
new light. She saw him as a man of strength. A man who could protect his family, not just whine about it to others the way he had been
doing all year. And yet he was also flawed, wasn't he? Yes, Bob probably would have died anyway, but Tom did nothing to save the man.
He was not perfect. And this gave Charlotte the permission to finally
let go of good Charlotte the way she had done with bad Charlotte.

As for Tom, seeing Charlotte's flaws allowed him to finally feel deserving of her, of his family, and of his life.

Things don't always happen this easily. But most couples don't
have these kinds of life-altering events to shake them up. Inertia,
stagnation, routines—it is hard to change in the face of these powerful forces.

Bob Sullivan's death had changed them both.

*I was mad, of course. Furious. Hurt. Devastated. I walked around
with this pit in my stomach that just sucked up everything inside
me. I couldn't look at her for days. I made her tell me the details,
where they would meet, how often, for how long. I made her tell me
about the day she found Jenny. She apologized just once. She told
me about her childhood. She was so calm about it, not pleading for*

forgiveness, but just wanting me to understand. She said you had helped her to understand herself, how she needed to have her two selves, the good and the bad, because of the shame she carried with her. She cried when she told me about her stepfather, about the first time it happened. I listened, and when she was done telling me, she just got up and left me alone in the room. She didn't say anything else about any of it for two weeks.

Charlotte said those were the longest two weeks of her life, even longer than the weeks after Jenny's rape.

It was because there was nothing left for me to do. No action to take. No calls, no errands, no nothing. I just had to sit and let my husband know me, all of me, and decide whether he still loved me. It was very hard because after I told him, I knew I loved him more than I ever had before. Or maybe I should just say that I knew I really loved him, period.

Tom came to Charlotte on a Thursday night. They were alone in their bedroom; the house was quiet.

I walked in, and she was standing at her dresser, looking in the mirror. I could see her reflection from where I was standing. And I saw her for the first time. I mean I really saw her. She was not the woman I thought I had married. But God, she was beautiful! I'm sorry . . . I've been crying a lot lately. She was just so beautiful, that vulnerable girl, and that strong woman—they were all there in her face. And I just wanted to hold her.

Charlotte remembers that night well. I doubt either of them will forget it.

I didn't notice him in the room until he was almost standing behind me. He reached his arms around my waist and rested his head on my shoulder. He told me he loved me. He told me he thought I was the most beautiful woman he'd ever known, more beautiful now than ever, now that he could see all of me. I fell into him. I felt this wall crumble to the ground. There was nothing standing between us anymore. We made love and then I slept all night in his arms.

Sean also found a reconnection with his wife after the death of Bob Sullivan. He came to see me the very next day, the day after he almost killed the man himself. The day after he had the recall.

I drove home like a wild man. I couldn't get there fast enough. I wanted to tell my wife that I had not killed Bob Sullivan. That I had not killed Valancia. That I had tried to save him. It's not just that I remember it. I could easily have remembered it only to learn that I had been the one running for that door, driven by arrogance that no amount of reason could ever contain. That's how I felt about most of life. Living with the anxiety—it made me do so many crazy things. I could have been the one, maybe even wanting to die, finally, after so much suffering. Don't you see, Doc? I know now that I'm not completely fucked up. That I'm not so fucked up that I led a man to his death.

"No, Sean. You are not so fucked up. In fact, you ran after him. You tried to stop him. And you were willing to die for him. You are a hero."

I wanted to be a hero. I thought if I killed Sullivan, I would be saving Jenny. Can you imagine if I had not remembered that night? If I had killed an innocent man? I came so close.

"I don't think you would have shot Bob Sullivan. It's not who you are."

Maybe. Sean sat staring at the ground. He nodded slowly. *Maybe, Doc. Guess we'll never know.*

Sean continued to see me for his anxiety, and to finish our work putting the ghosts to bed. Having found those few memories from that day in Iraq, it was a seamless task and deeply satisfying. The trauma from the blast, from the injury, found its home and stopped roaming. Sean went back to college that year. His wife had a daughter, and they named her Sara. And he remained a close friend to Jenny, the man who could hold her black bag full of garbage.

Those are the happy endings. I cannot take all the credit for what these extraordinary people did to change their lives. I will simply say that I am grateful for the small part I was able to play.

And now I must tell you the ending for Glenn Shelby.

It was seven days after the death of Bob Sullivan that the body of Glenn Shelby was found swinging from that metal bar in his apartment. The weather had turned quite warm, and he had started to smell.

When the Cranston police sorted through his things, they found the black ski mask, the black gloves, and a notebook describing in detail the rape of Jenny Kramer.

Glenn had been in property maintenance before his coworkers grew uncomfortable around him. I told you that earlier. Maybe you had forgotten. The last job he did for them was caring for two homes in Fairview. He did everything for them, weeding, lawn maintenance, tree pruning. And cleaning their pools.

Detective Parsons called me with the news.

It's crazy, isn't it? He's a real sicko, this one. Two stalking convictions. Numerous complaints from coworkers. In and out of prison. Crazy bastard. Looks like he was planning to rape someone at that party. He was following several teenage boys on Instagram. Used a fake profile. Fucking idiot kids. They're so caught up in their "likes" and "followers." I bet they don't know half the people they let into their world. We found the chat about the party in one of the hashtags. They started talking about it a week before. Gave him plenty of time to prepare. Looks like he was targeting a boy. We're still trying to identify where it started, which kid let him into the circle first. That might tell us something.

I already knew the answer. I had been through Jason's account to

clean it of photos with the blue sweatshirt. I do not use Instagram.
But one of my son's "followers" kept appearing and appearing, "liking" his posts, trying to start conversations, and prodding my son to
"like" things back. It's hard to explain why it jumped out at me. This
follower's picture and posts never revealed the face of Glenn Shelby.
But I just knew. The desperation oozed like a toxic chemical from the
screen, page after page after page.

Shelby had taken to stalking my son.

Shelby had gone to that party to stalk my son.

Now you understand the debilitating fear that was provoked when
I found out my son had been in those woods.

I did not tell Parsons.

"That is something, Detective. Really something. I have a request.
You said there were writings? About the rape?"

*Oh yeah. This guy kept detailed notes. They match everything
we found and more. It's sick stuff, I'll tell you.*

"I know this will sound strange. But I think I could use them to
help Jenny with her memory. Do you think I could see them, or copy
them?"

*Jesus Christ. That is strange. Is that what she wants? To know
everything he was thinking and feeling while he did those things to
her?*

"I will speak to her and her parents. But I don't want to get their
hopes up if we can't get the writings."

I can get you the writings.

"Thank you."

*Oh—and I almost forgot. That old-timer from Oregon? Remem-
ber?*

I remembered.

*Says he found the file. The report was from a school. A teacher
saw the blood coming from the kid's shirt. Made him go to the nurse,*

and she reported the cut. Said it didn't look like an accident. It was too clean, like someone had cut him on purpose.

"Well, Detective. I guess that's not relevant anymore, is it? Glenn Shelby would have been a child himself back then."

Yeah. I told him we didn't need the file anymore. Thank God. This whole thing is finally over. Think I'll take my vacation time.

"You deserve it." I did not mean this.

So do you, Alan. You have been a godsend for the Kramers. I know they are very grateful to you.

"Well, I was more than happy to help. I just hope I can finish the job."

Chapter Thirty-five

Empathy is defined this way: "the ability to share and understand the feelings of another."

Women talking for hours at a lunch. Men walking the golf
course together every Sunday morning. Teenage girls glued to their
phones. This is when we tell our stories, sometimes in meticulous
detail, watch the expressions in others as they take in the words. We
extract from them their sympathy, their joy, their understanding. We
do this so we are not alone as we walk slowly toward our death. Empathy is at the very core of our humanity. Life is pain without it.

These are the last few strands of sugar.

Detective Parsons gave me Glenn Shelby's writings. The Kramers
discussed my plan and agreed that it was worthwhile. So one evening in early summer, just over a year after the rape, Jenny Kramer
came to my office to finally learn, one way or another, exactly what
had happened in those woods behind Juniper Road.

She wore the clothes from that night—the duplicates we had been working with at the office. She wore the same perfume and makeup. Her hair was down except for one small braid on the right side.

Jenny had taken the events of the past two weeks extremely well. She said it was comforting to her that the man responsible was not Bob Sullivan, but instead a man with a serious mental illness. I facilitated this with a very generous description of Glenn's condition. I know if she had met him and seen how normal he presented to the world, she would have felt differently. Given his conditions, she said it felt more like an accident, like she had gotten in the way of a wild animal in the jungle, or a shark. Or that powerful wave in the ocean. It was not about whether she forgave Glenn Shelby for raping her. It was about her ability to understand, and to place what happened into a context that made life possible to live. Some things are not like that. Some things are so incomprehensible that they rip out our floor, our foundation, and we hobble through life with fear of falling through with each step taken. That was how it would have been with Bob Sullivan—the man who smiled at her when she went to her father's work, who could have any woman he wanted. To think that he could have done those things to her would have left her devoid of reason, and incapable of trusting anyone ever again.

"Where do you want to start?" I asked her.

She was nervous and, I think, a little embarrassed.

I don't know. Should I be on the ground? Or should I just sit here and close my eyes?

"Why don't you sit and close your eyes. Let's see if that's enough."

I let her smell the bleach disk. I played the music. I had a Baggie with some debris from the woods, and I opened that as well. Jenny took a long breath and exhaled slowly. Then she closed her eyes. I pulled out the writings that Detective Parsons had given me. I began to read the words of Glenn Shelby.

I parked several blocks away and walked to Juniper Road. From the woods, I could see everything. The house was lit up in every room. Kids were drinking and laughing. Some of them went to be alone in bedrooms. They met the drug dealer by the back door. I saw the boy inside. I knew it was only a matter of time. I could see his car parked in the driveway. It was near the edge of the woods. I knew I would take him from there.

I looked from the pages to Jenny. She was concentrating. There was no emotion yet.

The boy left, but he did not go to his car. He kept walking down the driveway and out to Juniper Road. I lost sight of him, and this made me angry. The girl came then. I heard the ground crackle as she ran. I heard her tears. I was easily distracted by her. She was so sad.

I could hear Jenny's breathing quicken. I wanted to know what was happening, but I didn't want to interrupt it, whatever it was. I knew these words were leading her back. I could sense it.

I walked up to her. She was startled. I realized then that I was wearing the mask. People usually smile when I walk toward them. People like me. I reached to take it off, but then I remembered I couldn't. "Don't be scared. I didn't come here to hurt you. I was waiting for someone else." She started to walk backwards, her eyes were wide like she was looking at some monster. "I told you not to be scared! Why are you looking at me like that, girl? Can't you see I'm trying to be nice to you? Girl! Don't you walk away from me! I'm not a monster. Girl! Girl!"

I heard a mumble then, a very quiet mumble. I looked at Jenny. Tears rolled down her face. Her mouth was dry as she whispered the word. Girl. Girl.

Through the woods I could see the boy again. He went back inside the party. My chance was gone. I couldn't stay here with this girl knowing. And I was not going to leave without doing what I'd come here to do. She would have told someone, and then there would be no more parties, no more chances. It was not easy to do, but I have had the benefit of seeing a brilliant doctor, and I know how to stop myself from obsessing. I know how to be flexible. And this girl was making me angry. I was trying to be nice to her. I was trying to help her. She was being cruel to me. I know what that feels like. She had no right to make me like her and then push me away. Someone else did that to me, and I would not stand for it again. I slapped her hard across the face and watched her fall to the ground. I climbed on top of her and started to do what I had planned to do to that boy. I did not need to use any drugs. She was so weak and I was so strong. I did not have to put her down to finish my work. I ran my hand under her shirt. Her skin was so soft. I had not felt skin for a long time.

Girl . . . girl . . . Stop yelling. . . . Girl . . . I like your skin. I really like your skin.

Jenny was saying the words now—the words that were on the page, words I had not yet read. My heart was exploding! She was back there, that night. She had found her way back!

I took off her clothes. I put on the condom. It was so easy. She was so small, I could hold her with one hand. I made love to her then. She was crying, but I was being very gentle. But then I remembered it was not the plan to be gentle. I came here to follow a story. And that story would not be right if I was gentle. "I'm sorry, girl." I stopped making love to her and started fucking her, hard. I tried to picture the boy, and that made it easier. I took the stick from my bag. I did not forget one word of the story. I started to scratch her. I remembered where to do it.

I stopped reading. I knew what was on those pages.

It was my story. I closed my eyes and remembered. There is so much pain as he rips into me.

It is the story I had told to Glenn Shelby, the boundary I had crossed. The bright Oregon sun is on my face. I can see my house so close. He laughs when he hears my cries.

It is the story he had remembered and savored and then inflicted on this beautiful young woman. He laughs at me and calls me a bitch.

I wiped tears from my face. I opened my eyes and read on from Glenn's writings.

I took some of the skin from the stick and rubbed it in my fingers. It was slippery, and it began to break into little balls of flesh and then fall to the ground. I scraped some more.

Jenny opened her mouth, and the memories came out on the wings of her words.

I think he's tickling me at first. He's holding me down so hard with his forearm on my neck. And I think maybe he'll stop and just do that for a while, the tickling. Maybe it's over. But then the tickle starts to burn and then burn more and I realize he's carving out my skin.

Yes, Jenny. Yes! And the blood starts to trickle down my back. I can feel it, warm and sticky. He tells me he's making his mark. He tells me he's going to eat my body, this small piece of my body like a cannibal.

Jenny continued as if she could hear my thoughts, as if we were one. And in that moment, we were one, sharing the same story. My remorse was profound. But I did not let it in.

Jenny continued telling our story.

I feel the nerve, he's reached a nerve and I cry out again. He stops and then . . .

I picked up our story then, reading on.

"I'm sorry, girl." I have to follow the story. I stopped carving her and I fucked her more. She yelled again. I wasn't enjoying this.

This was not an easy story to follow. It was not the boy, and I didn't like how long I had to do this. I started to wonder if the story had been remembered wrong. An hour is a long time. My arms were getting tired. And there was so much yelling! "Girl! Stop yelling!" *I had to stop many times so she would calm down and be quiet.*

Jenny joins in. We are like an orchestra, two instruments playing the same song.

Girl . . . stop yelling. Girl . . . Oh God!

I think quietly to myself. I know, Jenny. The pain is unbearable as he thrusts into me. I am only twelve years old. My body is small. He is seventeen. He is a man. He brought me here to look for snakes. He told me I would catch a snake. *See,* he says. *You caught a snake.* I cried then. I just cried. It wasn't an hour. Glenn had asked me how long it went on, and I told him it felt like an hour. I did not say it was, actually, an hour before we saw my mother's car pulling into the driveway. He pulled himself out of me and left me there to bleed.

I read another passage.

I took a long break, checked my watch. I let her catch her breath.

Jenny spoke more words, more memories. They came out quietly, almost in a whisper.

It's almost over. Only seventeen minutes and eight seconds left.

Jenny opened her eyes and met mine, just inches away. We were both crying, our memories now fully before us.

I remember it. Jenny said, *I remember him.*

"I know. I can see it in your eyes. I can see it!"

And I could. I could see everything. I could see myself. I was no longer alone.

Chapter Thirty-six

My parents did not want to report the rape. They did not take me to a doctor until the school nurse made them, and then it was just to stitch up the carving. They were afraid the state would remove their foster children, including the one who had taken me into the woods behind our house. My mother said this was something that we could work through. That this boy had a very sad story and needed our help. His behavior—that's what she called it—was a result of his difficult life, and we should not judge him too harshly. The school nurse saw blood from my shirt, and I told her it was from a fall. There was a report, but that was it. The pain of this secret, of having shared it with no one, was brutal.

I remember the day I shared my story with Glenn Shelby. We were having a session at the prison in Somers. He was telling me about a boy he had stalked. How he'd stood outside his house, watching him from the woods. How he had thought about touching him. I started to tell him that these urges were bad. That they could hurt people. He asked me how this could be when it felt so good to imagine it. He recounted examples from the inmates. He recounted things that they did to each other and to him. He had been with hundreds of people, men, women, teenage boys. They were mostly prostitutes. Some were just heavily intoxicated. A few had been drawn in by his charm and so desperate for love that they failed to see the psychosis in his attachment to them.

I had been trying to explain to him that boys should be off-limits, even the ones working as prostitutes. I did not want him to develop a taste for youth, so I started to tell him the story. About the boy lured into the woods. About the fear and the pain. He asked me for details. He asked me why it hurt this boy. I shared my story in great detail. I had not told anyone this story. Not one person. Not in my entire life. Before me was a wide-eyed consumer of my tale of horror. I could not resist the urge to finally say the words out loud. He was so very skilled at luring secrets from their vaults. And I had been so pathetically weak. I told him about the physical pain. I told him how it stole this boy's will. And I told him about the carving. I told him that I was that boy.

Glenn followed this story like a road map when he stumbled upon Jenny in those woods. The rest of it—how he knew the ways to protect himself, the shaving, the condoms—he learned from the other inmates and the endless stories they divulged. I try not to dwell on the fact that he had gone there to rape my own son. That he had gone there to punish me, but then perhaps to give me a gift, the bond of empathy with this girl he had stumbled upon in the woods. With Jenny. How he thought this gift would bring me back to him. The gift in lieu of the punishment. This is what he told me that day in his apartment. That he had been flexible.

I was honest at the start of my tale. When I began to treat Jenny, my desire to give her back her memory was grounded in concepts of justice, and in my belief that it would heal her. Everything changed the moment I read about the carving in the police report. I have described how shocking information enters the brain and wreaks havoc. How it takes time to make the adjustments to the new reality. It was that way for me when I read those words. When my mind adjusted to the facts, the truth was undeniable. It could not be a coincidence. I knew with absolute certainty that Glenn Shelby had raped Jenny Kramer. And I knew he had done so because of me and the story I had shared with him.

Why, then, did I not run to Detective Parsons? Why did I not give Tom the vengeance he craved? Why did I deny my new patient her justice? How can I explain it now if you don't already see? I had been alone for so very long. Yes, some of my patients are victims of assault. Of rape. But none of my patients had been so young. None of my patients had been carved, branded like an animal. There was no one else on this planet who could understand. I walked alone. Until Jenny Kramer. The sudden need to have her remember was more powerful than my conscience. And they would have taken that from me if I had told them the truth.

I went to see Glenn at his apartment when I thought I might need another plan to save my son. And to make sure he never came near my family again. There was more than one way to accomplish this.

It was not until I went through my son's phone that I realized Glenn had gone to that party to harm Jason, that he had been stalking him through social media. Before that moment, I had naïvely believed that he had simply gone where there were children so he could find a victim, any victim. It had even crossed my mind that Teddy Duncan, the twelve-year-old boy next door, had been the target. Glenn knew I was twelve when I was attacked.

I am a better doctor to borderline patients now than I was when I first met Glenn. I understand the depths of the disease, the extent of their obsessions with an individual. And the lengths they will go to affect us. Before I left Glenn alone in his apartment, I told him poisonous things. And the poison is what killed him.

"You failed, Glenn. You did not hurt my son, and this gift you think you gave me was unsatisfying. Jenny is a girl. I was a boy. She was fifteen. I was twelve. I will not see you again. After today, I will not see you. There is nothing you can do that will ever change that. There is nothing you can do that will ever make you important to me."

There was another story I had told Glenn. It was about a patient at New York–Presbyterian. It was not my patient. I was doing my residency, which involved more observation than actual treatment. One of the patients I had been observing killed herself. I recall being concerned about her but saying nothing to her primary doctor. I did not want to be wrong and look foolish. She tore her gown into long pieces, tied them together, and hanged herself from the hinge of the bathroom door. I told Glenn that I had never forgotten this woman, even though she was not my patient. I told him that she would weigh on my conscience until the day I died.

Glenn Shelby was a dangerous man. A monster. My monster. I know that I helped to create him with my indulgence. With my carelessness. And then, I suppose, I killed him.

I could not cure Glenn Shelby. Maybe God can.

I am guilty. Hate me if you must. I have tried to show you the mitigating facts. Charlotte, Tom, Sean. I gave them back their lives, and none of that would have been possible if we had not had the collision. If I had not told my story to an unstable patient. If Jenny had not been in those woods with him. If I had confessed the moment I learned the truth. Hate me. Despise me. But know that I have weighed everything on the scales. And know that every night I fall asleep. And every morning I wake up and look in the mirror without any problem whatsoever.

I do not see the Kramers for therapy anymore. After a productive summer with Jenny, she was able to go back to school. Like Sean, the memories she found hiding within her helped to put the ghosts to bed, and she began to respond to more traditional trauma treatment. By that fall, she was ready to move on with her life.

I always find joy and pain when a patient is cured. I miss them.

I see the Kramers in town. We are all very friendly. Tom and Charlotte seem happy. Jenny seems happy, normal. I see her laughing with her friends.

Sometimes when I am with my wife, when she wraps her arms around my waist, she will touch the scar on my back. Sometimes when she does this, I picture Jenny and I know I'm not alone anymore. The pain is gone. I have healed myself.

My practice has picked up now. I have become a memory-recovery expert of sorts, and I sometimes get patients from across the country. I am thinking of opening a clinic. The trauma treatment continues to be used. I have written papers, spoken at conferences. I have become somewhat of a crusader against its use, and I have done my best to curtail its administration. I see its appeal. It seems so easy, doesn't it? To just erase the past. But now you know better.

I always say the same thing to these patients when they first come to me, convinced they are doomed to a life with their ghosts, with their lost car keys never to be found. It gives them comfort when I tell them. It gives them comfort to know that all is not forgotten.

Author's Note

While the drug treatment in this novel does not currently exist in its
entirety, the altering of both the factual and emotional memories
of trauma is at the forefront of emerging research and technology in
memory science. Researchers have successfully altered factual memories and mitigated the emotional impact of memories with the drugs
and therapies described in this book, and they continue to search for
a drug to target and erase those memories completely. While the original intention of drug therapies to alter memories was to treat soldiers in the field and mitigate the onset of PTSD, its use in the civilian
world has already begun—and will likely be extremely controversial.

Acknowledgments

It would require an entirely new novel to recount the journey that resulted in the writing and publication of *All is Not Forgotten*. While the actual writing time was about ten weeks, it also took me seventeen years, four other novels, two screenplays, one legal career, three children, and enough angst to fill Dr. Forrester's calendar for many years. Writing can be hard. Knowing what to write is even harder. I feel blessed, humbled, and grateful that I found my way to telling this story.

To that end, I begin my acknowledgments with my agent, Wendy Sherman, for knowing what I should write, and for her patience while I got my head around a new genre. Her abilities to read a writer and know the market are truly spectacular. I owe many thanks as well to my editor and publisher, Jennifer Enderlin, for her unwavering enthusiasm, and to Lisa Senz, Dori Weintraub, and the entire team at St. Martin's Press for their extraordinary efforts to publish this book with precision, but also with genuine passion for the project. It has been such a joy for me to work with so many talented professionals. On the West Coast, my gratitude goes out to my film rights agent, Michelle Weiner at CAA, for knowing we would be in such good hands with Reese Witherspoon and Bruna Papandrea at Pacific Standard Films, and Warner Brothers. And for placing the book with some of the finest publishers quite literally around the globe, thank you to foreign rights agent Jenny Meyer.

While I accept full credit for all liberties taken in my description of memory science and psychology, I am indebted to Dr. Felicia Rozek, Ph.D., for providing brilliant insight into the psychological dynamics of the characters and events, and to Dr. Efrat Ginot, Ph.D., and author of *The Neuropsychology of the Unconscious: Integrating Brain and Mind in Psychotherapy*, for educating me on the science behind memory loss, recovery, and reconsolidation.

On a personal note, I owe many, many thanks to my fellow writers, who courageously stare down blank pages every day and still managed to read my work, assuage my doubts, and lend a hand—Jane Green, Beatriz Williams, Jamie Beck, John Lavitt, and Mari Passananti; my trusted readers and "plot testers," who balanced honesty with encouragement—Valerie Rosenberg, Joan Gray, Diane Powis, and Cynthia Badan; my beloved friends who support me unconditionally; my patient partner, Hugh Hall; and my courageous, complicated, and beautiful family, who believe in hard work and big dreams.